509ers

Cariboo is a small fictitious city in the eastern part of Washington State located on land that was once part of the Cariboo Cattle trail that ran from where the Snake River joins the Columbia, to the Canadian border just north of Oroville Washington. The trail was used only from 1859 to 1868, but you can still find traces of it if you know what to look for. A hub for diverse farms and ranches, it is the largest city in Adams County with a population of about seven thousand, five hundred with another seven thousand folks living outside the city limits, but making good use of city conveniences. With a distance of twenty miles or more to the nearest interstate and surrounded by roughly a thousand square miles of irrigated farms and ranches, it has become a Mecca for hunters, most of whom drive a hundred and fifty to two hundred miles from the big cities of western Washington just to shoot a few pheasants and water fowl.

1.

"God damn! Unless you want this old truck to smell worse than it already does, you better pull over for a minute.

"You gonna piss or puke, you dumb ass?"

"Maybe both or neither, but let me outta here before somethin' bad happens."

Nate bolted out the door just a little faster than Jeremy could get the truck stopped and loosely rolled onto the shoulder of the gravel road. "Damn good thing I'm drunk or that mighta killed me," Nate thought or said. He wasn't sure which.

The air being a little fresher out here than in the cab of the truck, Nate decided that a piss was all he really needed, and being the gentleman that he was, walked unsteadily across the shoulder to water the ditch beyond the light emitted by the open door.

"Hey Jeremy, come 'er." slurred Nate, as he did his best not to wet himself.

"What the hell, you want me to hold your hand or somthin'?"

"No, no. I just need to know if I'm seein' things. You know, like them hallucinations."

"I doubt it. I think those things happen while you're dryin' out and I don't see that happenin' soon.

"Now, what is it you spy with your drunken eye?"

"Jeremy, is that a hand sticking out of that bunch'a weeds down there in the ditch?"

"Oh shit! Let me grab my flashlight. Now be careful where you pee. In fact, why don't you go lean on the truck while I take a better look.

"This damn old flashlight's almost worthless," Jeremy thought as he walked back to the shoulder, " but it's better than nothin'."

He pointed the feeble beam down toward where they had seen the hand.

"Oh God! There's a whole person lying under that brush. I gotta go down there and see if they're alive."

2.
SUNDAY, OCTOBER 29

"You look like hell, Hal," said my friend and boss Sam Ryan, the captain in charge of the Cariboo satellite station of the Adams County Sheriff's department. "Wild Saturday night? You should know better at your age."

Of course he knew that for me a wild Saturday night would be staying awake long enough to watch the eleven o'clock news.

"That's right, Sam. I got up out of my warm bed and climbed into my ice cold county issued oversized under powered Ford death trap at three o'clock this morning just to take a hell raising drive through town and out east on Fletcher road."

"That have something to do with you sitting here at your desk on a Sunday morning?"

"You don't miss a thing, do you?" I said while I was rubbing my eyes, stifling a yawn and debating whether to drink the last of the cold black semi liquid in my coffee cup.

"You gonna tell me about it or do I have to wait and read your report?"

This wasn't really a question, but rather a subtle order to fill him in now, not later.

"Two of our local boys were headed home on Fletcher Road after last call at the Thirsty Dog this morning," I began. Going over it out loud to Sam always helped me to see things clearer in my own mind.

"They stopped to relive their over worked bladders and damn near pissed on a body covered with weeds in the ditch."

"You sure they didn't put it there?"

"I really doubt it. Those two are completely harmless as long as Nate does the drinking and Jeremy does the driving."

"Oh, those two. Yeah, I got to agree with you there. They might be a little rough around the edges, but I can't see them hurting anyone."

"No. In fact, Jeremy slid down into the ditch to try and help her out, but it was way too late.

"Then, they drove over to old man McPhee's place, got him out of bed, used his phone, called us and met our car back at the body. A lot of involvement for anyone who would rather not be associated with a crime."

"Maybe they did all that just to make you look for someone else. Besides, why didn't they just use a cell phone to call it in?"

"Number one, they're not that bright and number two, they don't have a cell phone between 'em. Nobody gives them to farm hands, and if they did I don't think those guys would carry one. Would you if you didn't have to? Besides, out where they spend most of their time they probably couldn't get a signal anyway."

"Have you made a positive ID on the body and notified any kin folk yet?"

"Everyone who has seen it agrees that it's Cheryl Collins."

"You mean that sweet little gal that waits tables down at the Swept Wing Inn?"

The Swept Wing was built about twenty years ago and named as such hoping to lure some business from the Boeing flight training facility up in Moses Lake. That never really materialized because of all the places that sprung up much closer and didn't require a forty five minute drive down highway 17. Somehow though, the Wing as the locals call it, has managed to survive in this rural community. It's a popular venue for wedding receptions and a meeting place for local service organizations. The in-house restaurant is appreciated for its down to earth menu, a well stocked bar and a well stacked bartender that always managed to keep things lively while never letting it get out of hand. And a band that did a fair job on rock music as well as country on Friday and Saturday nights. Sunday brunches serving the after church crowd rounded out the weekly routine most of the year.

However, during hunting season each fall, the locals tended to find other places to go as the prices always crept up a little and the clientele seemed to be mostly 206ers, 425ers and 253ers, what they called the influx of hunters from those area codes, Seattle, Tacoma and Bellevue, over on the other side of the mountains.

I said, "I'm afraid so. And, as far as next of kin, we haven't found a thing as yet. She lived by herself in a double-wide up on 12 South West. I'm heading up there as soon as I finish writing up what we know so far."

"Isn't that swanky hunt club bunch stayin' at the Wing this week end, Hal? Did you stop and see any of them this morning?"

"Sure, that was my first stop after I found out who she was."

"Any thing come of it?"

"There were about twenty guys with shotguns standing in the parking lot waiting for their guides and at least ten I knew to be high end lawyers. As a small county sheriff detective I decided to let them be for the time being."

I grabbed highway 26 and headed west as far as SR- 262, turned right and then left again when I reached 12 SW. About three miles west on 12 SW, I spotted a Grant County Sheriff's patrol car parked in a driveway on the right. I pulled in along side and was greeted by a dog barking somewhere nearby. I made the call to Grant County before I left my office and explained the circumstances. They told me a deputy would meet me, help me gain access to the residence and then secure the area if it appeared to be the scene of a crime. Otherwise, for now, I was on my own. Jurisdictional jealousy is extremely rare out here where a hand-full of officers do their best to keep the peace in an area that measures about a hundred miles by a hundred miles. Any of us could need help fast at any time and the closest officer may not be a member of our own department. We tend to do what we think is necessary at the moment and sort out responsibilities later.

As it turned out, the deputy waiting for me was someone I'd had the privilege of sharing a little single malt with from time to time. We lied shamelessly to each other about our proficiencies at various manly pursuits but never about our homes or our jobs.

"Hear you've got a homicide on your hands, Hal. Figure it happened here?"

"Haven't figured much of anything yet, Jeff. I'm told this is where she lived though. I guess I'll look around, and if it doesn't look like it happened here, at least I might get to know a little bit more about her and what might have led to this kind of an end."

The place was locked up tight and we couldn't locate a key hidden in any of the normal places. This in itself is a little strange out here. Most folks living in this area never lock their doors and those that do always have a key hidden somewhere to be found with just a little looking.

"You got one of those lock picks like all the TV detectives, Hal?"

"No, but I've got a nice flexible credit card that'll probably slip that old lock faster than a key."

I was right and we hesitated just long enough to put on our rubber gloves before walking into Cheryl's home.

The furnishings probably came with the mobile home when it was bought some time in the early seventies. It was the quickest way to replace a home that had burned to the ground with a cold winter right around the corner. The family that lived here and worked the farm probably intended to re-build, but that never did happen. Times were hard for the small farmers, as always, and the insurance policy probably hadn't accounted for inflation. All but one acre of the original two hundred was sold, when a year after cancer took the dad, the mom married a farm implement dealer and moved into town. The kids weren't going to keep farming but they had a weird sentimental attachment to the place where they spent time as a family with all the joys as well as the hardships that went with a small spread. None of them wanted to live out here in that old double wide though, so they rented it out and divided the small income between them.

Everything appeared to be well cared for. How she kept that “pop corn” ceiling looking so clean was a mystery I’d have to work on after we found the who and why regarding Cheryl’s death.

“I didn’t see no car in the driveway or back of the house. Had she come home after work, Hal?”

“Everyone I’ve talked to so far thought she was headed here right after she left the Wing. She worked the breakfast and lunch shift from six AM to two PM. and had said she needed a nap before coming back to town for a little Saturday night fun. Take a look in that old barn. Maybe her car’s in there.”

While Jeff headed out to the barn I gave the place a pretty good look. There didn’t seem to be anything indicating a struggle. The bed was made and no dirty dishes in the sink. There was a stack of magazines on a table next to a recliner that faced a 30” flat screen TV. This might’ve been where things began to tickle my brain a little. Great Expectations, Nurture with Nature and Modern Motherhood were the most recent publications in the stack.

“Hey, Hal," Jeff said as he came back into the home, "did she drive one of those gutless old Blazers like maybe an ’84 or so?”

“1983 according to the DMV. I guess she needed four wheel drive but speed wasn’t necessary to get from here to work and back.”

“Well there’s one of them in the barn, and funny thing, the hood feels warm.”

8

~

"Where the hell were you this morning, Charles? We waited out there in the parking lot till it was damn near light out and still you didn't show."

"I guess I over trained a little last night. Had a headache and the trots this morning."

"I don't doubt that. You sure looked like you were havin' fun with that little waitress gal. Like you really had something goin' on. The hell of it is that you cost me one hunt, and that isn't refundable."

"Sorry Robert. Can I slip one of the guides a C to get it reinstated?"

"Nah, I've just about run out of clients I can run over here to get a write off for my membership anyway. I'll be barely able to use up the rest of my hunts with friends. Other than you it doesn't seem like I've got that many."

"You're the one that wanted to be a lawyer. What the hell did you expect?"

"Careful what you say. Some day you might just need me."

I spotted them sitting at a table against the far wall. They both sported hundred dollar haircuts but looked like they hadn't shaved in a week. Just like a lot of the locals except for the hair cuts. When did it become stylish to look like you over slept and didn't have time to clean up?

I grabbed a nearby chair and as I sat down in it at the end of their table I said, "Good afternoon gentlemen, okay if I join you for a minute?"

They both looked at me as if I had just asked if they had heard about Amway. I pulled out my badge, showed it for a second and asked, "Mr. Crawford?"

"I'm Charles Crawford," the one to my left replied. "And this is Robert Langley, my attorney."

I did my best to stifle my amazement as I asked, “Just why do you think you need a lawyer Mr. Crawford?”

“I...I didn’t mean it quite that way officer. Mr. Langley is the attorney for our company, and I’m here as his guest on a hunting week end. I should have introduced him as my friend.

“Just what is your purpose for interrupting our lunch?”

“This is a small town, Mr. Crawford and not much happens that isn’t seen and talked about. I heard that you and Cheryl Collins were tearing up that dance floor pretty good last night,”

“Surely a little Saturday night dancing isn’t a crime here in Cariboo, is it?”

“No, not at all. Otherwise I’d have put half the folks in the county in jail at one time or another.”

“May I ask what this is all about, officer?" This from the unusually silent till now lawyer.

“Actually it’s Detective Halverson, and Cheryl was found in a ditch out east of town early this morning.”

“Was she hurt? Had she been hit by a car? How is she?”

“She was dead, Mr. Crawford, and she hadn’t been hit by a vehicle.”

“Oh God, and I was with her just last night!”

“That’s why I’m here, Mr. Crawford. When did you see her last?”

“About ten, ten thirty, She’d been drinking soda water all night and I’d been doing Jack Daniel’s. We quit connecting on the floor about that time and she said she was going home.”

“And then what did you do, Mr. Crawford?”

“I had a few more shots of Jack and headed to my room.”

“You had your own room, Mr. Crawford? Did anyone see you go there?”

"To tell the truth, yes I had my own room but I kinda hoped to share it. No. I don't remember seeing anyone else on my way to my room."

"According to my resources, you and Miss Collins looked like you knew each other when you met here last night."
"Yes. We met when I was here on business last summer."
"And, what is that business, Mr. Crawford?"
"Agricultural and off road fuel. My father in-law owns Wholesale Fuel. We specialize in diesel fuel to be used only on private property. No road taxes. I was over here helping to set up a new bulk plant for local distribution."
"So, you are married, Mr. Crawford. Is your wife aware of your fondness for dancing when you're away from home?"
"What do you think, detective?"
"There is a chance that Miss Collins was pregnant. Would you mind coming down to the city hall and letting us do a swab to check your DNA?"
"I've got to step in here as your friend and as your attorney, Charles. Detective, are you prepared to arrest my client on some charge or will you please excuse yourself so we may finish our lunch and head home?"
"Just one more thing. Please give me the number for your cell phone in case I need to talk to you, Mr. Crawford. And make sure you keep it with you at all times. If I fail to reach you in say, ten minutes time, I'll have to call your wife or your father in-law and explain your relationship with Cheryl."

3.
MONDAY, OCTOBER 30

Checking in Monday morning with the Coroner up in Ritzville, the county seat, I was told that I was correct in assuming the victim was pregnant. She had been that way about three months, so to my way of thinking, this was actually a double homicide. The cause of death, asphyxiation by carbon monoxide, surprised me though. A fairy common method of doing one's self in, but I'd never found a suicide covered by brush at the bottom of a ditch.

I'd tried to talk with several of the Latino employees at the Wing yesterday afternoon but none of them seemed able to speak English. If I was one of those modern TV detectives I'd of just switched to Spanish and gone on from there. Unfortunately I took Latin in high school and our Spanish speaking detective was watching his son play football over in Boise this weekend, and wasn't due back until Tuesday. I decided this morning to find out how Jerry, the Wing's general manager communicated with his staff.

"Hey, Jer', got a minute?" It was nine AM and Jerome Dumas was just entering his office with a cup of coffee in his right hand and a napkin wrapped danish in his left.

"Sure, Hal, what can I do for you?"

"Jer', I've got a little problem here."

"Really? One of my employees was killed and you've got just a little problem?"

"Well there's little problems and then there are bigger problems. Maybe you can help me with a little problem and that might lead to a solution to our larger problem."

"Sorry, Hal, I guess we're all a little on edge this morning. Sit down. Want me to call down for another coffee and Danish?"

"No thanks, I'm fine."

"So, what little problem can I help you with?"

"Your Latino staff Jer'. None of them seem to speak English. How do you manage to run this place so efficiently when I know you are about as bilingual as I am?"

"Ramón."

“Ramón?”

“Ramón is kind of like my Department of Human Resources for my Latino employees. He is an American citizen and supplies me with legal aliens, at a very fair price, to do the jobs that don’t require interaction with the guests.”

“So you have a record of all of their green cards?”

“I have twenty green cards on file for twenty employees. They’ve all been working here for at least fifteen years.”

“You’re sure about that? The girl cleaning rooms over by the pool can’t be more than twenty, twenty five years old. She started when she was five or ten?”

“Ramón takes care of all that. As far as I know they're all the same people that supplied the green cards fifteen years ago. Who can tell if some changes are made? They won’t speak to me, and they will hardly even look at me. I can’t really tell one from another and every thing works smoothly. I just let Ramón do his thing.”

“Are you serious, Jerome? If the INS really decided to do their job you could be in a world of trouble here.”

“This arrangement is one of the main reasons this place is successful, Hal. Are you going to blow the whistle on me?”

“Nah Jer'. Our instructions are to turn a blind eye to anything like this. But, if the political climate changes next November, you better have a pretty good lawyer.

“Now that we’ve settled all that, I still would like to question some of your employees as to what they saw last night. What would you suggest?”

“I’d talk to Ramon. He should be able either translate for you, or get those who do speak English to answer your questions.”

“Okay. So how do I find Ramon?”

“He has his office in room 151, one of our suites on the first floor at the far east end of the hotel.”

"He has a suite for an office? You're the hotel manager and your office here is barely big enough for the two of us to sit here. What the hell is the deal here?"

"I'm not going to lie to you, Hal. Without Ramon and his people, this hotel would have folded years ago. I manage the stuff everyone sees and Ramon does the rest."

"So if I question any of Ramon's people they are likely to say what ever Ramon has suggested."

"That may be so regarding more people than you realize."

With this new information in mind I left Jerome's office and found the corridor leading east to room 151.

"Hola, senor. In what way may I help you?"

"I take it you're Ramon?"

"Si. Ramon Martinez. And you sir?"

"Detective Haroldson, Adams County Sheriff."

"Am I in trouble detective?"

"Should you be?"

"No, but somehow I doubt that this a social call. Am I correct, sir?"

"Mr. Martinez …"

"Please sir, Ramon."

"Okay, Ramon, I need to talk with some of your staff regarding a homicide. So far none off them seem to speak English even though, according to the hotel records, they have all been working here for fifteen years or more. Is there something I'm missing here? Should I call the INS for some help?"

"Oh, no, senor. I have told them to listen in English and Spanish, but speak only in Spanish. You would be surprised how effective that can be.

"If I understand you completely, if they make an exception for you we will be allowed to continue business as usual?"

"Only so long as my ass doesn't end up in a sling. No promises beyond that. Now, do you have a roster of your staff that were working Saturday from noon to closing time?"

"They are the same as are working right now senor. And they are working the same jobs as then."

At that he pulled what looked like a cell phone from his belt, pushed a button and said something rapid fire in what I guessed was Spanish. The only words I recognized were detective and Halverson.

"I think you will find that my staff will be quite obliging, senor."

"Would any of them tell me anything bad about you, Ramon?"

"Ask them yourself, Detective. I am sure they have nothing bad to say."

I decided to cut back across the parking lot and start at the other end of the hotel with my inquiries, when I saw a beat up old pickup pull in. Jeremy Chambers, one of the pair that discovered the body, climbed out slammed the door twice to make it stay, looked around, and spotting me, headed my way.

"Hey, Jeremy, what brings you to town on a work day?"

"Aw, we're 'bout done for the season with nothin' pressing 'till we get the first snow. Thought I'd check with you, see if you know any more about what happened to Cheryl."

"You knew her? You never said anything the other night."

"I really didn't know her. She just used to come down to the "Dog" once in a while on Saturday night, have a few, and dance with some of the guys. Seemed like a real nice gal. Never did the tease on anyone, and all the guys liked and respected her. Last time I saw her there was some time in July or August. She came in with some dude who was wearin' fresh jeans and polished boots. They danced a few, and when one of the regulars tried to ask her for a dance, he got all pissed off and they left."

"You remember what the guy looked like?"

"Didn't pay that much attention. Maybe five ten to six foot, dark hair. Looked like he had some kinda perfect hair but damned if he didn't look like he needed a shave. Good dancer though."

"You ever dance with her?"

"Naw. Drinkin' and dancin' are Nate's things. I just keep him out of trouble and drive him home."

"If you don't mind my asking, just what's the deal with you two? Is it like a "Broke Back Mountain" kinda thing?"

"Broke Back…shit! Is that what you think? Is that what people around here think? No! In fact, hell no! Damn, no wonder we get those looks. Oh God!"

"What is the deal then? Tell me and maybe I can help straighten folks out."

"Okay, this is what the deal is. I grew up over in Colfax, you know that's about fourteen miles north of Pullman where the State University is. At one time, before I was born, it was the richest town per capita in the United States. Of course there weren't that many people there then so a few dry land wheat ranchers with tens of thousands of acres of land kinda tilted the statistics.

"My dad worked for one of those ranchers doing what ever needed to be done and my mom cooked and cleaned the main house. We lived in a nice double-wide overlooking miles of wheat land and nothing else. From the time of my mid-teens I knew I had to get out of there or I'd go nuts, or worse yet, end up just like my folks. Either way, I just couldn't see that happening.

"Then, on a shopping trip to Spokane I happened to see a recruiting poster that said I could see the world if I would join the United States Navy.

"I had just turned eighteen, was about to graduate from high school and could hardly wait to see the world they were talking about. Two weeks later I was in San Diego starting boot camp. I did well there and in all of my testing and was assigned to Hospital Corpsman school. From there I was sent to Camp Pendleton to train with a Marine Corps Infantry Company soon to be shipped out to who knows where?

"Who knows where, happened to be Iraq just after we were supposed to have everything there under control. Just a little mopping up to do and go home in a year.

" I was sent to a Marine company that had been there since the start of this version of Desert Storm, rotating personnel in and out as their tours of duty began and ended. Some of the guys were old hands and some were green just like me.

"One week after I arrived, the first squad of the platoon I'd been assigned to was sent out to reconnoiter an area that was suspected to house several un-friendlies. Out and back two hours tops. No problem.

"Fifteen minutes out our lead vehicle was hit on the right front quarter by a RPG and rolled over on it's left side engulfed in flames.

"There was screaming from that vehicle as ours stopped and the four of us vacated to our left side seeking cover and pouring rounds of ammo into the area where the grenade had to come from. Well, three were shooting but I was frozen with fear, had soiled my pants and was lying face down under our vehicle with my arms under my face. The noise was terrifying and I was completely disoriented. I had no idea what to do.

"That's when this scrawny assed little buck sergeant crawled under the vehicle, whacked the side of my helmet with the but of his M-16 and calmly said, "We need you Doc. Let me help you outa here. I know you're just a little confused but let's go take care of the guys that are hurt.'

"Only the driver had made it out of the lead vehicle and he appeared to have had his bell rung as well as being badly burned. One of the guys from our vehicle had taken a hit in the right arm from small arms fire, and the driver of the third and trailing vehicle had broken his left wrist when he bailed. I somehow managed to do what I was trained for and hardly noticed when the other two squads of our platoon showed up and the bad guys disappeared.

"No one seemed to notice the stench of my clothes as we headed back to base, and the next day, Captain Swain, the company commander, called me in to congratulate me on my fine performance under my first combat experience. He said that Sergeant Mathews told him he was proud to have me attached to his squad and that for a God damn Swabby I had done okay. 'Coming from that tough little bastard,' he said, 'that's a hell of a compliment.'

"As they say, the rest is history. Nathan Mathews had just returned to Iraq for his second tour and looked out for me while I looked out for his squad for the next year.

"Why," I asked, "after all that trying to get away from here, did you end up almost where you started?"

Jeremy kind of paused for a minute and then, looking a little sheepish he replied, "To tell the truth, I guess this is the place I really wanted to be. I just didn't know it until I saw a how bad things could be elsewhere."

"How did Nate end up here with you," I asked "Was he from around here?"

"No, Detective. But when he got back to the states he just couldn't adjust to civilian life. No structure to keep him grounded. The VA called it PTSD and tried to get his family to help him. Trouble was, his family didn't believe in any kind of violence and had pretty much disowned him when he joined the Corps. We had corresponded a little by mail and someone in the VA Hospital found one of my letters. His Doc wrote to me explaining the situation and I just felt I had to try and help. I drove that old truck to San Diego, picked him up at the hospital and brought him home with me. I thought out here he could slowly re-adjust to civilian life, but it's been damn near ten years. I guess he's about adjusted as he'll ever be.

"Broke Back Mountain my ass! I may be a little shy around the girls but I never…Jesus!"

"Well Jeremy, I'm pleased to hear that you have such an enlightened view on such things. So tell me, does Nate seem to be adapting to life stateside or are there some issues that I should know about?"

"I don't know. He doesn't seem to want to grow up. It's like he just turned twenty one, but hell, he's in his thirties, about four years older than me and I get kinda tired of the so called carefree life style. Maybe it's time to cut him loose and see if he can survive on his own. He sure as hell did over in Iraq when we were all depending on him to keep us alive."

I told him that I had been trained at Camp Pendleton by guys like that back in 1957. They where in high school when they joined the reserves and as soon as they graduated they were activated, run through boot camp and combat training, and then sent to Korea. Never had a chance to be a kid before they were forced to grow up over night.

"He ever have any black-outs? You know, not remember where he's been or what he's done?"

"Only when he's been drinking, and I've pretty much kept track of him then."

"Always? You've never lost track of where he was?"

After a moment's hesitation he nodded and said, "Yeah, pretty much always."

This little extended detour through the parking lot had probably cost me any advantage of surprise I had hoped for in interviewing Ramon's staff in a reverse direction. While the suddenly acquired language skills of the Latino staff were impressive, I learned nothing new except for one odd item: According to the man who kept an eye on the parking lot at night, Cheryl left the premises around ten thirty and headed east toward highway 17 instead of west on highway 26, the shortest route home.

State highway 17 runs from the little town of Mesa, down on I- 396, north past Cariboo, then past the town of Warden, crosses I-90 where there is a park and ride lot courtesy of the Grant County Transit system, through Moses Lake and on north till it meets US 97 just north and east of Brewster Washington. US 97 then continues north to the Canadian border. Of course, just because Cheryl had left the parking lot and headed that direction didn't necessarily mean she was intending to use highway 17. After all, Fletcher road is also east of town.

By now lunch time had come and gone and my ample gut was telling me it needed something to work on or it would keep making unpleasant noises. I headed to our local Mini-Mart-Deli-Gas station to pick up a packaged ham and Velveeta on rye left over from the last millennium.

Mama San, the name everyone around here used when addressing the small aging Korean lady stationed in her usual place behind the cash register, gave me a half nod, half bow and full smile and asked, "You look'n for free apple, Sheriff?"

"Not today, Mama San, how about a nice young obedient daughter that would make a good wife?"

"Oh, fresh out of those. How about a day old doughnut?

"I hear about Miss Cheryl. So too bad. Nice girl, always talk when she come in to buy gas. I think that old car of hers was giving trouble though. Last two, three months it use lot more gas than before. She have to fill once every three days. Used to be once every five days. Used to be all credit card, now alternate card and cash."

I paid for my sandwich and orange Gatorade and thanked Mama San. She said," Say hello to Missus Sheriff, poor lady," as walked out the door.

I made the call to the station and asked Sam if he could get a crew out to Cheryl's barn to pick up her Blazer and bring it in for the tech guys to go over. I not only wanted them to check for prints and anything that seemed out of place, but to see if there was anything mechanically wrong that would cause a sudden drop in gas mileage. I then headed out to Cheryl's myself to dig through any receipts I could find for service work done on the Blazer.

According to the few work order/invoices I found, Cheryl had been taking her Blazer to Leon's for routine maintenance and repairs just like most of us in Cariboo. Leon was a local genius that could use all of the modern computer diagnosis tools required for today's vehicles but still knew how to rebuild a carburetor, haywire something together when parts where no longer available, or when called upon, weld together old wood stoves and a flat bed trailer to make a wood fired barbeque for the local service clubs to use for fund raising picnics.

The most recently dated invoice was for a lube, oil and filter in September. It also showed exhaust work done but didn't specify exactly what that was. This service was performed two months after the previous. Older invoices averaged three months intervals. I decided to go have a talk with Leon. Maybe this was nothing unusual for Cheryl or maybe it was.

Leon had a car up on the lift and was welding on something that I thought was way too close to the gas tank. He tilted his welding mask up with his left hand while setting the "stinger" down on a nearby work bench.

"Hey, Hal, come to see if we can make a real pursuit vehicle out of that sorry old Ford?"

"No, Leon. Just came by to ask some questions about Cheryl Collins."

"Yikes! That's a little scary. I heard she was found murdered out on Fletcher Road the other night"

"That's right, Leon. Did you do it?"

"Just a minute, let me look at my schedule for last week. No, it's not on here. According to this I was digging up old grave sites that night looking for gold fillings. Sorry."

"Well, I had to ask, just in case.

"Seriously, I need to ask some questions about her car."

"That old Blazer is questionable all right. We've done just about everything possible to keep it alive but as it approaches three hundred thousand miles it might be time to let nature take it's course and just let it die. Sorry, I guess that was a poor choice of words considering the circumstances."

"Leon, can you tell me when you last worked on that car and what was done at the time?"

"Sure, let's go into the office and I'll pull her file."

Leon's office was about fourteen feet square, had a state of the art computer, four sets of two drawer filing cabinets, a microfiche viewer, two chairs and a roll top desk that was probably a hundred years old with a bottle of single malt scotch in the right hand bottom drawer. Cheryl's file was in the top drawer of the far left filing cabinet.

"Everything we've done to that Blazer since she first brought it in two years ago should be in here. Let's see, we last worked on it on September 14th. We did a lube, oil and filter as well as some exhaust work."

"What was the exact nature of the exhaust work Leon?"

"We illegally removed a nearly plugged catalytic converter and replaced it with a straight piece of exhaust pipe. Are you going to cuff me now?"

"Why would you do something like that?"

"First, a new converter would run close to a thousand bucks. Second, that old car needed to have all the extra junk removed so it could just function as transportation. All she wanted and needed was a reliable four wheel drive rig with a heater that would keep her from freezing in the winter while she drove back and forth to the Wing and did a few errands around town. We removed the AC compressor a year ago so the bearings on it couldn't seize. I wasn't too worried about her polluting the air out here. Christ, the potato plant puts out more stink than a thousand cars and no one says anything about that!"

"Okay, you're off the hook for that. Tell me, would that pipe make her gas mileage drop?"

"Hell no. It should have given her at least one or two more miles per gallon."

"Can we look to see how many miles she was driving on average per month?"

"Well, looking through her records, she was bringing the car in about once every three months and that was a forty five hundred to five thousand mile interval. Except, when she brought the car in for service in September it was a little over five thousand miles and only a two month time span."

4.
TUESDAY, OCTOBER 31

The techs had taken the Blazer up to the County seat, where our headquarters and crime lab was located, so Tuesday morning I drove the sixty five miles to Ritzville and checked in at the Sheriff's motor pool garage. They had dusted the complete car inside and out for prints and were in the process of separating and cataloging them before sending them to the Washington State Patrol lab where they would be checked against a national data base. An officer in a green County Sheriff jump suit was carefully running a vacuum over surfaces inside the car looking for traces of anything that may tell us something about Cheryl and her activities prior to or, even after her death. We exchanged the usual pleasantries cops do, insulting each other's ancestries and sexual habits, and I went right to checking the odometer. According to the figures Leon had supplied, prior to her servicing the car in September, Cheryl was averaging between sixteen and seventeen hundred miles a month. It appeared now that during the two months since the servicing she had driven over five thousand miles. That meant an increase of seven or eight hundred miles each month. Whether that had any bearing on the case I didn't know, but any variation of a victim's life shortly prior to a murder had to be looked into.

I decided, now that we knew Cheryl was pregnant, it was time to find out who was the father of the fetus. My first guess at this point would be her dancing partner with the great hair, Charles Crawford. I Called the State Patrol Crime Lab over in Seattle and asked to speak with Sergeant Ross Taylor. I had worked with Ross on several cases previously and I thought he might understand my thinking regarding Mr. Crawford. When he got on the phone I explained the situation and he said he would be happy to be of help.

My next call was to Mr. Crawford.

After about four rings a flat sounding female voice told me that Mr. Crawford was not available at this time and that I could leave a message after the tone.

"Mr. Crawford this is Detective Halverson of the Adams County Sheriff's department. It is presently 11:04 A.M. I expect a return call at 509-___-___ prior to 11:25 A.M. If not, I will make a call to your residence and explain to whoever answers the phone why I need to talk with you. I will then call Mr. Wayne Jordan, owner of Wholesale Fuel and do the same thing."

At 11:15 my cell phone rang.

"Detective Halverson, this is Charles Crawford returning your call."

"Thank you for being so prompt, Mr. Crawford. I have a request to make of you."

"What is it, Detective?"

"We have confirmed that Miss Collins was pregnant at the time of her death. I need to identify the father. Now I can go through a lot of legal crap to do this but of course that will mean a lot more people will know about your relationship with Miss Collins."

"Just what is it you want me to do? I'm not the father for God's sake!"

"I'd like to confirm that, Mr. Crawford. The easiest way would for you to be at the Washington State Patrol Crime Lab tomorrow between 11:00 A.M. and noon. Ask for Sergeant Taylor. He will take a swab of the inside of your mouth for DNA testing. If you aren't the father you have nothing to worry about at this time."

"The State Patrol Lab? I don't even know where that is. I think I better call my attorney and ask about this."

"The Lab is located at 2203 Airport Way South. Go ahead and ask your attorney and at the same time you might ask him what a divorce goes for these days. If you fail to show before noon tomorrow I will start the legal crap and it will be necessary to inform your wife and your father in-law the reason for our interest. Your choice. Good by Mr. Crawford."

God this job is fun at times!

If this had happened in one of our state's big cities there would have been uniformed patrolmen questioning all of Cheryl's neighbors for blocks in any direction from her home, but the only neighbor within a mile happened to be right across 12 SW from her place. Time for me to canvas the neighborhood.

Before I went visiting I stopped by my office to go on line and see what I could learn about Cheryl's only neighbor. According to the County assessors site, the home was owned by The Light and the Truth, LLC and the tax statement was sent to a Post Office Box in Bellevue Washington. So much for being prepared.

12 SW runs east and west along the southern slope of The Frenchman Hills. Cheryl's house is on the uphill side of the road, and the driveway I was looking for was about twenty five yards west, across the road, and went downhill for about a hundred feet before ending up in a turn-around with a dried up water feature in the center. The Golden Retriever lying on the porch picked up some kind of a stuffed toy with it's mouth and proceeded to bark a muffled bark as it wagged it's tail and walked unthreateningly toward my car.

Apparently alerted by the dog, a woman opened the front door of the rambler and looked over my radio car. She looked to be about fifty and very well groomed for Tuesday afternoon in this part of the country. By now I was out of the car and she approached me with the grace of a model on a runway.

"I'm Grace Mallory and you are?"

I showed her my I.D. and gave her my business card while attempting to hide my surprise at her sophistication.

"And, to what do we owe your visit today, Detective Halverson?"

"Were you acquainted with your neighbor across the road, Miss Collins, Ms. Mallory?"

"Mrs. Mallory. But please, call me Grace. We would occasionally meet when at the mail boxes at the same time, pass the time of day, so to speak, and walk back to our respective homes. No, we really were not acquainted. Again Detective, why these questions?"

"Miss Collins was found in a ditch out east of town early Sunday morning apparently having been murdered sometime after about eleven thirty the night before. I'm trying to find out by whom and why."

"My God! Where did it happen? Not here at her home I hope. This always seemed to be such a safe area. Are we in any danger?"

"I don't believe so ma'am, but until I have some more answers, I can't be sure.

Did you see her coming and going much? The driveway is almost right across the road."

"Not really, but old Buck over there," she pointed to her Golden Retriever, "sheds so bad that he is strictly an outdoor dog and barks at any car that slows down or pulls into our driveway and maybe hers. Some nights for the last, oh, maybe three or four months, he has been barking more than usual. Maybe three or four times a night."

"Could Mr. Mallory possibly have seen anything that you may have missed?"

"That's Dr. Mallory, Detective."

"Oh, really, it's always nice to have another doctor out here. What is his specialty?"

"Divinity, Detective, he is a man of God."

"Well it's always nice to have them out here too. Do you think he might have a few minutes to talk with me ma'am?"

"He has nothing but time since they sent us 'out here' Detective. Please come in and I will introduce you."

We went in through the front door and I was immediately impressed by the view of the Saddle Mountains through what appeared to be a wall of glass on the south side of the house. Also visible was a large tiled patio surrounding an oval swimming pool that, in spite of the cold, was uncovered and steaming like a hot spring. The Doctor, or

Reverend, was sitting cross legged on the floor in an almost trance like state staring out over the steaming pool and seemed unaware of our presence. He looked very fit with a tan that was still fading this late in the fall. His haircut was another one of those hundred dollar jobs but was just starting to get a little shaggy. He was clean shaven though, probably on orders from his wife.

My first thought was that maybe he was conversing spiritually with his boss, but then I picked up the scent of marijuana and decided otherwise.

"Dear, this is Detective Halverson from the Sheriff's office. Can you give him a few moments of your time? He is inquiring about a matter of great importance."

He slowly turned toward the sound of her voice, paused and then said, "Please be seated, Detective. How may we help you?"

I was a little uncomfortable with the 'we' part of that response, not being on very close terms with his boss, but I decided to just plow along, and took a seat on a nearby footstool. I decided to try and satisfy my personal curiosity first and asked, "How long have you folks lived out here?"

He responded with, "Six very long months, Detective with at least six months left to go."

"Oh? You make it sound like a prison sentence. What were the circumstances that brought you here?"

He gave me a piercing look that probably intimidated most people but only made me want to laugh at his apparent sense of self importance. "I am the youth minister for a Mega Church in the Bellevue area across the lake from Seattle. We have a congregation of nearly three thousand and are still growing. Because of a small error I made concerning some of our youth, I have been sent here to rest and review my commitment to the church. I wish to discuss the matter no further."

I told him, “That’s fine with me but I would like to ask you a few questions regarding your neighbor across the road, Miss Collins.”

“I know nothing about any neighbors across the road or otherwise. Why are you asking?”

“Miss Collins was found in a ditch early Sunday morning. She had been murdered sometime between eleven thirty Saturday night and two o’clock Sunday morning.”

“Do you think I had something to do with it just because I have made one little error of judgment?”

“Not until just now,” I said.

“Please show the detective out Grace. I know nothing about the girl and I must get back to my meditation.”

It was good to get back out into the fresh air. I thanked Mrs. Mallory for her time and told her that there was a chance that I would be back, depending on what other information I may accumulate.

It had been a long day and I had a lot of information to ponder. I decided to head home and see “Missus Sheriff, poor lady," my trophy wife. She is nearly twenty years younger than me and teaches English at Cariboo High, home of the “Brahma Bulls.” The live mascot hasn’t been a bull since his first spring but no one else seems to notice. I guess that’s why I’m the detective. Also, the way the football season has gone so far this fall, a free range organic chicken would be a more appropriate mascot. Most of the big strong farm kids around here are too busy helping out at home to be able to spend time before or after classes doing extracurricular activities. That leaves the “townies” that will put down their Game Boys and smart phones long enough to run up and down the field for a couple hours a day. Most of them are as out of shape as I am. But then – if you have been doing the math you have figured this out – I’m closer to eighty than seventy.

So, why do I still work? Other than we can use the income, the main reason is that I don't want to find myself some day sitting in my Lazy Boy with a drink in one hand and my service revolver in the other wondering which one to put in my mouth. Divorce and suicide, the things most cops have in common. I did one. I don't want to do the other.

Well, I do have a drink in one hand but my notebook is in the other as I sit in my Lazy Boy and smell the onions sautéing. I don't know what Shirley is making but if it contains sautéed onions it has to be good.

I don't have any real idea who the murderer is as yet but if I had to make a choice based on the people I have interviewed so far, I'd say the Seattle wife cheater or the medicated meditating minister. That is solely based on them being jerks. But then, nice guys don't often kill people.

5.
WEDNESDAY, NOVEMBER 1

Here it was Wednesday morning and I still hadn't figured out who did in Cheryl Collins. They say that if a crime like this isn't solved within the first forty eight hours the chances of catching the perpetrator drop to about twenty five percent. I didn't bother to count the hours because that sure as hell wouldn't help.

When I arrived at my office at seven thirty, there was a note on my desk with a phone number and asking me to contact officer Carlos Cruz, a patrol officer with the Moses Lake P.D. I punched the number into my desk phone and was connected to Cruz's voice mail. I left my name and cell number and forgot about it.

I then took out my pocket calculator and opened up a Washington State road map that I carried in my brief case, and spread it out on my desk.

I knew that it was twenty five miles from the parking lot at the Wing to Cheryl's home. Making that round trip five days a week accounted for two hundred and fifty miles. Add, oh say, one hundred miles for other running around, meant she was probably driving about three hundred and fifty miles a week. That old dog of a Blazer probably got no more than fifteen miles to the gallon and that meant about twenty three to twenty four gallons a week. Filling up every five days would mean about fifteen gallons at a time. Three months ago she started filling every three days. That meant about one half fill extra each week or an extra one hundred and thirty to one hundred fifty more miles. I think.

My head was starting to hurt when I was saved by the bell. Well, not really a bell but the buzz of my cell phone. I groped through the stuff on my desk, found the phone and managed to push the thing that lets you answer before it went to voice mail.

"Detective Halverson."

"Detective, this is officer Cruz from the Moses Lake PD."

"What can I do for you officer Cruz?"

"Please start by calling me Carlos, sir."

"You got it. Now, why the call?"

"Yesterday was an off day for me and as I was returning from a shopping trip to Spokane, I stopped by the Sheriff's garage over in Ritzville to see an old hotrodding buddy of mine. He was examining an S-10 Blazer that I understand belonged to a murder victim down your way."

"That's correct, Carlos. Do you know something about the car?"

"It looked familiar to me so I noted the tag numbers and when I got home I went through my notebook and found a match.

As a part of my beat up here, I check the park and ride lot on SR-17 just south of the intersection with I-90. On 4, August I saw that Blazer in the lot with an occupant in the driver's seat. As this is a common way for car prowlers to watch for their next victim, I took the tag numbers and approached the occupant. She identified herself as Cheryl Collins and told me she was waiting for someone who should be arriving shortly."

"What time of the day was that Carlos?"

"Fifteen thirty, sir. Three thirty in the afternoon. I did see her there several times after that including one night about eleven thirty when I had the four PM to midnight shift. I didn't note those times or dates because I figured I knew who she was."

"Is there anything else that stands out in your memory Carlos?"

"Just this sir. When I saw her the first time and questioned her being there at the park and ride she actually thanked me for my concern. Then after that, every time I saw her there, if she saw me she would give me a big smile and wave. She seemed like a really nice girl and kinda reminded me of my kid sister. If I can help you in any way to catch the bastard that did the deed please call me."

"You've already been a great help Carlos. I think now I understand her change in driving habits over her last few months. I promise I'll be in touch if I have anything else that you might be able to help with.

"And Carlos?"

"Yes sir?"

"If I have a viable suspect in your jurisdiction you will be called to help bring him in."

"Thank you sir. And one other thing sir."

"Yes?"

"Are you married to Mrs. Halverson the English teacher at Cariboo?"

"I am the lucky man."

"Please tell her: If it don't rhyme it aint a poem. I think she'll remember me."

My next call was to GTA, the Grant County Transit Authority. I used my desk phone for this because I had an idea I might have to wait for a real person to be available.

"Thank you for calling the Grant County Transit Authority. All of our representatives are answering other calls at this time. Your call is very important to us so please stay on the line and your call will be answered in the order it was received. Your expected waiting time is estimated to be ten minutes."

I cursed silently, just in case this call wait was being recorded, and put my phone on speaker.

After listening to "Eleanor Rigby" as played by a symphony orchestra three times a disinterested sounding voice answered, "GTA, my name is Greg, how may I help you?"

"Greg, this is Detective Halverson of the Adams county Sheriff's office. Can you connect me to your security department please?"

"Sure, but why didn't you just punch in 613, their extension?"

"I didn't know the extension and even if I did your answering recording didn't give me the opportunity before putting me on hold."

"Well don't take it out on me. I just work here."

"Extension 613 please, if you don't mind, and Greg?"

"Yes?"

"You have a lot in common with a couple of my murder suspects."

Another half chorus of "Eleanor" and several beep tones later I heard the ring sound four times before, "Security, Morris speaking."

“Mr. Morris, this is Detective Halverson of the Adams County Sheriff’s office. I'm investigating a murder that took place last Saturday night or early Sunday morning.”

“How does that concern us, Detective?”

“I have reason to believe that the victim was a frequent user of the park and ride lot on SR-17 just south of I-90. Do you have security cameras at that location?"

"Yes we do. They're not very high resolution though. We monitor them real time, along with other cameras throughout our system, looking for unusual occurrences that might warrant sending one of our officers to the scene immediately."

"Do you keep any video received from the cameras?"

"Yes. They operate on a seven day loop so we have the last seven days available from that site. Want me to pull them for you?"

"Please do. If you'll tell me where they'll be, I'll pick them up this afternoon." I jotted down the information, thanked him for his help and hung up the phone.

I felt like we were getting a little insight to Cheryl's life, but there was a lot more to learn. So far I hadn't heard from anyone, other than Jeremy, Mama San and officer Cruz, who seemed to care that much about her demise. She must have had some friends in the area that were missing her by now and might have information that could be helpful. I decided to head over to the Wing for coffee, on the off chance that one of the other waitresses may have been acquainted with her other than as a fellow employee.

There probably is more breaking news being discussed at the Wing coffee counter during the ten o'clock break than at any small town newspaper at any time. Most of the regulars gather here Monday through Saturday about this time, pass insults to each other and catch up on the developments important to a small town, as well as gossip about anyone unfortunate enough to be absent. Generally you will find the local grocer, pharmacist, hardware store owner, Leon, and couple of mechanics from local implement shops, and retired folks hungry to participate in something that has been an important ritual in most small towns for years. Some people are sitting on the same stool at the same counter that a parent might have occupied before them. There is no one here from the big Wal-Mart super store out on Cunningham. I guess their grocer, pharmacist, hardware guy and mechanics might have someplace like this, but I doubt it.

Riding herd over the congregation is Mrs. Perkins. I have never heard anyone refer to her as anything but Mrs. Perkins, not even her husband Ralph. Mrs. Perkins, at least from what we've gathered, was a teacher in a one room school over in the silver mining country in Idaho until Ralph was injured and settled down to collect disability pay from the mining company as well as the State of Idaho. He is still able to lounge around the gathering places in town such as The Thirsty Dog but I've never seen him in the Wing. I think he has the same fear of Mrs. Perkins as the rest of us who feel like we're back in the fifth grade, with her as our 'no nonsense teacher.'

"Good morning, Mr. Halverson," she started. "I would have thought that you would grace us with your presence several days ago. I don't believe in better late than never, but it may apply in this instance. How are you progressing with your investigation?"

I was about to tell her that my dog had eaten my pages of notes when she suggested I move to an unoccupied booth where she would serve me with a black coffee, no cream. I asked her for a danish and she gave me that 'you know better than that,' look. I took a seat in the unoccupied booth that was the furthest away from the counter and did my best to regain adulthood before she approached carrying my coffee and another cup that was steaming and had the unmistaken string of a tea bag hanging down the side.

"Before I say anything else, Mr. Halverson, I wish you to know that I have only the interests of my friends here at the Swept Wing and throughout the area in mind. I may appear to be somewhat aloof and unaware of people's feelings, but that is only a façade I employ in order to keep myself from interfering in matters that are none of my business, but in actuality, bother me greatly. And, If you tell a soul that I really care, you will have to endure the wrath of a one time teaching nun. Do I make myself clear?"

"Yes ma'am, uh, sister, uh, Mrs. Perkins."

"Okay. Cheryl was a lovely, hard working, honest and cheerful girl, but to my way of thinking, she was a sexist. She had no female friends that I was aware of, but really loved the guys. I mean, really loved them as in she couldn't or wouldn't say no. Unless a guy was an unmitigated creep, like her neighbor, she seemed to have no boundaries."

"Her neighbor?" I asked. "What neighbor?"

"That pompous preacher from Bellevue that moved in across the road. She said he was always trying to get her to come over and meditate to rid her of her promiscuous ways. He was starting to bug her so much that she would go clear up to Moses lake, pick up one of her boyfriends and bring him to her house in her own car so he wouldn't see a strange car in her driveway. Then, she would take him back, after what ever, and come back home again. That must have wracked up a lot of miles on that old car of her's.

"This boyfriend in Moses Lake. Did she ever mention a name or anything about him?"

"No. Only that he was a pilot at the Boeing training center."

Two revelations in one conversation!

"Can you think of anyone else here at the Wing that Cheryl may have confided in, Mrs. Perkins?"

"None that I am aware of, Mr. Halverson. She seemed to just tolerate the other girls here. No enemies, but no friends either."

"Thanks, Mrs. Perkins." Handing her a business card I said, "If you think of anything else I should know please call this number regardless of the time of day or night."

"No need to thank me, Mr. Halverson. Just pay for your coffee and my tea before you leave. Oh, and say hello to Mrs. Halverson, poor lady."

I gave a five dollar bill to the cashier and she just said thanks. Didn't ask for more and didn't offer change. It must have been the right amount.

My cell phone buzzed just as I was opening the door of my radio car. The read-out said Ross Taylor, so apparently it wasn't going to be an official call from the State Patrol lab over in Seattle. I sat down in the driver's seat, hit what I hoped was the answer button and said, "Hello, Ross, did our boy show up?"

"You've really got him scared, Hal. Or, at least his wife does. He was here at eleven -oh-one asking for me. What a piece of work he is. I think he'd rather have you suspecting him of murder than have his wife and her dad know how he spent his time over your way. The way he was acting, I don't think he was the father you're looking for. However, that doesn't mean he isn't a murderer. We'll know about the paternity thing by next Monday. Incidentally, his hair looked so perfect that I had to ask him what barber he went to. He said that he didn't go to a barber. He has a stylist."

"Thanks, Ross. I've got another question for you if you've got a minute."

"Fire away."

"Have you heard anything about a Reverend Doctor Mallory? I believe he's associated with one of those Mega Churches over east of the lake, maybe in Bellevue."

"Wow! You really know how to ask 'em don't you. Yes, I have heard about the Reverend Doctor.

"Now none of this is on record anywhere, but I have a close buddy in the Fire Department over there who just happened to catch the call when this went down."

"Sounds interesting, what happened?"

"Well, it seems that one of the trainers at the Seahawks facility over in Kirkland is a member of that congregation and has a fifteen year old daughter who was active in the youth group. She was attending an evening class on meditation with other kids her age that was being conducted by our Reverend Doctor Mallory when her dad showed up a little early to take her home.

"He stopped at the reception desk, was told which room the class was in, and was assured that he could go right in and observe the last few minutes while he waited for his daughter.

"When he tried to open the class room door he found it to be locked. At the same time he detected the unmistakable odor of Marijuana smoke seeping from under and around the door. Doing what any father would do when smelling smoke coming from his daughter's class room, he walked down the hallway until he found a fire alarm box and pulled the handle."

"Just an alert citizen reporting a possible fire, Ross, I love it!"

"The alarm automatically called the fire department and started the sprinkler system.

"The door burst open and the first thing he saw was the Reverend Doctor running from the room soaked and naked as a jay-bird. He was followed closely by a dozen or so startled, wet, but fully clothed teenagers with dilated pupils. Our hero, the trainer guy, dashed into the room to make sure everyone was safe and just happened to come across the Reverend Doctor's clothes which he stuffed into the 'ditty bag' he was carrying that contained his own workout duds.

"The fire crew arrived while our man of the cloth was walking around with his 'wee willie' hanging out looking high and low for his clothes."

"What about the kids, how'd they handle them?"

"Apparently, when the fire alarm is activated in one section of the church building, it automatically seals that section off with a fire door, and unless smoke or extreme heat is detected in the other areas, the sprinklers don't come on. They moved the kids to the gymnasium, grabbed towels from the locker rooms and sat them on the bleachers where they questioned them first as a group and then as individuals, in case they had anything more to say.

"Meanwhile, the fire department was questioning the Reverend Doctor, completely ignoring the fact that he still had no clothes."

"Just what kind of meditation was the Reverend Doctor teaching?"

"Well, the kids were all still fully clothed but according to them, the Reverend Doctor told them that they needed to be 'as new born babes' and loose all inhabitations to deeply meditate and commune with God."

"What was the end result of all this?"

"That is where it gets complicated Hal. That Church has among its congregation some of the most wealthy and influential people around. People who would be extremely embarrassed if any of the happenings that evening were ever made public. Other than the Reverend Doctor's clothes gracing a tackling dummy and his being exiled to some remote area, nothing was done."

"Just in case you're wondering, Ross, that remote area is approximately twenty five miles from where I am right now."

After saying our goodbyes, I made a quick call to the HR department at the Boeing training center, identified myself, and asked for a list of their instructor pilots, including photo IDs if possible, to be e-mailed to my office. Next, I called Mr. Morris on GTA's extension 613. I asked if he had the security video. He told me I could pick it up any time at their E. Broadway office in Moses Lake.

Although The Reverend Doctor Mallory now had my curiosity buzzing, I felt he would probably sit tight for a while believing he had me convinced of his lack of knowledge regarding our victim.

I drove east, picked up SR 17 and headed to Moses Lake. So far, it had been an interesting morning and I felt like I was finally getting a little traction under my spinning wheels.

After an uneventful thirty minute drive, I pulled into the transit system's parking lot on E. Broadway and headed through the front door to the reception desk. I identified myself and was sent to Mr. Morris's office on the second floor. The door was open and I walked in to see not a Mr. Morris, but according to his ID tag and bars on his shoulders, Captain Morris starring at some kind of a ledger on his desk.

"Excuse me sir, I didn't know your rank when I called. I'm Detective Halverson of the Adams County Sheriff's Department."

"Aw, this is just a bull shit rank so I can tell a bunch of 'wanna be' cops what to do. You guys are the real thing. I can think of only about three of my twenty five officers that would make it in a real police department and I'm sure as hell not going to tell them. I put each one of them on a separate shift so I have one person on duty at all times that I can count on. The rest of them make ol' Barney Fife look like a one man SWAT team."

"You don't sound very happy with your job. Just why are you here?"

"My wife says that I'm one of those people who are happiest when they're unhappy, what ever that means. That could be true. I retired from the Portland Oregon PD five years ago and 'bout drove her crazy telling her how she should vacuum, load the dishwasher, organize her errands and shop systematically, and in general, run our home. Then I saw an ad somewhere for this position, interviewed with the GTA and was the only applicant that had ever been a real cop. I went from retired patrolman to captain in the blink of an eye. So, you can see how valuable these captain bars really are."

"Well, lets see how much of a real cop is left in that angry head of yours."

"Ya' know, this little project might just make me happy again. That would really piss me off."

He took a thumb drive out of the top drawer of his desk and slipped it into his computer.

"I hope you don't mind, Detective, I took the liberty of combining the last week of recording from all the cameras on that lot onto a single thumb drive to make it a little easier for you guys to review. I kept all of the originally recorded tapes in case you might need them in court, and replaced them with new tapes at our receiver. The original tapes are in that box on the floor to your right."

"Thanks, as long as we know which camera is which and the time stamp is on all the video that could really save some time."

"They all start from Wednesday one week before I received your call. The first sequence is from the lot entrance on SR 17. What kind of a vehicle are we looking for?"

"Our victim drove a nineteen eighty three Chevy S-10 Blazer." I gave him the tag number and we both started squinting our eyes and watched the scene at the lot entrance. Fortunately, the cameras are motion activated so things occur a lot quicker than in real time.

One beat up old Blazer showed up on that entrance tape for Wednesday but it had an Idaho plate and left within five minutes of arrival. The other cameras picked up the same vehicle making a quick tour of the lot.

Thursday's entrance tape was nothing special until 16:30, That's four thirty in the afternoon, when our subject vehicle entered the lot. There appeared to be one person, the driver, in the vehicle. At 17:07 the same vehicle exited the lot and appeared to have someone in the passenger seat. Checking the other cameras from 16:00 to 17:30 the same day we noted two local shuttle busses, a minni van full of a mom and at least four kids, a ride-share van and a BMW convertible. Except for the convertible, all those vehicles, plus at least ten others had exited the lot prior to 17:10. At 23:41 our subject vehicle re-entered the lot and exited again at 23:58 turning south on SR-17. The BMW exited turning north at 23:59. Bingo!

The BMW plate was one of the older ones with only three letters and three numerals. We could make out the first two letters and the last numeral from the recording. That should get us fairly close to the registered owner.

By now my eyes were getting crossed from looking at the video. I decided to head home with the thumb drives to see if I could make them work on my new HD TV. Captain Morris was okay with that because he had made himself a copy and figured he could spend the rest of the day holed up in his office checking the same stuff.

"Beats the hell out of listening to some old lady complaining about how the Latino population is abusing the transit system by sleeping on the seats," were his words as I left his office.

Shirley was home correcting papers at her desk space in our recently remodeled kitchen when I got there. We got the granite counter tops, new cabinets and appliances as well as a heated tile floor. Another reason I'm still working.

She asked. "How goes your newest case?"

"If it don't rhyme it ain't a poem," I replied"

"Well, in what way did you encounter Carlos?" she asked. "Nothing bad I hope."

"Would you expect bad?"

"I remember him as a little bit of a handful but really a terrific kid, as well as being drop dead good looking. If I was ever tempted to pull a 'Latourno' he'd be the one I'd have seduced."

"I'm glad you didn't. It would've been kinda awkward visiting you in prison wearing this uniform. Oh, wait a minute, I don't wear a uniform. I guess it would have been okay at that. He's with the Moses Lake PD and had a fairly significant lead for me regarding our murder."

"Well, tell him hello from 'Old Lady Halverson', when you next talk with him. And, tell him 'It don't gotta rhyme every time."

Before we could get any further on that subject my cell phone started to buzz and once again I managed to find the damn thing before it went to voice mail. "Detective Halverson," I answered.

"Detective, this is C. J. Morris, Grant County Transit and all that bull shit."

"Captain Morris, what can I do for you?"

"First, call me C. J. and second, I think I've found a real connection between your victim and the BMW. I've deciphered one more letter and one more number from the plate and ran what I had through the DMV. I come up with only two BMWs as possibles. One is registered to a Ronald Gregory of Seattle and the other to a George Thomas of

Mill Creek. Looking it up I found that Mill Creek is an upscale residential area between Seattle and Everett."

"Okay but what is the real connection?"

"The video shows the BMW entering the park and ride from the north at 22:45 Saturday night and the Blazer entering the lot from the south at 22:54. Then, the BMW exits the lot going north at 23:02 and the Blazer exits going south at 23:05. It appeared that there was only one occupant of each car."

Although I hadn't mentioned it to C.J., I was interested in finding Cheryl's Boeing pilot boy friend. It seems the Boeing Paine Field facility is located between Seattle and Everett also. This was starting to look interesting.

"You've out done yourself C.J. I should have a list of Boeing training center personnel waiting on my e-mail at the office. I'll head down there right now and see if we have a match. I'll call as soon as I find out. Thanks."

I know you're wondering. "Why doesn't he just log on to his e-mail right here at home and save a trip to the office?"

The answer is: Because our home is our sanctuary. In order to stay sane, or nearly so, I have to keep the world I deal with professionally as far removed from our personal life as possible. Once the camel's nose is under the wall of the tent the entire animal might as well be inside.

I explained the call to Shirley and told her that I might be late coming home. She just looked at me, nodded and very quietly said, "I love you, so be careful."

Seven minutes later I was at my desk where I woke up my computer and went to my e-mail. There was a message from the Boeing office of personnel explaining that the attached file contained the names, home addresses, local addresses and ID photos of all employees of the training center active there within the last six months. I clicked on the attachment, waited for it to load and quickly went down the alphabetized list to the "T"s. and called Captain Morris.

"Thomas, George C., home address on 150th St. SE, Mill Creek, C J. Does that match the DMV info you've got?"

"Exactly, detective. What do you have for his local address?"

"I show an address on North Shore Drive. Are you familiar with the area?"

"Yeah, upscale waterfront. Must be a long term lease over there or he owns the home. No apartments in that neighborhood."

"In view of the fact that he is a pilot, apparently has money and probably a current passport, I think we should go have a talk with him ASAP. I'm going to make a call to the Moses Lake PD and request a particular officer from their department to accompany us, that is assuming you haven't got something better to do."

"We can meet at my office on Broadway, head down 171, take a right across the bridge on Stratford and we'll be right there. And no, I got nuthin' better to do."

I made the call to Moses Lake PD, talked with the watch commander, arranged for an emergency back up car and got the okay to call officer Cruz at his home, since his shift had officially ended a couple hours ago. He answered on the third ring.

"Detective Halverson?"

"You should be the detective, Carlos. How'd you know...Oh yeah, caller ID.

"Carlos, would you like to go back to work for a couple of hours this evening?" I asked knowing what his answer would be.

"Did you find him detective?"

"I found a person of interest as they say in the big cities. He has a home in Moses Lake and I need a local officer to accompany me when I pay him a visit."

"I'm still in uniform 'cause I went to my eight year old's Pee Wee football practice after my shift and just got home. I don't have a radio car at home though. Should I check one out?"

"Not necessary. Meet me in the parking lot of the GCTA over on Broadway in about thirty-five minutes. C. J. Morris, a captain with the transit authority police will be there watching for you. He helped me ID the guy and the three of us will ride in my car to the subject's home."

"Are you expecting trouble detective?"

"I expect trouble every time I venture away from my own front door. Your job is to see that nothing bad happens to two old fart officers. That work for you?"

I called C. J. back and told him what was happening.

Thirty-six minutes later I was parked in the Transit Authority lot with officer Cruz in the right hand front seat and captain Morris behind the steel mesh screen in the back.

"While I was waiting, I Googled the address and got a satellite picture of the house," said captain Morris. "Looks like one door on the street side and one in the rear facing the water. There is a dock but I doubt anything would be tied there in the water this time of the year."

"Okay, good work, C.J. As I see it, we have a back up radio car at the north end of North Shore Drive just in case. The three of us will go in quietly, no lights, in my car and stop in front of the house. Hopefully he will be at home and maybe eating dinner or watching TV, and won't notice anything as officer Cruz walks to where he can observe the back door and I ring the door bell. Captain Morris will be with me, but if possible, will stay out of the line of sight from the front door. That way, there will be no uniforms to alarm him prior to my introducing myself. I will ask him politely if I may enter the house and if he says yes I will go in followed by captain Morris, who will beep officer Cruz, who will then come around to the front door and join us.

"If he doesn't want to let us in, I will politely explain to Mr. Thomas, that while I am away getting a warrant for his arrest a Moses Lake radio car will remain in front of his home and a Moses Lake Police boat will wait in the water behind his home. They will both, of course, have their light bars flashing until I return with you two, siren blaring and lights flashing."

"Any questions?"

"The captain is going to beep me? How?"

"Hell, he'll just holler for you. I don't know what I was thinking. You do have a way to communicate with the back up car don't you, Carlos?"

"Yes sir. Our shoulder mics are on the same frequency. The transit guys aren't."

"Then I'll leave it up to you to give them the all clear or May Day when I tell you. Any more questions?"

Assuming their silence meant understanding, I pulled out on to171 and headed south past Sporty's Steakhouse, the Pizza Hut and Taco Time, then hung a right on Stratford. I guess, having missed dinner, I noticed things a little differently. After we crossed the bridge, I turned left off Stratford, on to Knolls Vista Drive, and immediately left again on North Shore Drive. Our back up car was waiting there and I quickly brought the two officers in the car up to speed.

The house we were seeking had no exterior lights on, but we could see a glow through the front windows, as if there were lights burning in one of the rear rooms. I parked right in front, on the wrong side of the street, Carlos got out his side and quietly headed to his right to the back corner of the house where he would be able to watch the back door as well as see most of what was happening in the front yard. C.J. got out of the car and walked to his left as far as the front corner of the house where he could not be easily seen from the front door, but had a good view of the left side of the house as well as the front. I walked straight up the sidewalk to the front door and rang the bell.

For some strange reason, standing here on a crisp autumn evening ringing the doorbell of a complete stranger took me back to my youth. I almost laughed out loud when I imagined C.J. and Carlos loaded with eggs and toilet paper ready to decorate the house if the home owner didn't supply us with the candy treat part of the ritual. The spell was broken when a tinny sounding voice asked from a small speaker hidden somewhere near the bell button, "Please identify yourself."

"I am Detective Halverson of the Adams County Sheriff Department'" I said as I held my shield up to the peep hole in the door.

"I gave to the Police Benevolent society last Christmas as I do every year and will do again this Christmas. Your solicitation of funds isn't necessary."

"Mr. Thomas, I'm not here to ask for money. I am here to ask you some very important questions regarding someone whom we believe is an acquaintance of yours. Please open the door and let my associates and myself in. Otherwise, we can make this very difficult and embarrassing for you with a noisy arrest and a trip to jail where you will remain overnight or until bail, if allowed, is posted. Do you get my drift?"

"You have made yourself abundantly clear, detective." With this he opened the door and said, "Do come in."

C.J., observing the action at the door, walked to the right hand corner of the house and gave Carlos a shout.

George Thomas was a fit six foot two with dark hair starting toward a salt and pepper look. His piercing gray eyes matched the gray at his temples and he gave off an aura of cool confidence. In short, he looked like the ideal pilot to be in the cockpit if you were flying somewhere.

I walked into the home, asked Mr. Thomas to stand spread eagle against the wall of the foyer and frisked him for weapons. He was clean. This all happened so fast that he never had a chance to object. C.J. and Carlos, giving the all clear to the back up car via his shoulder mic, followed me in and closed the door behind them.

"Where would you like to have our little meeting Mr. Thomas?" As I said this I pulled an envelope from my breast pocket and handed it to him. "This contains a Miranda agreement for you to sign. I want you to do so before I ask you any questions."

"May I ask you a few questions before signing this affidavit, detective?"

"Sure, fire away." I replied.

"Please, if you will, explain the eclectic combination of officers that are suddenly in my home."

"The three agencies represented here worked together to identify and find you Mr. Thomas. Also my jurisdiction ends at the Adams County line. Thus the two agencies located in Grant County and Moses Lake."

"Just which of my acquaintances will we be discussing detective?"

"Miss Cheryl Collins."

"My wife didn't set this up did she detective?"

"No sir. We have had no contact with your wife...Yet."

"In that case, do you have a pen? I'll answer any questions you have regarding Cheryl so long as my wife is not involved in any way. In fact, I'll make note of that agreement on the Miranda affidavit."

Mr. Thomas escorted us into what must have been a den. There was a fire burning in a gas fireplace and above the fire was a flat screen TV about five feet wide with the local cable company's logo bouncing like a ping pong ball from top to bottom and side to side. Mr. Thomas must have hit the pause button before he came to the door. Two deep looking recliner chairs, a leather couch and several small tables comfortably furnished the room . On a table next to one of the recliners there was an open book and a half finished drink. Mr. Thomas took that recliner and motioned us to sit wherever, as he asked, "Is Cheryl in some sort of trouble, detective? If so how may I help her?"

I set my tape recorder on the table located in the space between Mr. Thomas and myself, turned it on and recited the date, time and place of the recording.

"When was the last time you saw Cheryl, Mr. Thomas?" I asked.

"Last Saturday night."

"About what time would that have been?"

"Eleven o'clock, I would say. Give or take a few minutes. Why?"

"We have reason to believe that you may have been the last person to have seen her alive, Mr. Thomas. That makes you a person we are very much interested in."

"Cheryl's dead? How? Why? What happened?"

"We came here thinking you might know how she ended up being found in a road side ditch early Sunday morning." I said as I watched him for any reaction to the news.

React he did! His healthy looking complexion suddenly turned as gray as his temples. He seemed to shrink into his chair and I could see tears forming in his eyes. He reached over and finished the drink that was on the table in one swallow. Was he shocked about Cheryl's death, or was he shocked that we had found him?

In the silence that followed I could hear the tic-tock of a grandfather clock I hadn't noticed when we entered the room. After about thirty seconds I asked, "Do you have anything you wish to say, Mr. Thomas?"

Another half minute of silence and then in a very small choking voice, "I loved that girl. How could I have let this happen?" Mr. Thomas paused again as if gathering his thoughts. "So far as I know, she has no living relatives. May I respectfully request responsibility for her proper internment. I'll pay for all funeral expenses as well as a nice plot in the Cariboo town cemetery. But, I must not be identified as her benefactor."

"I believe that can be arranged, but first, Mr. Thomas, will you please tell us exactly where you went after you exited the park and ride lot last Saturday night?" I asked.

"I came here, packed an overnight bag, threw it into my Land Rover and drove to my home in Mill Creek arriving there about three or three thirty Sunday morning."

"Do you have any way to verify that? Anyone that might have seen you?"

"Only my wife, but she was sound asleep and we have separate bedrooms. I woke up about nine thirty in the morning and joined her for coffee in the kitchen. She knew I had come home because my bag was there just inside the door to the garage. But she probably had no idea when I got home, and she didn't ask."

I did a little rapid calculation and said, "So you could have been in this area as late as five or six o'clock and still had coffee with your wife at nine thirty that morning. This isn't looking too good for you, Mr. Thomas. Can you think of any reason that you shouldn't be a prime suspect for Sheryl's murder?"

"I loved her detective and I feel so bad that I hurt her that night. I would do anything to go back in time and have a chance to change my decisions that evening."

"Are you confessing the to her murder, Mr. Thomas?"

"What? Oh no! I didn't hurt her that way. Although, my leaving her there alone may have contributed to her murder."

"Since you have nothing to substantiate your story about being headed west on I-90 at the time of the murder, I think we better wrap this up here and take you in and book you on suspicion of a homicide."

"Wait! I did stop for gas in Ellensburg. Hopefully I kept the receipt. If I did, it would be in my car out in the garage. May I go look for it?"

"You will stay right here while officer Cruz looks for your receipt. Where in the car would you expect it to be?"

"Probably in the jockey box between the seats, or maybe on the right hand seat or, maybe on the floor or,... God, I hope I didn't toss it."

"While officer Cruz is out there searching for your receipt, would you mind telling Captain Morris and me, a couple of older gentlemen like you, just what the deal was between you and Cheryl?"

He thought for a moment and began, "As you probably have realized by now, my wife and I are participants in a marriage gone cold over the last ten years or so. Partly my fault. My greatest passion has always been flying. Being on the ground and attending to everyday problems as well as fulfilling social obligations was making me a very sour individual. I took this job at the training center so I could be in the air again as well as be free of the boring, self serving, so called friends we had accumulated while living a life style that seemed expected of us."

I asked, "Had you been grounded for some reason before coming here?"

"Age and some obscure medical problems cost me my commercial license and the airline I was working for, of course, had to let me go.

"Then I was made aware of the position I now hold as a pilot instructor, where I could fly but always had an experienced pilot actually ready to do whatever was required should I somehow become disabled. A dream job really. And far enough away from my Mill Creek home that my social obligations could be forgotten. I bought this home and asked my wife to move over here, but as I expected, she declined the invitation. 'Too hot, too cold, too dusty, no social life, too many people of a different culture,' if you know what I mean."

"It sounds to me that you found yourself an amiable way to become separated without all the stigma that can be attached to such a move." I said.

"Exactly, detective. I found that I really liked a climate with such definite seasonal changes. And as I flew over the area I began to love the diversity of the land with the irrigated fields, the rugged wastelands, the farms and ranches so isolated and independent, and the small towns that had grown to support that independence. I began driving to these small towns on the days that I wasn't teaching. I enjoyed shopping in the mom and pop stores and eating in the cafes where most people knew each other and I was welcomed with polite questions or left alone if I wished to seat myself away from the crowd."

"I presume that is how you met Cheryl," I said.

"Correct. I was having lunch at The Swept Wing and she was my server. She asked the normal questions. 'What brings you to Cariboo? Where are you from?' And, when I told her I was a pilot she said, 'I've always wanted to fly but never have.'

"She was so vibrant and open that I found myself inviting her to take a ride in a small plane on my next day off."

"You own a small plane?" I asked.

"No, but they are easily rented at the Grant County air field and I still have my private pilot's license."

"About when did all of this take place, Mr. Thomas?" I asked.

"Just after the July fourth holiday. We set the following Sunday as a target, hoping the weather would be good and knowing we both had that day off. I obtained her phone number so I could confirm arrangements and finished my day in unusually high spirits. I rented a Cessna 172 at the Grant County airfield about ten A.M. that Sunday, and flew down to the Cariboo Municipal air field just south of town. Cheryl was there waiting for me, and had even packed a picnic lunch. The air was clear and still, and the countryside below us seemed to sparkle in the sun. She was so excited, pointing out landmarks below that she knew. She said that all of the crop circles made the land look just like a giant Chinese checker board. We ate lunch while in the air and she drank some of the wine she had brought. I never touch alcohol before or during a flight so I had bottled water. Yet, I felt as giddy as if I had imbibed. Her enthusiasm was infectious. The last time I'd felt that happy was when I took my first solo flight."

"How did things progress from there?" I asked.

"I couldn't get her out of my mind, Detective. I knew I had to see her again."

"So you began having an affair with her?"

"Not exactly. I naively thought we could be friends, have a plutonic relationship. Still, I couldn't have any of my neighbors or associates be aware of her, so we began, what I guess you might find a strange ritual, where she would pick me up at our rendezvous, the park and ride, and go to her home, where we usually made dinner together, ate and enjoyed each other's company for a few hours. She would then drive me back to the park and ride and, we thought, no one would ever notice anything different in our individual lives."

"Did that change at some point, Mr. Thomas?"

"It changed the evening there was a loud pounding on Cheryl's door. She opened it, and her creepy neighbor from across the road was there. He started ranting and raving about how Cheryl was living in sin and must come with him so they could meditate and have her sins forgiven. She merely said 'No thanks' and closed the door. Then she came to me, smiled and said, 'If people think we are sinning, maybe we should have a go at it'."

"Did you become intimate at that time, Mr. Thomas?"

"It wasn't as if I had made a conquest, Detective. I had fallen in love with Cheryl but had every intention of keeping our relationship chaste. In fact, I had encouraged her to see other men, and I know that she had gone out dancing on several occasions before and after we became intimate. I knew also that I would never be able to match her energy level, and I have never been able to dance without looking like a fool. But yes, that was the start of a much deeper relationship."

"So, did something happen that changed your relationship with Cheryl on Saturday?"

"During the previous week my conscience seemed to suddenly wake up and I was plagued with guilt over what I was doing. I began to think about my thirty some years of marriage, my daughter and mostly my grandchildren. How I had betrayed their trust. A divorce I could endure, but alienation of my daughter or not being a part of my grandchildren's lives would be devastating. When we met that night at the park and ride, I told Cheryl that I had to go home to my family and sort things out. We were both upset, and we parted on questionable terms. I will regret that parting for the rest of my life."

Officer Cruz came into the room shaking his head.

"Nothing, Detective. I scoured that Rover from stem to stern, under the seats, into every fold in the upholstery, the glove box, the jockey box, everywhere. Found a couple of gum wrappers a soda straw still in the wrapper, and less than a buck's worth of change."

"Mr. Thomas, would you like to call an attorney and have him meet us at the county jail in Ritzville?" I asked.

His reply surprised me. "No thank you, Detective."

"Why not, Mr. Thomas? Are you sure?"

"I could never have murdered Cheryl, Detective. I'm sure that if you are as diligent in pursuing the truth in this case as you were in tracking me down you will find the killer soon."

"Have it your way then. Would you like to put on a coat before I cuff you?"

"Please. There is a bomber jacket in the hall closet. May I get it?"

"Officer Cruz will get it for you and check the pockets for any kind of weapon," I said as I nodded to Carlos.

Carlos soon came back into the room going through the pockets of a leather bomber jacket.

"Just some papers and a lone stick of gum."

Carlos' expression went from bland to wide eyed as he checked one scrap of the paper. "Holy shit! This is a receipt for gas from the Chevron on Canyon Road in Ellensburg dated last Sunday morning at 12:48 A.M."

"Did you know it was there all of this time, Mr. Thomas?"

"No, Detective. But I think I would like to have another drink. Would you gentlemen care to join me. That is, if I'm now allowed to stay here."

"We'll have to turn you down on the drink and you can stay here. But," I handed him my card, "call me if you think of anything I should know and/or if you plan to leave town. I'll contact the coroner in the morning and tell him about your request regarding the internment. I'm sure his office will contact you about the details.

" One more thing Mr. Thomas. Cheryl was pregnant. Were you aware of that?"

"No detective. That makes it even a greater loss. I will presume the child was mine. If not, I don't care to find out."

"You seem to be a pretty square shooter Mr. Thomas. Don't let me find out I'm wrong. The consequences could be most disruptive to your lifestyle."

As I pulled a "U " turn from the wrong side of the street to head us back to the transit building, C.J. broke his long silence saying, "There, but for the Grace of God, goes you or me, Hal."

"Nah," I said shaking my head.

"Why nah?" He asked.

"Cause we're way too ugly. Now young Carlos here, he had better watch out when he gets a little more, ah, mature. And while we are on the subject, Carlos, Old Lady Halverson says, 'It don't gotta rhyme every time."

After I dropped C.J. and Carlos off at the transit building and called my wife to tell her I was on my way home, I had some time alone driving down SR-17 to think about George Thomas and his situation. I believed he was innocent of the murder but I couldn't rule him out entirely. He could have had an accomplice drive his Land Rover to Ellensburg and fill the tank while he drove his BMW down this same route and did the deed. Then he could have switched rides and driven to Mill Creek arriving in plenty of time to have coffee with his wife at nine thirty Sunday morning. It was a complicated scenario, and involved another person who may or may not have been aware of the reason for their trip to Ellensburg. Still, not impossible. I made a mental note to find out who his friends were.

The porch light was on but the rest of my house was dark as I clicked the garage door opener and parked as quietly as I could in the double garage. Stepping through the door into the kitchen I heard Shirley say, "I'm glad you're home.

Dinner is in the fridge. Warm it in the micro for two minutes and we can talk in the morning. G'night."

A long day for all of us.

6.
THURSDAY, NOVEMBER 2

As a detective, I get lied to on a regular basis. Some folks lie thinking they might be protecting a friend or a loved one. Others lie thinking they're protecting themselves. And some just can't seem to keep from lying even when the truth would serve them better. It was time I found out what kind of a liar the Reverend Doctor Mallory was.

The temperature was a couple degrees below freezing, the sky a dark gray and a few snow flakes were blowing like feathers in the shifting winds. I decided to check one of the new SUVs out of the sheriff department motor pool. The all wheel drive may come in handy before this day is over.

Twenty five minutes later I was pulling off of 12 SW into the Mallory's driveway, and was once again greeted by a Golden Retriever trying to bark through the green tennis ball lodged in its mouth.

The front door to the house opened before I got to the covered porch, and out stepped Mrs. Mallory, once again dressed and groomed as if she were on her way to meet the President.

"Detective Halverson, what a pleasant surprise. Won't you come in out of this dreadful weather?"

As we stepped into the foyer she went on to say, "I assume you have come by to tell us that you have apprehended Miss Collins' killer and we may once again feel safe here in our home."

"No ma'am. I'm afraid that isn't the reason for my visit. Is Doctor Mallory in?"

"Yes he is, Detective. He's out fiddling with the heating mechanism for the pool. May I get him for you?"

"Thanks, but if you'll just show me the way please, I'll talk to him out there."

We went out to the terrace by way of a glass door set in the middle of a wall of glass. About twelve feet or so beyond the door was the oval pool that, just like on Tuesday, looked to be heated to near the boiling point, considering the cloud of steam rising from the water. About twenty feet to the left of the pool and out of sight from the house stood a building that was around ten feet, by fifteen feet. It was finished on the exterior to match the main house and had a stainless steel chimney protruding from the roof. There wasn't any smoke coming out of the chimney but the heat waves in its vicinity made it pretty apparent that an extreme amount of heat was present. There was an open door on the near side of the building. Mrs. Mallory pointed and said, "He's in there, Detective. Now, if you will please excuse me, I want to make a quick trip into town to get a few supplies before the snow starts in earnest."

I thanked her and quietly stepped into a room filled with pipes connected to canisters, what I assumed to be a water heater radiating enough heat to make the room nearly unbearable, and more valves and dials than I would expect to see in the engine room of an aircraft carrier. The Reverend Doctor, wearing blue overalls with damp looking stains under arms and on the back was obviously perspiring heavily and not looking nearly so dapper as when we last met. He appeared to be inspecting the chimney and, being unaware of my presence, jumped like he had been poked with something when I said, "Hello."

Recovering his superior attitude in spite of the circumstances he asked, "What are you doing here, Detective?"

"I thought we'd have a little talk about honesty Doctor. But first, I'm curious about what you're attempting to do with your pool heater. Surely you have somebody who does the maintenance for you."

"Of course I do. But I thought I might be able to find out why the pool hasn't been coming up to the temperature I desire without having them traipsing all over everything."

"Well I don't know anything about pool heaters." I said, "But everything sure looks hot enough to me."

"And it is, now," he replied smugly. "I found that the chimney damper had somehow gotten jammed in a partly closed position restricting the exhaust and causing the heater to loose efficiency. It also forced exhaust into this room making the atmosphere in here rather foul. Fortunately the burner draws combustion air from the outside. Otherwise, it may have quit working altogether."

"How did you come to figure all of that out?" I asked.

"Prior to my being born again into The Church I was a mechanical engineering student at the University of Washington. I soon found that Theology was much more to my liking and there was no math involved."

"So you would be somewhat familiar with various petroleum fueled devises and the byproducts produced by combustion."

"Yes, somewhat. Why? Just what are you getting at detective?"

"I may tell you later. First, why did you lie about knowing your neighbor Miss Collins?"

"I'm dripping with sweat detective, may I please get out of these wretched overalls before you start badgering me with your irrelevant questions?"

"Nope. And if you are uncomfortable here in this room we can go into your house or down to my office. Your choice Doctor."

He pointed to a chair tucked into a corner alongside the maze of pipes and valves. "May I at least sit down over there?" He asked.

"Nope. I'll move it over here to the middle of the room where I can better keep an eye on you." I said as I dragged the chair to a position where I didn't think he could easily reach anything to use as a weapon.

"You treat me as if I where a suspect in that girl's murder."

"Yep. Anyone who lies to me automatically becomes a suspect. So far you're number one on my list. Tell me the truth now and tell me why you lied before. If I don't like what you say you'll be spending at least tonight in orange coveralls somewhere that isn't nearly as cozy as where we are now.

"I should tell you," I went on, "I know some of your background, and why you have been exiled to our fair county. Now start with your first encounter with Miss Collins and try not to leave anything out." This said, I placed my recorder on the floor between us and recited the time, date and place.

"I'd rather start with my reason for being less than truthful during your last visit." He replied.

"Okay, but I warn you, my bullshit detector is finely tuned, and so far I have no reason to feel like your friend."

"My chief reason for lying about Miss Collins, left just a few minutes ago to do some shopping. She can be an insanely jealous woman, Detective. For some reason beyond my comprehension, she interprets my interest in bringing young sinners to meditation, and through that to forgiveness and understanding, is in some way wrong."

"Really, I wonder why Doctor? Nudity in itself, I suppose can be tolerated. But when you are discovered undressed smoking marijuana in front of a group of teenagers, maybe she has a point."

"I am still of the belief," he said, "that only by coming to Our Maker as unclothed as a newborn, communicating through meditation are we able to be cleansed of our sinful ways. The marijuana helps to remove some of the earthly inspired barriers to such meditation."

"I would presume that in the future, should you have one, you will restrict such meditation to sinners over the age of eighteen."

"Yes," he replied. "Unfortunately some people interpret my methods as something sexual rather than purely spiritual."

Shaking my head at his logic, I then asked, "If that was your chief reason for lying, what were the others?"

"You may remember, Detective that when you called on us the other day, I was in the midst of meditating. As such, my mind is slow to react to things of this world. I knew I wouldn't be able to communicate with you properly and I was afraid you would then associate me in some way with Miss Collins' death."

"In other words, Doctor, you were stoned and paranoid. Now, let's go back to my original request. Tell me about your relationship with Miss Collins, starting with the first time you were aware of her."

The heat was still radiating from the mechanisms in the small room and we both had beads of sweat on our foreheads. Through the open door I could see the snow swirling around the steaming pool and beginning to stick to the surface of the terrace in an oval framing the pool, but about ten feet from the water's edge. By contrast, the warmth of the room felt good.

After a pause of maybe thirty seconds, presumably to collect his thoughts or concoct new lies, he began again. "I became aware of Miss Collins within a few days of our having moved here last summer. We had not yet shed our city habit of keeping our dog, Buck, indoors and walking him on a leash while carrying the requisite poop bag when he needed to go out. I was doing so one sunny day when I heard a voice from across the road asking me why I didn't just let the dog loose to do his own thing. I looked in the direction of the voice and there by the mailboxes was a very attractive young lady wearing immodestly short pants, and what I guess was a bikini top, barely covering her ample bosom. I will admit that I was taken aback, and may have appeared to have been staring at her as I formed my response to her question. After a moment, I told her that she was sinfully attired and that she should not be outside of her home without being more fully clothed."

"This from a man who advocates nudity and drugs during meditation." I said. "Unbelievable so far, Doctor. What was her reaction?"

"She called me an old creep, and told me to mind my own business. I responded by telling her it was my business, as I was a Man of God, and could help her find forgiveness for her dressing as a temptress."

"And she said?" I questioned.

"Stay away from me you lecherous old goat or I'll tell that snooty wife of yours that you came on to me."

"Go on, Doctor. What further contact did you have with Miss Collins?" I asked.

"Well," he said," I didn't mean to spy on her or anything, but I couldn't help but notice that she would often bring men home with her in the evening, and that sometimes they stayed rather late."

"You weren't spying on her, but although there are no windows on the north side of your house, you were aware of this activity?"

"The dog detective. By then we had started leaving the dog outside where he could attend to his own needs as well as alert us to anyone approaching our home. He apparently thought we should be alerted to any activity that took place within a hundred yards or so. I would hear him barking at all hours and get out of bed to check for intruders. More often than not, it was the arrival or departure of Miss Collins in that old SUV of her's. And, more often than not, she was accompanied by a man."

I was buying about half of what he was telling me. Standing on his front porch you could barely see the road let alone the driveway across the road and about twenty five yards to the east..

He went on to say, "One night about two or three weeks after our first encounter she brought home a man, and I just could no longer keep my silence. I knew I could help her rid herself of the demon that was bringing her to spiritual ruin. I went to her door, knocked and when she answered, asked her to come with me so we could meditate and through meditation absolve her of her sins and she could once again be within the 'Grace of Our Lord."

"What was her reaction to that, Doctor?"

"She said no thanks and slammed the door in my face."

"What contact have you had with her since that happened?" I asked.

"None, Detective and I will swear to that by all that is Holy."

"Okay. Now, where were you from about ten thirty last Saturday night until say, noon on Sunday?"

"I was here at my home. I went to bed after the eleven o'clock news, and slept 'till just after seven o'clock Sunday morning. Then I did my exercise laps in the pool and settled down in front of the TV to watch the service being broadcast from my church."

"Is there any way you can verify that, Doctor, anyone who was with you or may have seen you here?"

"Mrs. Mallory returned home sometime after midnight Detective, but she would be able to vouch for my whereabouts after that time."

"Where had Mrs. Mallory been prior to her returning home, Doctor?"

"It must have been one of her many charitable functions. She attends so many these days, trying to fill the time that our exile has brought us, that I no longer bother to ask where she is going or where she has been."

"Just one more question, Doctor. When and where did you meet and become acquainted with Mrs. Mallory?"

"Back when I was at the University. She was a fellow mechanical engineering student. Needless to say, she never had use for an engineering degree after we married."

I thanked him for his time, handed him one of my cards and warned him against leaving the area without notifying me.

The weather had really turned nasty and I had to brush snow off the windows of my county owned SUV. 12-SW was slick and I congratulated myself on my forethought in checking this rig out of the motor pool earlier in the day. Even so, it was going to be a slow trip back to my office.

Just a little less than an hour later I pulled into the department parking lot and found a car already in my spot. Damn! I thought. Then I realized it was my radio car, right where I had left it earlier today. I drove to the visitor's lot and parked, hoping no one would ticket me for not being a visitor, and waded through two inches of snow to the front door. I had picked the right ride for today but I had neglected to put on the right footwear this morning, and as I sat at my desk pulling the wet shoes off of my freezing feet, I had one of those random thoughts.

Something was bothering me about Mr. Thomas' story the other night. Why would you leave your overnight bag by the kitchen door and not take it into the bedroom with you? I decided to make a quick phone call.

She picked up and said, "Hello," after the third ring.

"Is this Mrs. George Thomas?" I asked.

"Yes this is. Why is the Adams County Sheriff Department calling me?"

There you go! Caller ID again. "Mrs. Thomas, there is a possibility that your husband George may have been in a small collision involving a parked car last Sunday morning," I lied. "He claims he was in Mill Creek with you at the time. Can you verify that?"

"I wasn't even home last Sunday morning and I haven't seen that lying son of a bitch in months."

"Thank you, Mrs. Thomas. We may contact you again regarding this matter."

As Inspector Clouseau said in *The Pink Panther*, 'The thought plickins.'

I decided it was time to bounce some of the stories I'd heard in the last few days, off my boss, Sam Ryan. Captain Sam Ryan, that is.

He was in his office, the one with a window, looking intently at something on his computer screen. "What'cha got there, Sam, some hot porn to be used in a future investigation?" I asked.

"I'm afraid not, Hal. Just reading some daily reports from the guys who do the real work around here. Speaking of which, I haven't heard much from you regarding the Collins case. Care to fill me in?"

As usual this sounded like a request but was really an order. I hadn't typed anything official on the case into our computer system but I had my usual lined yellow 8-1/2 by 11 pad filled with notes as well as my trusty cassette recorder.

I started by telling him everywhere I had gone and everything I had done since we talked on Sunday morning. I may have left out the details of my coercing cooperation from some of the people I talked to because I didn't want to have their transgressions muddying the waters right now. Then, I played the recordings of my sessions with Mr. Thomas and the Reverend Doctor Mallory.

When I looked up after turning the recorder off, Sam had his eyes closed. For a second I was afraid I had put him to sleep. Or worse, he had died of boredom listening to me drone on with the details of the case. You can imagine my relief when he opened his eyes and asked, "When you have to drive over to western Washington do you usually fill your tank here in Cariboo or Moses Lake where it is somewhat reasonably priced or do you wait and fill up at those highway robbers in Ellensburg?" Then he asked, "Do they have security cameras at that Chevron station over in Ellensburg?"

"I'll call right away and ask them." I replied

"Also, do a little checking. See where Mrs. Mallory has been spending her time, and find out if she can account for her whereabouts late Saturday and early Sunday morning." He suggested.

"And, while you're at it, find out where Mrs. Thomas was if she wasn't home Sunday morning.

"And why the hell are you walking around this office bare footed?"

My call to the Chevron station that had printed the receipt Mr. Thomas had come up with, was just as frustrating as my first call to the Grant County Transit Authority.

"Canyon Chevron. Can I help you?" that was a pretty standard way of answering a business phone.

"This is Detective Halverson of the Adams County Sheriff's department." I started. "I am inquiring as to whether you have security camera on your property."

"I'm not at liberty to tell you. How do I know you're from the Sheriff's Department and not just someone who wants to know about our security?"

"Look at your caller ID ma'am."

"We don't have caller ID on this phone."

"Then call this number," I gave her the main switchboard number, "and ask for Detective Halverson."

"How do I know that isn't just your phone number and not the Sheriff's office?"

"Okay. Dial information and get the number for the Adams County Sheriff's office. Call that number and ask for Detective Halverson"

"Will you reimburse me for the long distance call?"

"If you don't make that call within five minutes I will have an Ellensburg police car with siren and flashing lights pick you up and take you to the Ellensburg Police station where I will meet with you tomorrow to ask the very simple question about your having or not having security cameras. Have I made myself clear?"

"You don't have to get nasty. I guess it would be easier to just tell you that we do have security cameras."

"Thank you. Now, do you still have any activity recorded by those cameras between ten P.M. last Saturday and six o'clock Sunday morning?"

"No. They are on a twenty four hour loop when they're working, but they haven't been working for about six months or so."

"The Adams County Sheriff's Department thanks you for your help ma'am." I said between my gnashing teeth.

At this point I was tempted to call the place again, tell them I was from the Ellensburg police and warn her about someone posing as an Adams County Sheriff obtaining security information from area businesses. Maybe they'd get their cameras fixed.

When I gave Sam the news about the cameras he merely asked, "Does Mr. Thomas know that they don't work?"

Good point. Could be it's time for me to try out lying the liars. Nah, maybe just not tell them everything. When you outright lie you gotta remember too much. That reminded me...I called our local newspaper and told them that they could release the name of the victim now, as we believed there was no next of kin. We won't release the cause of death until we have a viable suspect in custody. Then I called the motor pool and told them the keys were on my desk if someone could pick up my radio car and put it in their garage. The way the weather was looking I'd be wanting to drive the SUV for a few days instead of that damn oversized Ford sled.

My socks, hanging off a chair over the heat register in my office, were still damp and my shoes felt slimy as I slipped them on my feet. I poked my head into Sam's office and told him I was headed home for a change of footwear, and then I thought I'd go find Mr. Thomas. I knew they wouldn't be flying in this weather and I doubted that he would be expecting me.

A call from my private cell phone to the personnel department at the Boeing Training Center provided the information I needed. I admit, once again I lied a little when I told them I was from Fed-X and had a package for a George Thomas that was to be delivered to him personally. He would be in room 112 in the ground school section of the giant hanger that housed the center until at least five P.M., giving a final written test to pilots he had instructed during the last training period. Allowing for the snow I should arrive there about four or so. I planned to be waiting outside the classroom door as he exited. I called the Moses Lake Police Department, cleared the way as far as jurisdictions, requested and was provided officer Cruz who would meet me at the main entrance to Grant County International Airport.

The snow was still swirling and whirling, not being driven by a strong wind. This meant fair visibility as I drove north toward Moses Lake in the SUV. The all wheel drive was doing it's job but I had to remind myself that even with that and the anti lock brake, stopping suddenly could be a problem. It was four P.M. on the dot when I pulled through the gate to the airport and spotted Carlos in his patrol car, which turned out to be another SUV. He jumped out, walked through about four inches of snow and joined me, sitting down in the right front seat. I noticed he was wearing high top shoes with heavily cleated soles. Smart kid.

I told him about the my brief conversation with Mrs. Thomas, and my suspicions about Mr. Thomas' having someone else provide the receipt from the Ellensburg gas station. Then we decided to take both cars to the Boeing building just in case something unexpected happened. He went back to his car, followed me to the reception door of the hanger, and as instructed, called and reported our location to Moses lake dispatch..

It took a few minutes to explain to the receptionist that we didn't wish to have Mr. Thomas paged, and have her direct us to room 112. We were waiting at the door when it opened and people started filing out, some looking at us quizzically while others seemed to be completely unaware of our presence. I think I would rather ride in the airplane piloted by one of the folks who noticed us. Following the exiting crowd was our Mr. Thomas who was quickly put spread eagle against the wall, frisked and cuffed by Carlos.

"What the hell is this? I thought you were through with me!" Mr. Thomas shouted as Carlos sat him on a desk and I closed the door.

"Someone lied to me, Mr. Thomas and I don't like that." I said as I invaded his space and was almost nose to nose with him.

"Your wife says she wasn't even home last Sunday morning."

"You talked to my wife? I think that negates the Miranda agreement I signed detective. I have nothing further to say to you."

"Fine. Officer Cruz, will you please escort Mr. Thomas to my car and lock him in the back seat. I'll take him to the county lockup at Ritzville where once again he will be made aware of his rights and be allowed to call an attorney. I do have my doubts about any of the lawyers in this area venturing out in this snow, so he'll probably have to spend at least the night in one of those cold cells. Although, there might be someone in the cell that will cuddle up and keep him warm."

"What did you tell my wife, Detective?" he asked

"You're not gonna talk to me, I'm not gonna talk to you, Mr. Thomas. Let's go officer Cruz, before the snow gets any deeper."

"Wait, wait, wait! Do you have another copy of the Miranda I could sign? I'll date it for today and that will nullify the previous one. I'd really rather not go to jail."

"You're probably still going there, Mr. Thomas, but, that would provide me with some options."

I didn't have a signable copy of the Miranda but I noticed a computer terminal and a printer on a table at the side of the room and asked Mr. Thomas if I could use it. I Googled Miranda rights and printed two copies. Mr. Thomas noted the date and time on both and signed them. I took one, let Mr. Thomas have the other, and started my trusty little recorder. I stated the date, the time, the names of all present and told him about my telephone call.

He was visibly relieved when I told him about the ruse claiming to be a traffic officer. However, when I told him what his wife said regarding his absence from her sight I thought he might have a stroke.

I gave him a minute hoping that little blood vein on his forehead wouldn't burst and then wondered if one ever had.

"Well Mr. Thomas, what do you have to say?" I asked and then threw in, "We don't believe it was you who bought gas in Ellensburg either. The security tapes should be in my office tomorrow morning. Did you loan a friend your credit card and bomber jacket?"

"I'm not worried about those tapes detective. I was there when I said I was. Besides, the cameras I saw at the station that night were such low quality that I doubt you tell if it was me or a gorilla in my jacket."

Well, so much for trickery on my part.

"Not wanting to wake anyone with a noisy garage door opener, I didn't try to put my car in the garage when I got there early Sunday," he said. "so I didn't know she wasn't home. I let myself in the front door and carried my overnight bag to my bedroom. I went to bed leaving my bedroom door open so when Clarice, my wife, walked down the hall toward the kitchen in the morning she could see that I had come home.

"I woke up about nine thirty or so, went to the kitchen, made coffee and went to knock on my wife's bedroom door. The door was ajar and when I knocked, it opened partially. I called my wife's name, and received no response. I called louder, thinking she may still be asleep, and still nothing, so I opened the door completely and found the room and the bed to be vacant.

"My first thought was where the hell was she and who the hell was she with? Then I let a little reasoning creep into my mind. I hadn't told her I was coming home this weekend and she could be at my daughter's house babysitting and doing an overnighter.

"I made a call to my daughter's home, and when her husband Jim answered I exchanged pleasantries with him and asked if I could speak to Leah, my daughter. When she came on the phone I once again exchanged pleasantries and then asked her if she had spoken with her mother in the last few days. Leah said no and that she was starting to worry a little because she had been unable to reach her mother by calling our home or her cell phone. Then she asked, 'Is everything all right with you two?'

"I assured her that everything was just fine, and we were just miscomunicating a bit because of my living in Moses Lake. I told her that I loved her and her family and that I hoped to see them all soon."

I asked, "Did you make any further attempts to locate your wife?"

"I had no idea where to look. I decided I'd stay for the day and see if she came home. I made myself a late breakfast and watched the Seahawk's play the Red Skins back on the east coast. After the game, I got tired of waiting around and headed back to my home over here. I still don't know where my wife was. I even thought about how ironic it would be if she were having an affair. How it would make divorcing her much less expensive for me and would allow me to pursue a life with Cheryl without the burden of guilt I had been carrying. And, I have to admit, I thought without remorse, how everything would be even better if my wife was completely out of the picture."

"How fortunate for you, Mr. Thomas that I spoke with your wife today or you could be a suspect in more than one murder."

"Detective, those thoughts occurred prior to my being suspected of Cheryl's killing. Had I known then how upsetting an experience this would be the subject would never have crossed my mind."

"Now that you have told us a completely different version of last Sunday morning, one that I have no reason to believe, would you please tell me why you lied the first time, and how you thought we wouldn't find out?" I asked.

At this point the class room door opened and one of the local 'Rent- a -cops', apparently building security, stuck his head in the door, did a double take and asked if we would be leaving soon. I told him to give us ten minutes and then he could go ahead and lock up. But be sure that we had left the building before doing so. He gave me a 'Yes sir' and closed the door.

"Mr. Thomas?" I said.

"I guess I was hoping you wouldn't be talking to my wife. I see now I was being naive. The truth is, I didn't want to admit that I wasn't in complete control. My affair with Cheryl had caused me to neglect every other aspect of my life and I regretted my estrangement from most of my family."

"Most of your family Mr. Thomas?"

"As I'm sure you are aware by now, my wife and I have nothing binding us together besides a marriage contract. But I love and need my daughter and her family. I'm so afraid that if I divorce my wife, I'll be separating myself from those I love. My denial of the true situation, including my lies to you during our last meeting, enable me to carry on, do my job and live day to day."

"Bull shi, Mr. Thomas. I don't think I have quite enough to charge you with as yet so I'm going to let you go home tonight. But don't be surprised if you see a Moses Lake PD car every place you go unless you decide to leave town. In which case we will have you incarcerated and lost in the system until I have sufficient evidence to lock your ass up for good."

"What about Cheryl's Memorial service on Sunday, Detective. Will I be able to attend?"

"We will send a police escort for you, Mr. Thomas. You have become a V.I.P."

Mr. Thomas went left going toward the employee parking lot as we exited the room and Carlos and I went to the right toward the front entrance. As we walked, Carlos turned to me and asked, "If the tapes from the gas station clearly show someone else pumping gas at that time from that pump can we finally put that bastard where he belongs?"

"Nope," I answered.

"Why not?" he asked.

"'Cause there are no tapes," I said

"You mean you lied?" He asked

"Yep"

"Christ, am I the only honest man in the world?" he asked.

"Could be," I answered.

7.
FRIDAY, NOVEMBER 3

Friday again and the gun clubbers would soon be pouring into town and the bar at the Wing would be pouring into them. I was at my desk wondering if there would be any helpful information floating around the bar tonight when lips became loose. The ringing of my desk phone jarred me back to the present.

"Detective Halverson, how may I help you?" My standard answering line just rolled out of my mouth without any thought necessary.

"Detective, this is Doctor Mallory. I'm becoming quite concerned. My wife left home yesterday to do some shopping and has not returned."

"Doctor, she left while I was there yesterday and you are just now calling to say you're concerned? Have you called anyone else?"

"No sir. I didn't realize she hadn't come home until I couldn't find her this morning. I was meditating all yesterday afternoon and apparently fell asleep and slept the night through."

"In other words you got stoned and anything could have happened to anyone while you were checked out of the real world. Stay right where you are, and stay away from the grass while I do some checking around. If I find you stoned again I'll drag your sorry ass out on to the road in front of your house and arrest you for being under the influence of a narcotic in a public place. With your history it'll stick."

"Please detective, find my wife for me and I will be eternally grateful. I'm worried about her safety, especially considering the recent demise of our neighbor."

"Tell me the license number of her car, hang up and stand by your phone, asshole." I was pissed!

He gave me the tag numbers and letters, and as quickly as I could hang up and redial I called traffic. Mrs. Mallory hadn't shown up on any reports so far but the dispatcher put out a call to all units for any information that may not have been recorded as yet.

My next call was to the hospital to find out if she had been admitted for anything. Nothing there. Then I called the jail and again had a negative response.

Then some evil thing in my mind made me call the Swept Wing Inn.

"This is Detective Halverson from the Adams county sheriffs department. Will you please connect me to Grace Mallory's room."

"I know you, Hal and this is just your way to find out if we have a Grace Mallory registered here," was the reply from the girl at the switchboard.

"You got me again, Karen. But if she is registered will you please ring her room?" I asked meekly.

"205, her usual room, Hal. Want me to ring her, or do you want to come over and talk to her?"

I was beginning to feel like I was the only one around here that hadn't a clue about what went on in my town.

"I'll come over and see her. Please don't let her check out before I get there."

"You got it, Hal. She is sort'a creepy."

The guys at the motor pool had done as I requested yesterday afternoon so I was able to park in my spot close to the front door of our offices. Even so, I had worn wool socks and my heavy boots with cleated soles this morning. The snow was still falling lightly but not so much that I had to clear my windshield before I drove the few blocks to the Wing.

I entered the Inn, waved to the girl at the front desk and took the stairs to the second floor. Once there, room 205 was the second room on the right side of the hallway to my left.

There was movement to be seen through the peep hole in the door within seconds of my knocking. I heard the safety chain being removed and the night lock clicked loudly before Mrs. Mallory stood in the doorway looking just as elegant as she had yesterday afternoon.

"Why Detective Halverson. How unexpected to see you here. To what do I owe the pleasure?"

"You owe it to the worry you've caused your husband, Mrs. Mallory. He obviously doesn't know where you are and is concerned with your well being. He even referenced the death of your neighbor, fearing something terrible has happened to you." I guess I had raised my voice a little because I could hear doors opening along the hallway and when I looked I could see people staring at me with suspicion in their eyes. I pulled out my badge, flashed it around and muttered something about everything being okay. They bought it and returned to their rooms.

I didn't want to enter her room without a witness so I asked her if she would join me downstairs for a cup of coffee.

"Just let me grab my purse detective." She said as she tried to close the door but stopped when my heavy boot with it's cleated sole blocked it open. "I'll be just a moment."

We took the elevator down to the main floor and walked into the coffee shop. I saw a table against the far wall near the entrance to the bar, and with a light pressure on her elbow, guided Mrs. Mallory toward it.

I then took out my cell phone, handed it to her and said, "Call your husband and tell him that I've found you and that you're alive and well. Then we'll have a little talk."

She looked at my phone and said, "No thank you detective. I would prefer to use my own."

When I saw the rose pink thing she pulled out of her purse I could understand her not wanting to use my ugly black phone. In fact I became a little ashamed of it myself and quickly put it back in my jacked pocket. I didn't see any buttons on her phone and wondered how she would be able to dial a number when she merely said "home" and placed the phone to her right ear.

After about five seconds she said, "Yes, yes I'm fine...I didn't want to drive home in that blizzard so I checked into The Swept Wing for the night...I did call but you didn't answer the phone...Well I decided that if you were too busy to answer my call I was too busy to leave a message... Yes, I thought you were probably meditating dear. When did you notice that I wasn't home?...My, you must really have missed me...Later today if the snow stops... Yes, I'll call before I leave. Good bye."

"Do you think it might be time to face the Doctor's drug habit head on?" I asked.

"And have him constantly asking where I'm going, what I'm doing and when will I be home? I think not detective. I find it refreshing to have my occasional freedom from piety. And when he's 'meditating' he usually just stays home and doesn't bother anyone or cause further embarrassment to himself or me."

"I have been told, Mrs. Mallory, that you stay here often enough that you have, what the staff here refer to, as a regular room. Would you mind explaining that to me?" I asked.

"I'd rather not," she replied. I've broken no laws so, as I see it, it is none of your concern."

"Where were you last Saturday night, Mrs. Mallory?" I asked.

"I had checked in here at the hotel and met with some friends from our old congregation. I began to feel unwell just after we had dinner, excused myself and drove home."

"What time did you arrive at your home, Mrs. Mallory?"

"It was a fairly late dinner so I would think around nine thirty or ten o'clock."

"I see. Do you have anyone who can vouch for your whereabouts from say, seven P.M. to two A.M. on Sunday?"

"If it becomes absolutely necessary, detective, I can provide witnesses to my being here at the times I claim. Doctor Mallory will do the same regarding my being at home the rest of the night. Why do you ask? Surely I'm not a suspect in that girl's death."

"Everyone is a suspect until I solve the case, Mrs. Mallory. Especially those folks that tell me lies.

"The snow has stopped. I suggest you call your husband and go back home. The girls at the front desk will let me know if any of your 'friends' come looking for you and I will relay the message. Please give me the number of your fancy phone."

So, who was lying about when Mrs. Mallory arrived home that night? Or was she telling the truth and he was too far gone to know what time she got home. Doctor Mallory was looking less and less reliable and Mrs. Mallory was looking less and less creditable. I talked to Karen at the front desk and she assured me that if anyone asked about Mrs. Mallory (actually Karen called her Grace, something I could never do) she would give me a call.

By this time the snow had stopped falling, the sun had come out and a beautiful blanket of white covered the area. As I drove through town I could see shop keepers shoveling snow off of the sidewalks in front of their establishments. It reminded me of a Norman Rockwell painting and I came close to being in a good mood. Then I thought of all the debris buried under the snow and that reminded me of my suspects and the crap that was buried just beneath the surfaces of their lives. Most of my friends and people that I work with are just like me, struggling to make ends meet, and we don't have enough time, money or energy to screw around corrupting ourselves. I guess the meaning of success depends on your point of view.

When I got back to the office, the parking lot had been cleared of snow except for the piles in the corners that would grow throughout the winter and probably be there until March. I parked in my reserved spot and had a nice dry walk to the front door of our building.

I tapped on the door frame to Sam's office, walked in, and without waiting for an invitation, took a seat in front of his desk.

"Come on in and sit down, Hal." This was his usual response to my usual entrance. "I can see you've got something on your mind. Spit it out."

"The Reverend Doctor Mallory obviously is a stoner," I started. "Where is he getting his stuff and, do you think that could have anything to do with Cheryl's murder?"

"He could be getting it from that medical marijuana shop up in the mall, I suppose," he said. "But I doubt that he could have a prescription that called for the dosage you've described."

Unexpectedly, Sam got up from behind his desk, walked to the door and closed it. "Or," he went on to say, "he could be getting it from Ramon over at the Wing."

"Ramon? He's dealing grass as well as running an illegal alien employment scheme? And you know about it?

"I know you Sam, and I don't believe you're on the take here. What's going on, and why have I been kept in the dark?"

"Okay, here it is Hal. I am aware that folks of your generation have very strong feelings toward the use of marijuana. Some are like you and regard it as a dangerous and destructive drug. Others have used it in moderation as you would alcohol, since the late fifties and early sixties. My generation is a little more tolerant of it as a recreational drug, if you will. Personally I prefer a good single malt scotch, as I know you do. As we work our way down to the folks now in their twenties and thirties, they regard a stoner much as we would regard a drunk. So long as their peers use it in moderation and don't progress to more lethal drugs it is as acceptable as alcohol. In fact, I'm certain that it will soon be made legal and sales will be controlled and taxed by the state just like alcohol and tobacco are now."

"But it's illegal Sam. Aren't we supposed to uphold the law and arrest people who break the law?"

"It's illegal to cross the street in the middle of the block without a crosswalk. It's illegal to drive on tires with less than a sixteenth of an inch of tread. Hell, it's illegal to spit on the sidewalk. If we arrested someone every time a law was broken there'd be more folks in jail than on the streets.

"If someone is under the influence of alcohol, marijuana or any other drug in public I expect them to be arrested. What they do in the privacy of their own homes, as long it is not harmful to anyone else, is none of my business."

"So where does this stuff come from Sam, Mexico?"

"No, it's grown locally and the grower as well as Ramon are fully aware that if I find that any of their product is ever sold to anyone under the age of twenty one, or if any of their customers become a problem because of use in public, I will come down on them like the proverbial ton of bricks.

"I know I could very well lose my job over this but I feel we're better off allowing Ramon to control the market in our area than we would be with an unknown outsider with no connection to the community."

"Since you're baring your sole to me on this subject, would you mind telling me who the grower is?" I asked.

"How do you think Nate and Jeremy make it through the winter without going on unemployment?" He asked.

"That makes me wonder if their discovering the body was really coincidental. What if she knew about the growing operation and had threatened to tell us?"

"Why would that be a threat? I told you they knew we already were aware of their operation. Unless they started selling the stuff up at the school they had nothing to fear and I know those boys well enough that I'm sure that wasn't the case. They're a little rough around the edges but still smart enough to not spoil our deal."

While Sam once again got up from behind his desk, walked to the door and opened it, I thought to myself, "There goes my theory about my friends
and co-workers not having things hidden just below the surfaces of their lives."

I was wondering if I was being dismissed or if the opened door was just the signal that the marijuana subject was now closed when Sam, sitting once again behind his desk asked, "How did your little missing persons case go this morning?"

I proceeded to tell him about all that had transpired this morning including the differences in the Mallory's time lines. We agreed that it could be due to Doctor Mallory's muddled condition, but that I should establish which version was correct.

Sam asked, "So far Hal, do you have any sense of a motive for Miss Collins' murder other than your drug ring theory?"

"My first thoughts were that someone wanted to do away with her because she was carrying their baby and was threatening to reveal an affair," I replied. "But now, I'm beginning to wonder about jealousy of a spouse that may have learned of an affair."

"Considering the cause of death, it could have been an accident combined with fear of discovery that lead to her being dumped in a ditch. Have you thought of that, Hal?"

"Not really." I said. "But, I'll run that idea through my head and see what happens."

"Speaking of the jealousy angle," Sam asked, "Have you found out where Mrs. Thomas was last Sunday morning?"

"No. I haven't given it much thought yet. How do you think we should pursue that angle Sam?"

"I'll clear it with our office up in Ritzville and the Mill Creek police department. You can have a nice little trip to western Washington this weekend, see what you can find out."

"I'd rather stay here and, talk to some of the hunters that were here last week, and attend Cheryl's memorial on Sunday. It may be interesting to see just who shows up for that."

"That's right. That Thomas fellow is anonymously covering all the expenses. Are you going to let him come down here from Moses Lake?" he asked.

"I have a couple of officer friends that have volunteered to bring him down for the services and pretty much sit on him while he's here. I don't see any problems there."

"Have it your way, Hal but, if you find nothing that narrows down the scope of your investigation over the weekend you gotta go over and see what Mrs. Thomas has been up to."

By now it was late enough in the day for some of the weekend hunters to be arriving at the Wing. I'm sure many of them thought noon on Friday was the proper time to end the work week during hunting season, or golf season, or what-ever. I don't think any of the hunt club members punched a time clock or actually kept track of their hours. Well, maybe the lawyers, but I'll bet their noses grew a little whenever they noted their time.

I decided to head back to the Wing and see if Karen, at the front desk, had anything interesting to tell me, and then maybe I'd grab a happy hour snack in the bar.

With the clear skies and the rapidly lowering sun the temperature had dropped to the point where my ears stung a little as I walked once again to my car. Or maybe I was being talked about. The pavement sparkled with salt crystals that had been scattered like chicken feed in the areas where today's sun had caused the snow piles to bleed their moisture, and the normal late afternoon sounds of the town were muffled by the snow. I damn near slipped into a good mood. Then I almost went on my ass when my feet hit a spot that hadn't been salted and my attitude returned to normal.

Karen saw me as I walked through the main entrance and waved me over to the desk. "I was just going to call you,

Hal. I got an inquiry about the whereabouts of your Mrs. Mallory."

"And who was doing the inquiring," I asked.

"Another of our regular guests. I think he belongs to that snooty hunt club bunch. Not only that but I think he's also a lawyer. That makes him extra smarmy."

"Smarmy? Is that an actual word?"

"Sure. It means something like yucky only worse. Doesn't your wife ever use today's vocab when she talks to you?"

"No Karen. We still use a lot of thee's and thou's. Now, do you have a name for me?" I asked.

"Robert Langley, he's a 425er from Bellevue."

"425er?"

"Yeah, you know. Worse than a 206er from Seattle."

I finally realized she was referring to the telephone area codes from the other side of the state and asked, "And where would a 509er find this 425er at this time do you suppose?"

"Hey, you're catching on fast. He's in the bar doing the four to seven."

"Four to seven ?"

"Yeah, happy hour. All you can eat ors devours, as they say, from four P.M. to seven P.M."

"Thanks Karen. Maybe I'll go there and find happiness. Or, Mr. Langley."

After the brightness of the lobby it took a few seconds for me to spot Mr. Langley sitting alone at a table in the dimly lit bar. When I did, I sauntered over to the buffet, grabbed a plate and filled it with things that I didn't recognize. I guess I've gotta get out more.

He was facing away from the serving area, so when I sat down across the table from him he showed for an instant a look of surprise on his face that was soon replaced with a look of annoyance.

"What the hell, Detective. Are you going to try harassing me the way you have my friend. Haven't you found your culprit yet?" he said before I even had a chance to say hello.

"No harassment intended today, counselor. I just wanted to have a little snack and mention that we have a mutual acquaintance."

"And who would that be?" he asked looking more irritated all the time.

"Mrs. Mallory or, I suppose you probably call her Grace."

Did you ever see a tire go flat when punctured by a large sharp object? Except for the sound of air escaping, Mr. Langley's demeanor bore a close resemblance.

"Would you like to enlighten me as to your relationship, Mr. Langley, or should I draw my own conclusions?"

"I'd rather that you would just go away, but I suppose that would be only wishful thinking on my part."

"Good," I said. "I think we're beginning to understand one another."

"My ex-wife and I were members of the congregation of a large church located on the east side of lake Washington. Mrs. Mallory was the wife of one of the Pastors of that church and we had become friends, Grace and I, over a period of several years. Don't read anything into that, Detective. We simply had a few things in common. Her stoner husband and my clueless wife.

"As a successful young lawyer I couldn't have my wife working in anything but a high end socially accepted position, and quite frankly, she would have been lucky to land a job flipping burgers at McDonalds. She became quite bored with the life of leisure, and I was working eighty hours a week trying to keep up the facade of a perfect life. I made the mistake of suggesting an addition to our home to occupy her mind while I was out slaying dragons. We hired a fine young man to do the work and soon I had not only an addition to my home but also an addition to my family. I had never told my wife about the vasectomy I had before we were married, but I held on to the hope that maybe one of my guys had bridged the gap and nailed one of her eggs.

"As you may have noted, Detective, I have very dark hair. My wife is of Italian heritage and likewise has very dark hair. The carpenter doing our addition had the very same flaming red hair as the baby. We were divorced, and so far as I know, my ex and her carpenter are living happily ever after.

"Enter Grace and her soothing sophisticated way of saying 'every thing will work out Robert', you're young and so strong. I know we can overcome our problems.

"She has become a crutch that I should cast aside, but so far I haven't been able."

I let this all sink in and then asked, "Where were you between ten P.m. last Saturday and two o'clock Sunday morning?"

"I had a late dinner here with Grace during which she seemed to become more and more agitated. She left to go home about eight thirty or nine. I went into the bar and watched that fool Charles dance with your victim a while, and then went to my room and watched TV until I fell asleep."

"You call Charles a fool. I thought he was your friend."

"A lawyer really can't have a client as a friend and vice versa. He and the company he works for are clients. I get to know too many things about my clients to be comfortable with them as friends. As for being a fool, he's married to a bright beautiful lady who's father just happens to own a very lucrative business that will some day belong to Charles and his wife. That is, if Charles doesn't fuck it up like he almost did with Miss Collins. I'm a lawyer. I do sneaky things like pretending to be friends with someone in order to keep them as clients. Hell, I'm even being friendly with you."

"I think we both know that being friendly with someone makes it easier to catch them off guard," I said. "Hence our friendly conversation this evening."

"Not to change the subject," he said. "I noticed a small placard by the front desk with a date and time of a memorial for Miss Collins. Is the hotel springing for that.? I was under the impression that she had no living relatives."

"She has a gentleman benefactor," I told him.

"The father of her unborn baby?" he asked.

"Could be," I replied.

"Sounds to me like a likely suspect. Maybe I should go to the memorial and slip him my business card."

"You really are smarmy," I said.

"It goes with the job detective."

"Now about your relationship with Mrs. Mallory..."

"I have nothing more to say concerning Mrs. Mallory, except this: Please do not tell the good Doctor about our relationship. Believe it or not, we are not sexually involved. Doctor Mallory would never believe it because deep down inside that pious facade he is a lecherous old goat. If necessary, I can relate to you some rather interesting stories about the man."

"That won't be necessary Mr. Langley, I am aware of some of his less than desirable traits.

"Thank you for an interesting happy hour," I said. "And good hunting."

"You too detective."

I was leaving the bar to look for other folks that might have been here last weekend when my cell phone buzzed in my jacket pocket. I found the right button apparently because when I answered there was a voice saying in Korean accented English, "Mr. Sheriff, this Mama San over at Mini Gas. Come quick. I have very important information for you."

"Can it wait?" I asked. "I want to question some more people over here at the Wing."

"No. Can't wait. Very important!" she said.

Well, it sounded like she may have a lead for me so what could I do but jump in my car and rush over there?

I parked the SUV right next to the door and rushed in expecting to find answers to some of my questions on the case right here in this most unexpected place.

"Okay, Mama San, what have you got for me?" I asked somewhat franticly."

"It's your anniversary Mr. Sheriff. Why you not home?"

"Oh God," I thought. "It's a good thing I didn't go to western Washington like Sam suggested."

"Are there any of those nice roses left, Mama San, over by the front door?" I asked desperately.

"Not for you Mr. Sheriff, they all reserved for someone else."

"I guess I can run up to the mall and find something," I said.

Mama San hollered something in what I guess was Korean and a young man that I hadn't noticed stocking shelves, jumped like he was poked with a stick and ran into the back room. I was about to thank her and head to the mall when she said, "Wait a minute sir. I save your neck and trip to mall."

The floral arrangement that preceded and nearly hid the young man as he re-entered the room can only be described as beautifully extravagant. At least with my limited vocabulary. There must have been a large vase somewhere in the white wicker container with its fan shaped back. It was overflowing with fresh flowers and greenery that could only have come from the tropics.

"What is this?" I asked.

"When you working on tough case you have only one track in your mind sir. Some times train going wrong way and you forget about other important things. Give this to Mrs. Sheriff. Don't tell how you got it."

"I don't know what to say, Mama San."

"Say nothing sir. Just give me credit card. You think I do this because I like you?"

I managed to get the arrangement into the SUV and out again when I parked in my garage, without doing it much damage. When I walked through the door into the kitchen I heard a gasp that I hoped was not the sound of Shirley dying of shock.

"Hal, you remembered!" she gushed. "I was sure you had forgotten and would be working late again on that girl's murder case."

"How could I ever forget anything as important as our anniversary?" I lied.

"All I got you was this card I picked up at Mama San's the other day. I didn't want you to feel bad if you had forgotten." Then she added, "Like you have the last five years."

It was too cold for the barbeque so we broiled a couple of rib steaks in the oven, tossed a nice green salad and poured glasses of local red wine from the box on the counter. Then we sat in front of the propane fireplace and reminisced about our time together. Miss Collins had left my mind for the night.

8.
SATURDAY, NOVEMBER 4

I woke to the sound of the wind brushing the shrubs against the house. Pulling the drapes aside a little, I could see the snow blowing by the neighbors yard light. It should provide good hunting today for the gun club boys. The pheasants would hunker down in the snow and hold until they were found by the dogs and the ducks would be congregating on the few ponds that weren't frozen over.

Shirley could sleep in but I needed to start paring down my list of suspects and find an answer.

I started the coffee maker, washed down my daily medications with the dregs of a water bottle that was in the fridge and sat down at our eating bar with my trusty yellow pad and ball point pen. I was reading my notes thinking how much less complicated life would be if we all would just tell the truth, when the beep of the coffee maker brought me back to reality and the fact that I may not have been completely truthful myself the last few days and life had been more enjoyable because of that. Well, so much for simple solutions.

As I poured my coffee I thought maybe I should have something to eat with it so the caffeine wouldn't hit me too hard and give me the jitters. Looking in the fridge again, I spotted a piece of leftover pizza that I thought would do the trick. Funny, I didn't remember having pizza lately. Was Shirley holding out on me? I hoped those were green peppers there on top.

Once again settled down at the bar I began writing the names of the suspects I had so far.

First there was Charles Crawford. Charles had dated Cheryl last summer when he was over here on business. Had they been intimate at that time and had she told him about her relationship with Mr. Thomas when they met again last week? Had he killed her in, as they say, a fit of jealous rage? How could he have accomplished that? Could he have somehow gotten her into a vehicle or some other place, run a hose from a source of carbon monoxide to where ever she was and gassed her? Then taken her body in his car and dumped her in the ditch?

Her body had shown no signs of struggle, but I wondered if we should have the State Patrol lab go over his car. I decided to call and spoil his Saturday.

I punched the numbers into my cell and, as expected, got his voice mail.

"Mr. Crawford, this is Detective Halverson. You know the drill. call me back within the next twenty minutes at this number. I'm giving you the extra time because of the early hour. Don't screw yourself up by being late."

I was just topping my coffee off when my phone buzzed. Fifteen minutes a fair compromise.

"This is Charles Crawford. What is it now?"

"I want you to take your car, the one you drove over here last week, in for service this morning."

"What? You called to tell me to have my car serviced?"

"The service station is located at 2203 Airport Way south. You know where that is. Please have it there at ten o'clock sharp. Is that clear Mr. Crawford?"

"Anything else, Detective?"

"No, Mr. Crawford. Just don't wash it or do anything to clean it up before you go because that would look very suspicious."

As soon as I hung up I dialed my friend Ross Taylor on his home phone hoping everything could be arranged with the lab. His phone went to voice mail and I left a message telling him it was important that I talk with him sooner rather than later. He returned the call ten minutes later, and when I explained things he informed me that it was his day off and without overtime authorization he couldn't go in. But he agreed to make the calls necessary, and said he would make a social call to the lab in his civvies about eleven this morning. He'd call me on his own phone then. I thanked him and went to the next name on my list.

The Reverend Doctor Mallory had lied to me right from the start by saying he was unaware of Cheryl's existence.

He had definitely met her on at least two occasions and had probably spied on her many other times. His living just across the road provided easy access should he wish to harm her. The question is 'why would he wish her harm?' Was his pride so great that she angered him with her rebukes? Most people smoking cannabis are pretty laid back while under its influence, and from what I've observed, that would be most of the time with the Doctor. However, on those rare occasions when he was not stoned, the clarity of the real world may have driven him to violence.

I came to the conclusion that I needed to find out more about the Doctor's past actions when confronted with situations not to his liking. As to the discrepancies about the hours, one of the first indications of being under the influence of alcohol or drugs is the loss of one's sense of time.

Then there was George Thomas: Possible father of her unborn child, wayward husband and prolific liar. A seemingly intelligent man when he wasn't thinking with his private parts. If I could be positive of his whereabouts Saturday night and Sunday morning I could either nail him for the crime or cut him loose. He appears to feel some responsibility for Cheryl's death. Was it because of the way they parted on Saturday, or was he totally responsible? And what about Mrs. Thomas? More work to do there.

As far as that goes, what about Mrs. Mallory or even her friend Robert Langley?

More questions came to mind as I saw the light of a stormy dawn outside my kitchen window. How exactly was the murder committed? If it was meant to look like a suicide, dumping her in a ditch was sure to spoil that illusion. Had someone, unknowingly, interrupted the killer causing panic and a rapid change of plan? Or was her death accidental as Sam suggested, and was she dumped to hide a relationship that I have yet to discover?

And a seemingly small detail, why was her car still warm when I visited her home mid morning on Sunday?

As I looked at my notes I felt as if I knew less now than when I first saw her in that ditch.

Okay, I thought, lets put some of this in order. The results of Mr. Crawford's DNA test should be available on Monday. If they show that he isn't the father of the fetus, I think I better identify who is. I should have taken a swab from Mr. Thomas when I interviewed him the first time. If neither of those two are the father, I've wasted a lot of time and may have blown the whole thing. I'll make sure Mr. Thomas pays a visit to our offices while he is in town tomorrow, and supplies us with a sample of his DNA.

The more I thought about it the more concerned I became. If neither Mr. Crawford nor Mr. Thomas are the father, it would mean the murderer could be someone I have yet to meet. Actually, even if one of them was the father, it could still be someone I hadn't encountered.

I couldn't imagine Doctor Mallory having an intimate relationship with Cheryl but stranger things have happened. Another phone call seemed in order. I punched the number for Mrs. Mallory's pink phone into my old black relic.

"Hello," she actually answered her phone.

"Mrs. Mallory, this is Detective Halverson. How are you this morning?"

"I knew it was you when I answered my phone, Detective. Are you really calling to inquire as to my well being or is there something less social on your mind?"

"I merely wished to ask if you and Doctor Mallory would be so kind as to stop by my office tomorrow on the way to Miss Collins' memorial."

"We have no intention of attending the memorial for that woman, Detective. We have no ties to her whatsoever."

"It would be the neighborly thing to do, Mrs. Mallory. Oh, by the way, I had and interesting conversation yesterday with a friend of yours, a Robert Langley."

"I see, Detective. What time is the memorial?"

"Two o'clock at the Logan and Sons Funeral home."

"Would one o'clock be convenient, Detective?"

"Perfect Mrs. Mallory. Thank you, and I'll see you then"

I was about to make my next call when Shirley came into the kitchen, and without saying a word, grabbed a cup from the cupboard and filled it from the coffee maker. After three good healthy sips she acknowledged my existence with a grunt and a nod aimed vaguely in my direction. She isn't a morning person and I knew there wouldn't be any further conversation before she finished this cup and poured a second.

On any given school day, Shirley is up and raring to go at least three hours before it is time for her to drive the one mile to her classroom. She will have gone through the entire day in her mind and be pacing the living room waiting impatiently for the ding from her kitchen timer that signals it is time to back her car out of the garage and start the voyage of another day.

Non-school days are different.

I entered C.J. Morris' number into my phone and pressed call.

"Good morning, Hal. What's happening?"

"Good morning to you, C.J. Are you set to do the big favor for me of escorting Mr. Thomas to the memorial tomorrow?"

"Ready as can be. Carlos and I are going to pick him up at his home at one PM. We'll be in civies but armed, and I'll be driving my personal SUV so we won't arouse any undue attention."

"Just one change, C.J. if I may. Can you pick him up at noon instead and have him at my office at one o'clock?"

"Are we finally going to book him? Hot damn!"

"Afraid not C.J., I want to get a DNA swab from him and It might be interesting to see his reaction to another guest that will be here at that time."

"Okay, Hal. I'll call Carlos and Mr. Thomas and tell them about our change of plans."

"Call 'em but don't tell Mr. Thomas why the time change. Let him stew a little wondering about it."

"You got it, Hal. See ya tomorrow."

I still wanted to nose around The Wing a little today, but since the people I was most interested in probably wouldn't be there until around noon, I decided to try and score some more points on the home front.

Without smiling, because I knew that might be pushing it a little so soon after her waking, I asked Shirley if she would like me to make a nice omelet or something for our breakfast. She nodded, took a sip of her second cup and said, "That would be nice."

Now we were having a real conversation.

I looked through the fridge trying to discover something that would inspire me toward gastronomical success, but other than another slice of leftover pizza, found nothing at all breakfast like.

"Lets go out for breakfast." I suggested. "How about the Swept Wing Inn and one of their fabulous weekend breakfast buffets? I'll shower and shave and you do what ever is necessary and we'll head on out and eat like the rich folks."

After only an hour's time and three more cups of coffee Shirley was ready to join the elite of Cariboo at the Swept Wing's famous, at least around here, weekend breakfast/brunch buffet.

Snow had drifted against the garage door during the night and the electric opener struggled just a little pulling the door up. We climbed into my county SUV and backed down the driveway through a small blizzard as I checked to be sure the door closed again. The weather folks on TV this morning said this would last until about noon and then we could enjoy sunny but cold conditions for the rest of the weekend.

Shirley didn't question my use of the county vehicle so I figured she understood that this would be kind of a working breakfast/brunch.

We shook the snow from our coats and stomped it from our shoes as we went through the outer doors at the Wing. Once through the second set of doors the air was warm and welcoming with the aroma of fresh baked rolls. At the door to the dining room we were greeted by the hostess who took our coats and put them on hangers to dry.

"Good morning, Detective, Mrs. Halverson. As you can see, you have a lot of choices for seating this morning," she said.

The weather must have kept a lot of folks home this morning, because only about a quarter of the tables were in use. The buffet, however, was well stocked with steaming trays of almost anything you could imagine eating for breakfast. Well except, there was no cold pizza in sight.

"Thanks, Margaret," I said. "I think we'd like to sit way over there by the door to the bar. That way I can get some exercise walking back and forth to get my food."

My table of choice also gave me a full view of fellow diners, as well enabling me to see who was coming and going in the bar area. We made our first trek to the buffet and returned to our table with our undersized dishes loaded with enough calories to keep us warm for a week. Not bad for the first trip.

Looking around the room I was surprised by what appeared to be a number of mothers with their children. Shirley commented, saying, "It looks like all the dads are out hunting this morning."

"Too cold to take the wife and kids out today," I said as if I had figured it out myself.

Most of these families were not gun club hunters but were regular folks here for an outing that usually would involve the whole family. Hopefully the predicted afternoon sun would make it comfortable enough so they could all enjoy their weekend adventure.

One of the waitresses stopped at our table and asked, "Coffee, tea, Champagne, bloody Mary? The Champaign, at least the first glass, comes with the buffet as does the coffee or tea."

"We'll each have a Champagne," Shirley said smiling at me. And one cup of coffee, black, please."

As the girl went off to fill our order I said, "I can't drink any Champagne this morning. I have to keep as many of my wits as I can muster with me."

"I know," Shirley said. "The coffee is for you, the free Champagne is for me. Now, how about another trip to the buffet?"

The waitress brought our drinks as we were once again returning to our table with another truck load of food. She set the coffee in front of my plate and the two glasses of Champagne in front of Shirley and gave her a wink.

"How did you know to do that?" I asked.

"My mom's a teacher," she said. "And it's Saturday. And you should be working on finding Cheryl's killer, Detective. Not drinking Champagne."

"You were friends with Cheryl?" I asked.

"Probably the only real friend she had here at the Wing," she replied.

"Why do you say that?" I asked.

"Most of the girls resented her. She was no raving beauty, but for some reason she attracted the guys like she was a magnet and they were some kind of metal. Men would ask to be seated in her section of the dining room, and she always got the biggest tips. The other girls were afraid to bring their boy friends in, worrying that some how she would lure them away."

"But you didn't worry," I looked at her name tag," Sylvia, why not?"

"Because I was attracted to her also. Do I need to explain?"

"No, I guess not. Just how close where you two?" I asked.

"Just friends. I don't think she knew, or if she did, cared about my life style. We were friends and I miss her."

With this she turned away and walked toward the kitchen. I saw her bring her hand up to her face and could see her drying her eyes.

I was finishing up my second plate of food and contemplating a trip to the pastry section when Jerome Dumas, the Wing's general manager approached our table.

"Hal, Mrs. Halverson, I hope you are enjoying your breakfast. Be sure you take all you can eat. It's a small crowd this morning and I hate to have anything thrown away."

"If I keep eating like this Jer', I'll have to rent a room and take a nap," I said.

"No problem, Hal, we've got lots of 'em. Stay for the day and have dinner here tonight."

"And then what, Jer'? Stay for the night and have another breakfast tomorrow?"

"Sure, Hal, and then you could catch the Seahawks game in the bar...Hell, you'd never have to leave the place."

"Sounds like the perfect retirement. Unfortunately though, I'm not retired and Shirley has to prepare for another week of teaching. Maybe in a few years."

"Actually, Hal, I wanted to stop by and tell you the Wing is opening the High Flyers room for a reception after the memorial tomorrow. We'll have coffee, punch, some snacks and a no host bar. I hope to see you there."

"I wouldn't miss it Jerome. That's very thoughtful of you."

In my mind I'm thinking, "Good, more time to observe the mourners."

Soon after Jerome left our table, and before I could haul my posterior out of my chair and hit the pastry table, Sylvia re-appeared coffee carafe in hand, and asked, "Anything I can get you?"

"Maybe just a little of that coffee for both of us," I said. "And," I continued, "if you don't mind, one more question about Cheryl."

"Ask away detective, I'd like to help."

"Do you think there was enough dislike for Cheryl or, anyone working here jealous enough to wish her harm?" I asked.

"That's hard to say. Resentment can run awfully deep without it showing on the surface. I do know that my squeeze didn't like for me to get too friendly with Cheryl, even though she was obviously straight."

"Your squeeze?" I asked. "Who might that be?"

"Sorry," she said. "You're the Detective. You'll have to find out for yourself."

With that, she left our table without filling our cups. It seemed I had a knack for upsetting the girl.

Shirley spoke up at that point, "I think you may be pushing the girl a little too hard, Hal. I think she wants to help but it'll have to be at her speed. And I think she has more to tell you."

"So taking her down to headquarters and using the rubber hose is not recommended? You sure know how to spoil guy's fun."

"You have that gleam in your eyes, Hal, that means you've just thought of something," she said.

"Yeah, I just remembered the pastry table."

As I waddled toward the pastries I thought, "Maybe I already know her squeeze."

There seemed to be a rise in the noise level, and I looked up from my plate to see men entering the dining room from the lobby. Some joined families already eating, some took tables in numbers of two three or four, and others walked by our table headed for the bar. Looking at the number of red noses and ear tips, I had no doubt that the cold must have shortened this morning's hunt.

After giving the newcomers time to fill their plates and sit back down at their tables, I told Shirley I was going to leave her alone for a couple of minutes and not to eat my stuff while I was gone. She said, "We'll see. Depends on how hungry I get in your absence."

I started with the table of four nearest the entrance. "Gentlemen," I said showing my detective's shield. This got me four stares that said no to anything I was selling.

"You are no doubt aware of the death of one of the waitresses from the Wing last week." Still not a blink or a nod. I continued, "We have several persons of interest in the case but have made no arrests as yet."

I pulled a wad of business cards from my jacket pocket and at the same time fumbled my cell phone to the floor. After eating all I did in the last hour I hoped not to pass gas as I bent over to pick it up. First impressions are important, you know. Managing to keep everything within me, I gave each of the stone faces a card and asked, "If you were here last week, and can think of anything that may have any bearing at all on our finding her killer, please call me."

I repeated my plea, carrying my phone in a different pocket than my cards, at the rest of the tables occupied by men only. At the family tables I asked the man present if he had been here last weekend. If he said yes, I asked that if he was aware of the unusual incident that occurred Saturday night and had any information regarding it to please call me. The wives looked suspicious but the kids had no idea what I was doing there.

As I went by Shirley on my way to cover the men in the bar, she looked a little uncomfortable. "I told you not to eat my stuff," I said.

She just groaned and took a another sip of Champagne. Where did that come from? Sylvia must be plying her with alcohol. I decided to keep an eye on those two.

I was giving my spiel to the men in the bar when it occurred to me that I hadn't as yet encountered Mr. Langley. Why would he be skipping breakfast? Or had he just skipped altogether?

Exiting the bar, I saw that the check for breakfast was on our table. Shirley took my hand and asked, "Please help me up and take me home. I think I may have eaten enough for now."

I put enough cash on the table to cover the tab plus twenty percent and gently helped Shirley to her feet. As I looked down at her trim five foot two size, I knew judging from the cubic feet of food she had consumed, she had to be a little uncomfortable. Where could it be hidden in there?

By now my own load had somewhat stabilized so I was able to assist her with her coat and out the door with the minimum of internal turmoil. Once out in the cold air of the parking lot she turned to me and said, "that was fun. Lets do it again tomorrow,...Belch."

Once I had Shirley home, lying comfortably on the couch with the gas log burning and the stereo tuned to an oldies station, I headed back to the Wing to ask a few more questions.

Karen was on duty when I re-entered the lobby, and flashed me a big smile as I approached the front desk.

"Heard you and the Mrs. had breakfast with us this morning. Get enough to eat?"

"I'd groan but it wouldn't be very manly," I replied.

"A lot of guys do worse things than that and seem to think it's macho," she said.

"All flatulence aside, anything unusual or exciting happening here this morning?" I asked.

"With the exception of Detective and Mrs. Halverson having dined here, not really," she said.

"I didn't see Mr. Langley at breakfast. He hasn't checked out, has he?" I asked.

"No, but his friend that was with him here last week, Mr. Crawford, called looking for him. I put him through to Mr. Langley's room and the call was answered"

"About what time was that," I asked

"Just after all the mighty hunters returned this morning. You were still in the dining room with Mrs. Halverson."

"Would you mind telling me which room is Mr. Langley's?"

"Of course not. His usual, 207," she replied.

"Tell me Karen, does that room have a door connecting to room 205?"

"If we rent the two rooms as a suite we open the connecting doors. Otherwise, each room has its own locked door," she replied.

"So if I had keys to both rooms I could unlock the two doors and connect them?"

"I guess so, but that would be none of our business. We turn a blind eye to lots of things as long as no one seems to get hurt. The days of a hotel detective checking to see who is sleeping with whom disappeared way back when."

"One more question Karen. How well do you know Sylvia, the girl that waited on us this morning?"

"I know her but we aren't friends. She seems really nice but she belongs to, shall we say, a different social group than me."

"Do you recall ever seeing her with Mrs. Mallory?" I asked.

"Not that I can remember, but they're both around the hotel a lot, and I probably wouldn't have paid them any attention if I had," she answered.

After a second or two she exclaimed, "My God Hal, You're not saying..."

"No I'm not. And if I did it would be none of our business, just like the connecting rooms.

"Karen," I asked. "Do you ever worry about knowing the things you do about the people around you?"

"Do you think I should?" she asked.

"I don't know for sure. Does anyone else here know all the dirt on your clientele? "

"Probably. I think most of us entertain ourselves by seeing how people act when they think there's no one of consequence around. Ramon's crew probably knows more about the people that stay here than I do. A lot of folks act as if those silent Latinos don't even exist."

Guests were beginning to come through the lobby carrying and towing luggage from the direction of their rooms. Check out time, and Karen was going to be busy for a while. I thanked her and headed toward the stairs. Maybe using them would start the calorie burn needed after this morning's indulgence. Half way to the second floor I regretted my ambitious decision, but there was no turning back now.

As I did yesterday morning, I turned to the left at the top of the stairs. Today I knocked on the second door on the right, 207. As I waited, willing my heart beat and breathing to return to normal, I could hear muffled sounds of a conversation through the door. When the door opened, there stood Mr. Langley, dressed casually but not in the hunting outfit I would have expected.

"It sounded like you were talking to someone when I knocked," I said. "Am I interrupting something Mr. Langley?"

"I feel like you are interrupting my life every time I see you coming, Detective. But no, I just finished a telephone call."

"Clients Mr. Langley? Have they intruded on your weekend to the point that you didn't hunt this morning?" I asked.

"I chose not to freeze my ass off sitting in a duck blind this morning. I hunt for fun not to prove how much of a man I am, and it's not like I need to depend on the meat to survive. I'd rather be a Vegan than have to eat some of those damn ducks."

"You just enjoy shooting things?"

"Yeah, I'm not proud of it but we all do things at times that may seem uncivilized. I guess if they could shoot back, I'd find another way to escape the world of lawyering."

"While we're on the subject of lawyering, have you heard from your client Mr. Crawford lately?"

"Why do I think you already know the answer to that question, detective," he asked. "He was worried about getting his car 'serviced' today. I told him that as long as he was innocent of any crimes he had nothing to worry about. Then he told me that your victim had ridden in his car several times last summer and he was afraid that something might be found linking him to the girl. I told him that you already knew about the relationship, and that unless they found some sign of a recent struggle or something that could be positively dated for last weekend, his status regarding the case wouldn't change.

"Now, Detective, when are you going to stop badgering my client and me, and go find the killer?"

"All badgering will cease as soon as I have a conviction for this case," I replied.

"Is there anything else, Detective. The sun has come out and I'd like to go shoot something"

"Just one question, Mr. Langley. Is Mrs. Mallory a lesbian?"

"I'd like to think that's why we haven't been intimate, Detective. I think she's what's known as a 'switch hitter'. I just haven't been able to get her over to my side of the plate. Now, if you will excuse me," and, he closed the door without even inviting me in.

I have to say that I was glad that my next stop was down hill from my present position.

"Hola, senor Detective, you are back. How may I be of service?"

"Ramon, I have come to believe that you and your staff of workers probably know more about what goes on in this hotel than anyone else including all of the non Latino staff and management combined. Am I correct?" I asked.

"That could be a fair assumption senor."

"In that case, I want to prevail upon you to have a meeting of all twenty of your staff in the employee's lunchroom at three o'clock this afternoon . And I want you to be there assuring all of them that it will be okay to answer my questions truthfully without fear of reprisal. After you make that assurance, I intend to interview each person individually in private and then release them to continue their duties. They will not be able to talk with any other member of your staff until I have completed my interviews."

"That will be very difficult to arrange, senor. I doubt it can be done as you say."

"Then I will ask for help from the INS as well as the Washington State Patrol Narcotics Bureau. I'm sure they'll be interested in working with us," I replied.

"Oh, no need to do that senor. I will have them there at three."

I waved to Karen at the front desk as I slipped past and into the manager's office. I wanted to tell Jerome my plan for the afternoon, in case he had to rotate any of the hotel staff that wasn't involved..

"How the hell did you manage to set that up, Hal? I've never been able to get Ramon to assemble any of his crew for any kind of a meeting. He always insisted on handling all communications with them himself."

"Oh, I just smiled and said please," I said." Maybe you haven't been approaching him in a way that he understands. You know, language barrier and all that."

"You didn't threaten him, did you?" he asked.

"No," I said. "I only offered to provide some help if he didn't think he could accomplish what I was asking."

There was bright sunshine reflecting off the piles of snow in the corners of the parking lot as I walked toward my county owned SUV. I had just pushed the unlock button on the key fob when my cell phone started ringing. After searching the normal pocket of my jacket I remembered moving my phone this morning and grabbed it out of the other pocket just as it went to voice mail. I got in the car, started the motor and punched the 1 on the phone. It very politely told me that I had no mail in my mail box. Half way between the Wing and my office I heard the little chime noise that indicates I have a voice mail. I decided to show that phone a thing or two and waited until I was seated at my desk before I punched the 1 again.

It was Ross Taylor, my State Patrol friend over at the lab in Seattle, asking me to call him when I had the chance.

He answered before the third ring, "Hi, Hal."

"Hello again, Ross. I really appreciate you doing this for me. I owe you big time."

"An eighteen year old single malt should do the trick, Hal, and I'll even share it with you."

"You are truly a gentleman, Ross. Now, how did our boy do today?"

"According to the staff here, he arrived at nine fifty four this morning looking a little the worse for wear, you know, a bad hair day maybe. I guess he hadn't expected to have his car 'serviced' today. While they went over the car, he paced the parking lot talking to someone on his cell phone."

"Find anything interesting? I asked.

"A couple of moldy french fries under the front seat and some strands of hair on the passenger side head rest. We dusted the passenger side and the back seat area for fingerprints and there are some that may match your victim but they appear to be under others. My guess is that they were from last summer's little fling.

"If he's your guy, I doubt anything happened in this car. If it was completely clean I would be more suspicious."

"Thanks, Ross. I'll talk to you Monday. That's when we are supposed to hear about the DNA sample."

"Don't have to wait Hal, the paperwork is here and ready and I can tell you, unofficially of course, he's not the papa."

"In that case, your work is not finished, Ross. I'm getting two more samples tomorrow and we'll currier them to your lab by Monday morning."

"I'll be ready and waiting, Hal. Talk to you later."

After my conversation with Ross, I filled my time doing some of the dreaded paper work I had put off since the beginning of this case nearly a week ago. Actually, now that everything is entered in to the computer rather than being typed, corrected and typed again, the hardest part of the procedure is reading my own notes.

At two thirty I grabbed my trusty little recorder, checked to be sure it was charged up, and headed back to the Wing.

The employee lunchroom was alive with voices chattering loudly in a language I barely knew. So often when I hear a conversation in Spanish it sounds like someone is getting an ass chewing, but I've been told by my Latino acquaintances that it isn't necessarily so. When Ramon noticed me standing in the doorway he said just one word and the room became quiet. His control of these people was almost scary.

"Hola again, senor. We are all here as you requested and I have told them they may truthfully answer any questions you may ask without fear of any punishment."

"Gracias, Ramon," I said , revealing my total vocabulary.

Facing the gathering I began, "I wish to interview you one at a time in the pantry. The door will be closed so no one but myself will know the answers you provide to my questions. When I have completed your interview, you will exit through the kitchen door into the hallway, and leave the area without talking to anyone remaining in this room. With your cooperation we'll get this done quickly and you may go on about your business as usual. Any questions?"

Ramon spoke up. "In what order do you wish them, senor?"

"Completely up to you Ramon. As you see one exit, send in the next person. Now, may I have two chairs and that small folding table brought into the pantry?"

A couple of words in Spanish from Ramon and I had my interview room set up.

Each of Ramon's crew wore a picture ID tag with the employee's name and a corresponding number, as did the rest of the hotel staff. My notes and recording would take note of the number only. If needed, I could always have Ramon supply me with a name. I felt sure that he had many of them available.

My first interviewee was a young man that I recognized as the parking lot monitor who supplied me with the information about Miss Collins leaving the lot and heading east, rather than west toward her home. I explained my rules pertaining to this interview.

"I'm Detective Halverson from the Adams County Sheriff's Department. I am going to ask you a few questions about your work, and your observations here at this hotel. I'm recording our conversation on tape, as well as making notes on the paper pad you see on the table. Unless you tell them, none of your fellow employees or Ramon will know what you have told me during this interview. You may be completely truthful without fear of reprisal. However, should I find out at any time, that you have lied to me, I will come down on you like a ton of bricks and you will probably find yourself on an INS bus headed to Mexico. Any questions before we begin?"

"Senor Detective, what is this word 'reprisal,'' he asked.

"Punishment, just as Ramon explained to you earlier," I replied.

"Okay, senor," he said as I jotted his ID number on my note pad.

I then read his number aloud for the recorder and began the first of twenty interviews.

"Did you know Cheryl Collins? I asked"

"Si. She was a moza, a waitress in the dining room."

"How well did you know her?"

"Only to say hola, hello, when she went to and from her car, senor."

"Did you ever see her come or go other than when she was alone? I asked.

"Si. Three or four times last summer she left the hotel with that gas and oil man. Then later, return, get in her car and leave."

"Gas and oil man? What do you mean by that?" I asked.

"I was curious, so I ask Ramon about him. He said he was here to sell gas and oil to the ranchers around here. Ramon didn't like him. He said he not respect the housekeepers."

"Did you ever notice anything you would call unusual about her coming and going?"

"Only that sometimes on Saturday she would go after work and come back in noche, near dark. Most people work here go and stay away 'till they have to be back at work. She come back last Saturday, too bad. Maybe if she had stayed home..."

"Did you ever notice her with anyone else in the parking lot?" I asked.

"Only to say hello in passing someone she may know."

"Any that you would remember?"

"Only that preacher's wife."

"Preacher's wife? How do you know about her?"

"I can't say senor. Ask Ramon, he knows her," he said.

"This preacher's wife, did you ever notice her out there with anyone else?"

"Si, another waitress from the dining room, Sylvia. They would sometimes meet in the parking lot and talk. Sometimes it sounded like arguing. None of my business so I walk to other end of lot," he said.

"Do you remember when this happened last?"

"A week ago, maybe more, senor'"

"Do you recall ever seeing Cheryl and Sylvia together?" I asked.

"A few times. It looked like their shifts had ended and they were leaving at the same time."

"Did they ever leave in the same car?"

"No, senor. Not that I know of."

"Do you remember Sylvia ever leaving after her shift and then returning to the hotel later in the day?"

"Only once that I remember, senor."

"Do you remember when that was?" I asked

"I think it was last Saturday," he answered.

"What kind of shifts do you work?" I asked.

"There are three of us that watch the parking lot. We have twelve hours on, and twenty four hours off."

"Isn't that an awful long shift?" I asked.

"Its not really like working , senor. All we do is watch things. We don't have to pick crops or clean up after people. Pretty soft as long as nothing bad happens to anyone's car. If something bad happens, the person on duty will no longer have a job with Ramon."

"For your sake amigo," I said. "I hope nothing bad happened last Saturday night in your parking lot."

I gave him a business card, told him to call me if he thought of anything I should know, and dismissed him. One down, and nineteen to go.

My voice was worn out, the recorder batteries needed a charge and my ass felt like it had been sitting in this god-awful chair for days, when interviewee number eighteen came into the pantry and sat down. I wrote down her employee number, gave her my little talk about honesty and started my questions.

"What is your job here at the hotel?"

"I am doncella, maid, on second floor, sir," she answered.

"What exactly are your duties?" I asked.

"I take care of rooms 201 to 231."

"Isn't that a lot of rooms for one person?"

"No sir. I only have the odd numero rooms. Sixteen, enough for eight hours work."

"Did you know Cheryl Collins?"

"Si, she bring leftover pastries up to us each morning she work. I think she reason I'm so grande, fat, senor. Nice lady, very pretty."

"Did you ever see her visit any of the rooms in your area?"

"No sir. She only talk to us a little in our language, and go back to dining room where she work."

"Now this is a sensitive area," I said. "Remember, no one will know how you answer this question. Do you recall seeing anything unusual, or what you may think of as immoral in your area of the hotel?"

"What is this' immoral' sir?"

"Something that you may believe is sinful, such as married folks meeting with people other than their spouses," I replied.

"This is a hotel, senor. Things go on here that are none of my business. If it is not against the law, I think none of your business too."

Saying this she slid to the front of her chair as if to make me understand better her feelings on the matter.

" Okay, okay!" I said. "I admire your loyalty to your guests, and you're right. Normally, if it isn't against the law, it is none of my business. However, I believe that one or more of those improper relationships may have something to do with Cheryl's murder.

"Now, I'll ask you about specific persons. If you have any knowledge of them please answer my questions. Understand?"

"Si," she said, easing back to a more relaxed position.

"Mrs. Mallory," I said. Does that name mean anything to you/"

"Room 205 at least once a week," she replied.

"Mr. Crawford? Does that name sound familiar.?"

"I hear name last summer. He stayed here for several weeks but on first floor. Girls there say he big flirt. He had thing for Cheryl, I think."

"Sylvia, a waitress in the dining room?" I asked.

"She visit Mrs. Mallory sometimes. Mrs. Mallory a preacher's wife. I think she give Sylvia some kind lessons. Last Saturday she go home and come back to visit. Loud argument that day."

"Did you ever see Ramon go to Mrs. Mallory's room?"

"Oh no. She go to Ramon's office some times. Bring back package."

"Mr. Langley?" I asked.

"Room 207 each weekend this fall. Hunter, has shotgun in room."

"When you clean the rooms, do you ever find the connecting doors between 205 and 207 open?"

"None of my business and not against law!" she said.

I thanked her for her time and told her that she was the kind of person that would be a good friend.

The final two persons interviewed provided nothing additional to my meager accumulation of knowledge, and the only person left in the lunchroom when I exited the pantry was Ramon.

"I hope this was not a waste of our time, senor. Did you find out anything that may help find your killer?" he asked.

"Maybe, maybe not," I replied.

"While I have you here, Ramon, I'd like to ask you a question."

"Si, what is it senor?"

"How well do you know Mrs. Mallory?"

"We do business, Detective, that is all," he replied.

"And is that business confined to supplying her with a certain agricultural product, Ramon?"

"Si, I have no interest in becoming involved with anything else but my job here at the hotel, and my small marketing of farm products. I assume you are aware of my arrangement with Captain Ryan."

"Yes, I am aware of your, so called, arrangement, I answered. "But I don't necessarily agree with Captain Ryan's philosophy. Consider yourself as being on probation as far as I'm concerned. You help me and my opinion could be influenced."

"But Captain Ryan is your boss and your friend, senor. Shouldn't you go along and get along?"

"Who do you think would take Captain Ryan's place," I asked, "if he was to be found guilty of helping you with your business?"

"You, senor?"

"Si, Ramon. Think about it."

With that, I walked out of the room, down the hallway to the lobby and out the front doors. It was quite cold as I sat in my car punching in Sam's private number.

He answered on the third ring. "Hal, what's up.? did you learn anything useful with your interviews today?"

"Maybe, but I have to tell you about my conversation with Ramon just now, in case he comes to you with his version of the story."

I told Sam how I had bluffed Ramon into a corner and asked that he please back me up.

"No sweat, Hal. Although, sometimes you scare me with your ability to gain leverage on people."

I assured him that the leverage wasn't going to be used against him in any way, and that I wouldn't have his job under any circumstances. At least unless it paid a whole lot of money, and I knew it didn't.

Shirley was still on the couch when I got home, but now she was upright and wearing a pair of sweats.

"Hi, Shir'" I said. "How was your day?"

"I don't remember most of it. Must have been something I ate," she mumbled. How 'bout a nice light salad for dinner?"

"Sounds good to me," I told her. "And I stopped by Tony's Pizza on the way home and got a nice healthy chicken pizza to go with it."

"Perfect," she moaned.

9.
SUNDAY, NOVEMBER 5

Sunday morning arrived without a cloud to be seen. The blue of the sky and the pristine white of yesterday's snow were almost blinding when I opened the blinds at the kitchen window. What a fine day for a funeral. The ground will be frozen hard though, so Mr. Thomas' preference for cremation and plane lacquered pine box for her ashes seemed logical. Although I would rather have the body as a whole available until I had a conviction, just in case.

Shirley and I enjoyed an unusually relaxed morning, sleeping past dawn, reading the Sunday paper and eating the last of the chicken pizza.

About ten o'clock I broke the news to Shirley that I wanted her to accompany me to the memorial service at two this afternoon. She tried to beg off, claiming to have papers to correct and planning to do for school on Monday. I told her that I needed those 'school marm' eyes that she claimed to have in the back of her head. Besides, I saw her stuff all packed up neatly and standing by the door to the garage ready for tomorrow morning.

"No one likes to attend memorial services," I told her, "but you're so good at reading people that you could be big help to me. Also, It'll give you a good reason to wear that black dress that you look so terrific in. And since you'll be all dressed up anyway, we can dine with the 'in crowd' at the Wing afterward."

"You had hooked me at 'my ability to read people'. Then you reeled me in with the black dress bit," she said. "You didn't need to add dinner. Nice touch though."

"Just one little thing," I said. "I have business at the office at one o'clock and will have to meet you at the funeral home. Will you be okay with that?"

"Now dinner may be required, but okay."

There was a time, when I was younger, that I had what I called my wedding clothes, reserved for those times you got together with family and friends from near and far to celebrate with the new couple. Today backing the county car out of my garage at about noon, I was wearing my funeral clothes, worn more and more often as my generation aged.

The weekend duty rooster is small on Sunday afternoon, so there were only four people at the office needing to hear my plan. I told them about the suspects that would be arriving, one under an informal escort and the others, a man and wife. The men would have swabs taken to send to the lab for DNA testing. I told them that I wanted to be sure the two groups saw each other, but to keep them in separate rooms so they have no interaction. I asked them to observe the suspects for any reactions.

Mr. Thomas, wearing what must have been a thousand dollar charcoal suit, arrived with his escorts at about ten before one. CJ was wearing a slightly rumpled dark blue suit and Carlos had on black jeans, black cowboy, boots and a black sport coat over a black shirt and tie.

CJ and Carlos were immediately impressed when I showed them into Sam's office with his window and everything. When I told them that we were borrowing the boss's office and that my space was next door they seemed a little more at ease.

I seated Mr. Thomas on a chair that was facing the open door and opened up the DNA kit that I had put on the desk earlier. I thanked him for his cooperation as I was running the swab around the inside of his mouth.

"I did not agree to this, and it is a complete surprise," he exclaimed when I had removed the swab. "I told you that I didn't care to know who the father of Cheryl's baby was."

I explained that I wanted to know, and that I wouldn't tell him the results of the DNA test unless it became necessary to prosecute him. Then I asked him to sign an affidavit stating that we had his permission to take the sample. If not I would get a judge to work things out tomorrow or the next day. Meanwhile, he would be staying with us while we waited. He signed the affidavit with CJ and Carlos as witnesses.

We were sitting there in Sam's office exchanging more pleasantries when there was a commotion in the hallway and Doctor and Mrs. Mallory passed by the open door walking toward my office.

"What the hell is that lunatic doing here, Detective?" Mr. Thomas shouted. "Have you arrested him for Cheryl's murder? If you haven't you probably should. He's a creepy old pervert and shouldn't be allowed in public."

"He's here for the same thing you are, Mr. Thomas. I want to know if he could be the father. If he is, you could be off the hook."

"I'd rather be 'on the hook' than to find out that he was ever intimate with her, Detective. That's disgusting!"

"Thank you for your sample and your opinion, Mr. Thomas," I Said. "Your two friends here will take you to the funeral home now."

I guided them out of Sam's office, turning left so they would walk by the open door to my office on the way to the side door of the building. As we passed my door I thought I may have heard a gasp and some exclamations. I'd have to hear about them later.

After seeing them into the parking lot I went to my office where the deputy there was just finishing up with the DNA swab.

"Good afternoon, Doctor, Mrs. Mallory. Thank you for coming by on your way to the memorial. I know you are probably anxious to get to the funeral home, and I hope Deputy Jones here has been attentive to your needs. Do you have any questions?"

"Just why are we here, Detective, and what is the reason for the DNA sampling from Doctor Mallory?" Mrs. Mallory asked.

"I'm trying to determine the father of Miss Collins' unborn child, Mrs. Mallory, in order to either broaden or narrow the scope of my investigation."

"And you think that Doctor Mallory could be that person? That's absurd. He's been impotent for longer than I care to remember."

"Grace! Must we discuss private matters in front of these people?" the Doctor asked. "And, Detective, it is my opinion that the father is very likely the man that just walked by the door here."

"Really Doctor? Which man was that?" I asked.

"The tall, well dressed man with the mustache. I observed him several times at Miss Collins' home. It is my opinion that they were committing sinful acts while he was there."

"You observed them doing sinful acts Doctor?" I asked.

"Why no, of course not. I just assumed, with all of the comings and goings and what not."

"What about you, Mrs. Mallory?" I asked. "Do you have an opinion on the subject?"

"I know little about the girl, Detective and care less about her conduct as long as it doesn't have any bearing upon my personal life."

"So, she had no effect on any part of your life Mrs. Mallory?" I asked."

"None whatsoever", she replied.

"Doctor, please sign this affidavit that says you submitted to this test voluntarily and you folks are free to go, for now," I said. "I'll see you at the memorial."

Another affidavit in my file. These people are all so helpful.

Shirley was waiting just inside the main entrance to the funeral home when I arrived, and the look in her eyes would freeze salt water.

"Hi, Shir'," I said boldly. "Been waiting long?"

"Only long enough to check out the floral arrangements," she answered.

I stole a look into the room where the service would be held and saw only two bunches of flowers. Unfortunately, one of them looked kind of familiar.

The twenty or so people in the room were sort of milling around waiting for things to start, so it didn't seem too strange when Shirley led me to the familiar looking arrangement and showed me the card. 'For Miss Cheryl from Mama San'.

By now I knew where I had seen the same arrangement, and was working on a plausible story when Mama San herself walked up to us.

"Hello Mrs. Sheriff, Mr. Sheriff. You like flowers? After seeing flowers Mr. Sheriff order from me waaaay back last week for anniversary, I think they so pretty so I get same for Miss Cheryl. I hope okay?" she asked.

"Of course it's okay," my thawing wife said. "They are quite beautiful."

When Shirley stopped to talk with some of her past students that now worked at the Wing, she had her back to Mama San. Mama San pointed at me, made a small circle with her thumb and forefinger, pointed to herself and smiled. She then held up two fingers, then four fingers and then one finger. That woman should teach a sign language class.

We found seats in the rear of the hall on the right side where I could kind of see everyone, and as I settled in I couldn't help thinking that the person who said "The truth shall set you free," couldn't possibly have been married. Or maybe his wife did set him free. I'll bet that cost him.

I don't care if you barely knew the deceased, or didn't know them at all. If you are at all human, a memorial service has got to tug at your emotions. Maybe it's because as we look around at the other folks present, we realize that after a few days, or maybe a few weeks, most of them will go on with their lives as if the person being memorialized had never existed, and we're afraid that it will be the same at our own memorial. Fifty, sixty, seventy years or more, maybe less. Hard work, turmoil, sadness, accomplishments, happiness, all forgotten by but a few.

The gentleman conducting the service was a part time minister and full time employee of the local Farmer's Co-op. His small church, about ten miles east of town, was not financially capable of providing for full time clergy and by working with the funeral home occasionally he could bolster the coffers a little. As he talked about salvation and listed Cheryl's birth, death and other statistics, I looked around the room taking mental note of who was present, and by trying to read body language, who was mourning Cheryl's untimely death.

Mr. Thomas and his escort were the only people in the front row on the right. He was looking down and occasionally I could see him reach up and dab his eyes.

Front row left was Mrs. Perkins, Sylvia and three other girls that I recognized as Waitresses from the Wing. Mrs.

Perkins was nodding as if in full agreement with what ever the presiding reverend was saying. The girls were, from time to time, bringing handkerchiefs to their faces.

Second row left was Ramon, the girl that was in charge of rooms 201 through 231 (odd numbers only), and four other girls that I had interviewed yesterday. Immediately behind them sat the parking lot monitor who supplied me with so much information, and two other young men I reasoned were the other two lot attendants. All of the Latino males sat erect, crossing themselves at what must have been the appropriate times, and showing no outward signs of emotion. Very macho, while the girls were visibly a little shaken.

In the second row right, sat a man and a woman that I didn't know. Unusual for this small town and I decided I would introduce myself as soon as I could, after the service.

Leon, our local automotive guru, and his wife, were in the third row right as were two men I recognized as mechanics from his shop.

Sole occupants of the fourth row left were the Reverend Doctor Mallory and his wife. Impeccably dressed and checking her wrist watch from time to time, she seemed a little out of place among the mourners.

Much to my surprise, in the fourth row right, sat Mr. Langley and two men I recognized from my tour of the tables in the dining room yesterday morning. Call me a skeptic, but I could only assume they were all lawyers ready to pounce on anyone that I showed undo interest in. Or maybe they were here to defend each other. An interesting thought.

Mama San was in the fifth row left along with Jerome, the Wings general manager, and his wife, as well as Karen the girl from the front desk.

Directly in front of us in fifth row right, looking uncomfortable in their shirts and ties, were the two men who had discovered her body, Nate and Jeremy. Accompanying them were two equally uncomfortable but solemn young men. Hopefully I would have the privilege of meeting them before the day was over.

Shirley and I were the only occupants in the sixth row, left or right.

When the minister finished with what he wanted to say about Cheryl, he asked if anyone wished to add anything before he concluded the service. Jerome stood up and announced that the Wing had a meeting area set aside for the rest of the afternoon and everyone was welcome to come and share memories of Cheryl. After that no one else seemed to have anything to say, so a woman I recognized as the choral director at the high school, began playing the piano and singing Amazing Grace. Damn song. Now she had me wiping my eyes.

As we slowly filed out from the back of the room into the entry area I couldn't help but notice how quickly Mr. Langley and his two cohorts spotted Mr. Thomas and approached him. Hands were shaken and business cards were given within seconds of the completion of the service. Wolves attracted by what they thought was the scent of blood. Then, the three dropped back rather suddenly and I caught the last of something being said by Carlos as he stepped between them and Mr. Thomas. The word sounded like 'jackals', but I couldn't be sure.

Shirley sauntered over to talk with mama San and I thought "This may not be good," as I approached the couple from the second row right.

"Hi, I'm Hal Halverson," I said. " I don't recall seeing you folks before. Do you live in the area?"

"No sir. I'm Brad Amos and this is my sister Ellen. We're here to represent our family. We own the place where Cheryl was living."

"So you grew up in this area?" I asked.

"Yes sir. In fact, Mrs. Halverson over there taught both of us in high school here in Cariboo."

"So, what are your plans now for the place?" I asked.

"We really don't know how to proceed from here. What do we do with her stuff? Is the sheriff's office through with the place and can we move on? Will anyone want to live there knowing what happened to Miss Collins?"

"Okay," I said." Let me be a little more specific about who I am. I'm Detective Halverson and I'm conducting the investigation of Miss Collin's murder. I would prefer that everything remain as it is until I have a conviction in this case. However, if it is a hardship for you to tie the property up for that length of time, you could have the court return control of the property to you.

"As for being rentable" I said. "Right now, I don't think that the murder took place on that property, and it is a nice spot. I'm sure you must have great memories of the place."

"Good and bad detective. A lot of hard work without much return financially. Still, a lot of love and humor in the family. Then dad got sick and the world just dissolved around us. Too much history to walk away from I guess."

"I'll do everything I can to make this as easy as possible for you," I promised. "Now, may I ask you a few questions?"

"Sure, detective."

"How well did you know Miss Collins?" I asked.

"I'm afraid not well at all," he answered. "We put the place for rent on Craig's List. She was the first person to respond to the ad and all of her references looked good, her deposit check cleared and that was that."

"Sounds like you hit the jackpot with her. The place looked well taken care of when I was out there last week."

"Yeah, we're going to miss her, but that sounds a bit mercenary, doesn't it. From all I've heard, she was a really nice person."

I handed each of them a business card and went seeking Nate and Jeremy's friends.

Shirley and Mama San were still chatting, hopefully exchanging recipes or something, as I walked by them trying to catch Jeremy before he and his group headed back to God knows where.

"Hey Jeremy. Hold up a second," I asked

"Hi, Detective," he said.

Although Jeremy stopped and turned around, the other three kept walking toward the exit. In fact, I think they started walking faster than before.

"How 'bout introducing me to your friends," I asked.

"Uh, sure," he said. "Hey guys, come back here and meet Detective Halverson. He's working on Cheryl's murder."

"As if they didn't know," I thought.

"Detective," Jeremy said. "This is Todd Franke and Charlie Hamm, and of course you already know ol' Nate here. As I said, guys, this is Detective Halverson."

We shook hands all around and it became quite obvious that none of these guys sat around an office all day lifting nothing heavier than a ball point pen.

After all the introductions, I said, "At ease fellows, I'm not here to pry into any of your lives except for what you might know about Cheryl, and why she was killed. I presume you were acquainted with her or you wouldn't be here, and also, that you would like to see whoever murdered her punished."

There was short series of 'yes sir's' so I kept on going.

"Now I'm goin' to make another assumption, and that is," I continued, "that you knew her because she would sometimes frequent the Thirsty Dog and share a dance or two with you. Am I correct?"

Another round of 'yes sir's'

"Good, we're making great progress here," I said kind of in jest. No laughs from the guys though.

"Now," I went on, "can any of you think of anything that may help me figure out who wanted her dead and why?"

Surprisingly, it was Nate who spoke up and said, "Sir, we all liked her a lot. She was pretty and friendly and we liked just talking to her when we weren't dancing. We all respected her and kinda' watched to be sure no one got pushy or fresh, although, I think each one us would have liked to take her home or have her to himself for a while."

"That's right, detective," this from Charlie. "The only time I remember anyone not being polite to her was when she came into the 'Dog' one night last summer with this city guy, a dude in clean pressed blue jeans and a hundred dollar haircut. He apparently didn't like her dancing with us country boys, threw a little bit of a hissy fit and took her away with him. Come to think about it, that's the last I remember seeing her."

"Do you remember when that was, Charlie," I asked.

"I think it was around the fourth of July," he replied.

"Do you recall ever seeing the city guy again?" I asked.

"I think he might have stopped at the Paulson ranch one day in, I think, August. I was working on one of ol' man Paulson's tractors and they was lookin' at the fuel tank out back of the equipment shed. I just got a glimpse of him and his hair. No hat in that hot sun. Must be trying to catch cancer."

"Thanks Charlie. Anyone else have anything to add?" All heads shaking no.

I gave them each a card and Jeremy gave me his back saying he already had one. "If you think of anything you believe I should know about Cheryl, give me a call," I said. "And remember, we're on the same side on this and I'm not interested in the rest of your lives as long as you're honest with me."

I heard a four part sigh of relief as they walked out the door headed for their pickup trucks.

Just as I was about to look for Shirley, she walked up behind me and put her arm through mine. "I've been talking with Mama San," she said, quite unnecessarily. She tells me that you keep asking her if she has any nice obedient daughters that would make a good wife."

Relieved that this had been the subject of their conversation I told her, "Actually, it was a nice 'young', obedient daughters that I was inquiring about. Maybe if I had left out the young part..."

"Are you planning on replacing me?" she asked.

"No, just trying to be prepared for when you realize what a poor bargain you made when you married me, and tell me to take a hike," I replied.

"Well you're not gonna take any hikes without me buster. That is, unless they're real hikes. In that case my feet get sore awfully fast and you can go by yourself. But without any nice young obedient girl!"

We were crossing the parking lot when I remembered that we had come here in two different cars.

"I'm going to the Wing to see if I can gather any more information," I said. "If you want, you can go on home. You've done your duty for today."

"Hah! I'll follow you there. Dinner, remember?"

"Just slipped my mind. Ride with me then. We'll come back for your car on the way home."

I was surprised by the number of people in the High Flyers room when we arrived. Far more than the thirty seven, or so, folks that were at the memorial. Looking around I saw more of Ramon's crew than were at the funeral home. Maybe they had to wait until their shift finished. Or maybe they were still on duty, but allowed to attend this gathering because it was held in the hotel. Either way, none were making use of the no host bar set up in a corner of the room.

Noticeably absent were the Doctor and Mrs. Mallory.

Noticeably present, and surprisingly so, were Mr. Langley and his two friends who were making use of the bar.

CJ and Carlos had Mr. Thomas at a small table in the far corner from the bar, but I saw that Mr. Thomas had a drink in front of him while his escorts were sipping coffee from hotel cups.

Shirley walked immediately over to Carlos who stood up to greet her and was actually blushing when Shirley gave him a big hug and a peck on the cheek. I thought, "Maybe I need to get serious about Mama San and her daughters."

This time it was Mr. Langley who approached me.

"Detective Halverson," he said, "allow me to introduce my colleagues, Henry Harper and Sean Grogan."

Once again, handshakes all around but with 'how do you do and, a pleasure' and much softer hands.

"All attorneys I presume," I said.

"You are a detective," Mr. Langley replied.

I wanted to tell them that I got their scent but I didn't. Must be those sensitivity classes the county sponsors.

"Were you two acquaintances of Miss Collins?" I asked.

Mr. Harper spoke up. "Not really. That is, we knew of her as a waitress in the dining room here, but never had any other contact."

"So, did you come to me to tell me something of significance regarding her murder?" I asked.

"No detective," this time from Mr. Grogan. "We were curious as to who paid for the service and internment. We understand that Miss Collins had no relatives that could be found."

"So you actually attended the service with only that question in mind. That sounds a little suspicious. Maybe you gentlemen should come down to my office where we can better talk about the situation," I said.

Mr. Langley now joined the conversation. "Oh come on, Detective, you know why we we're there. We're lawyers looking for clients. We figured there might be someone attending that we could help. We tried to be of assistance to the man from the front row that was obviously being escorted by two of your people, but that latter day 'Zorro' interfered."

"I'll pass your compliment on to officer Cruz. Here is my business card for each of you two newbie's. If I may have your cards in exchange please? I will tell you this: The sponsor of the service is anonymous and will stay so. Good day sirs."

Shirley had by now left the embarrassed officer Cruz and was circulating among Ramon's crew. Because of her long career as a teacher here in Cariboo, she always found someone she knew wherever we went.

As I approached Mr. Thomas I couldn't help but notice the three empty cocktail glasses on the table. "I hope those are yours, Mr. Thomas, " I said.

"Sure are, Detective," he slurred. "I got my own drivers today so I figured I might as well drown my sorrows."

"How's that working out?" I asked him.

"Not so well, but I'll keep trying if you'll join me," he replied.

"No thanks, but thank you for what you did for Cheryl today. Now I think it's time for you to head back home and for CJ and Carlos to get back to their families."

Turning to his escorts I said, "I can't thank you enough for your help today my friends. I know you didn't expect it, but you'll find something in the mail from the county this week."

"If I can twist Sam's arm far enough," I thought.

"Oh, one more thing, Mr. Thomas," I said. "I believe I'll be going over to Mill Creek this week. I want to know where your wife was last Sunday morning even if you don't care. Any messages you wish to send along?"

He just looked at me with his mouth open. No words came out.

As I left them I caught Shirley's eye and nodded toward the door. She got the not so subtle hint, disengaged herself from her present conversation and joined me in the hall.

"Since this is going to be sort of a date night for us," I said, why don't I drive you back to get your car, follow you home, leave my county car there and return in your car. That way I can have a little wine with dinner and not have to worry about being in the county rig."

"I've got a better idea," she said,. Why don't you take me to my car and then I'll follow you home and we'll stay there. We've got a great box of wine and some frozen lasagna. And then we'll cuddle in front of the fireplace."

"You had me at great box wine," I replied.

10.
MONDAY, NOVEMBER 6

Monday morning I was waiting in Sam's office when he arrived for work.

"This can't be good," where the first words out of his mouth. "Or can it? Have you figured out who to arrest for Miss Collins' murder?"

"Not exactly," I said. "I'm afraid I have a request for you"

"And what would that be?" he asked.

"I've had a great deal of help from two officers that don't belong to our department," I said. And I'd like to see them compensated for some of their time."

"They volunteered. Volunteers don't need to be compensated."

"Were you in the service, Sam?" I asked.

"Sure," he answered, served four years in the Navy. Why?"

"Did you get drafted, or did you volunteer?" I asked.

"Damn right I volunteered. Thought it was my duty."

"Did you get paid for those four years Sam?"

"Okay, I see where this is going. Just what do you propose?" he asked.

"Double time for yesterday as well as mileage for CJ's private car."

"Where the hell am I gonna get that out of our budget?"

"I know you have discretionary funds available for snitches and that sort of thing. Use some of that," I said. "Also, no FDIC or any of those crappy deductions."

"I can't do that. It would be illegal," he said.

"So is crossing the street in the middle of the block without a cross walk, or driving on tires with less than a sixteenth of an inch of tread. Need I go on?"

"Your point is well made, I'll see that it's taken care of. "Now, what's your next move on this?" he asked.

I explained that I had two more DNA samples on the way to the State Patrol lab in Seattle because I thought knowing who fathered the fetus would either narrow down or add to the number of people on my list of suspects.

"That doesn't make much sense to me," he said, "but you're the one running this case."

"Also, I'm more and more curious about Mrs. Thomas' whereabouts on that Saturday and Sunday. I think I should go over to Mill Creek and see what I can find out."

"I'll clear it with Mill Creek PD and our office," he said. "When do you want to go?"

"I'd like to head over this afternoon so I can get started first thing tomorrow morning."

"That should be doable. Anything else?"

"Yeah, I'm not sure how to approach Mrs. Thomas without messing up Mr. Thomas' life if he is innocent."

"Screw him," he said. "He made his own bed. Now let him sleep in it."

I knew Sam was right, but hoped maybe I'd come up with something on the three to four hour drive to the other side of the state.

Going on line I found that there were actually no hotels in Mill Creek so I opted for the Residence Inn in the Alderwood mall just off I-5 a few miles to the west. I used my county credit card and made reservations for tonight and possibly a few nights to follow.

I'd discussed the possibility of this trip with Shirley last night so all I had to do was tie up a few loose ends here at the office, go home and pack a bag, leave a note and head west on highway 26 toward Vantage where I would hit I-90. If Snoqualmie pass was clear of snow, and traffic wasn't too bad on the 405 through Bellevue, I should have a little time to look around in Mill Creek before dark.

Traffic was light on I-90 and the pass was bare and dry over the Cascade Mountain range. I was thinking, "A breeze of a drive," until I hit the interchange with the 405 and turned north toward Bellevue. I thought I'd hit less traffic on the east side of lake Washington than I would going through north Seattle. Boy was I wrong! The freeway here seemed to change from three to six lanes and back to three again so often that I decided to get into the far left lane so I wouldn't mistakenly be led off at an exit and into the unknown. My county SUV must have had 'country bumpkin' written on it somewhere because in spite of my antennas and all suggesting a law officer was driving, cars were zipping by me on the right traveling at least twenty miles per hour over the posted limit. I was also subjected to a number of obscene gestures.

I eventually worked my way over to the far right lane, and as I exited the 405 in a giant loop, I could see my hotel off to the west, but I was now going south with seemingly no hope of reaching my destination. I finally exited onto SW 196th Street, took a left on 28th Ave. West, and ended up on the Alderwood Mall parkway. This took me back north under I-5, past the 405 - I-5 exchange and right to the hotel. If it wasn't for my GPS I may have ended up in Portland or Vancouver, BC.

When I checked into my hotel, I asked for and received a free map of the area which included the town of Mill Creek. Once in my room, I laid the map on the bed and found a route to the address I was looking for that included only surface streets. As it was starting to get dark outside and I was still suffering from freeway shock, I decided to exercise my expense account with a steak at the Keg, a restaurant shown on my map as within walking distance to the north. I had survived to fight another day.

11.
TUESDAY, NOVEMBER 7

Seven AM found me having the complementary breakfast along with about a dozen other men. Everyone had selected their own table and all were either reading the morning paper or watching a television channel that was alternating between local news and traffic reports, both of which reinforced my decision to live in a small town.

Back in my room with a final cup of coffee, I once again checked my route on the map I was given, brushed my teeth, checked my shield and my service revolver, and decided it was time to visit Mrs. Thomas.

After crossing highway 527, 164th SE became Mill Creek Road and I was in a very upscale neighborhood. I turned left on Village Green Drive and left again on Country Club Drive. I felt just a little out of place. The only country club I ever belonged to was called a grange. There were no homes actually on Country Club Drive and the lady on my GPS told me to take the first left turn, then a right turn. I did so, traveled about a block or so in what appeared to be a circle and found my address on the right.

This home was every bit as impressive as Mr. Thomas' place in Moses Lake. I guess the Thomas' must have been buying shares of Microsoft back when I was buying peanut butter and sneakers.

I parked in the driveway, got out of the car and started toward the front door. Before I reached the porch, the door opened and a lady in a designer sweat suit stepped half way out. She had a what appeared to be a cup of coffee in one hand and a burning cigarette in the other. My first thought was, "How'd she open the door with both hands full?"

"You may as well turn yourself around, get back in your car and leave right now 'cause I aint buyn' what ever you're sellin'."

As I continued toward the porch I pulled my shield out of my jacket pocket and said, "Detective Halverson from the Adams County Sheriff's department."

She squinted and tried to read the inscription on the shield, then stepped back and said, "You sure go out of your way to investigate a little fender bender. What the hell you want with me?"

"Could we please step inside, Mrs. Thomas, I have a few questions I would like to ask."

"Hell no. How do I know you're not some pervert with a fake badge come to rape and rob me?" she asked.

I took my photo ID out of my pocket and handed it to her. "Please call the Mill Creek Police Department and they will verify my identity as well as tell you that I am authorized to question you regarding an ongoing investigation in Adams County. Once you have done so, please come back to the door and let me come in. Should you not return to and open this door within the next ten minutes I will consider you interfering with an investigation and have you arrested by the Mill Creek PD. Do I make myself clear, Mrs. Thomas?"

She took my ID, closed the door and six minutes later the door reopened and I was invited in.

"Come on back to the kitchen, Detective. I've got a fresh pot of coffee. Would you like a cup?" she asked

"No thanks, Mrs. Thomas."

"Could be poisoned," I thought.

"Well then, sit here at the table and tell me why you've come so far to see me," she said.

As I was wondering if someone had switched people after the door was closed, she handed me my picture ID and actually smiled. Unfortunately, the tobacco stained teeth spoiled the affect as did the whiff I got of alcohol on her breath. I was beginning to understand Mr. Thomas a little better.

"I'm investigating the death of an acquaintance of Mr. Thomas', ma'am and trying to clear Mr. Thomas from my list of people who may have had some bearing on that death."

"In other words detective, my husband is a murder suspect and you are here to gather evidence against him," she said.

"Not so, Mrs. Thomas. At present I really don't think he had anything to do with it, but I need to be sure."

"Where do I come in on all of his?" she asked.

"You may recall a phone call from my department last week regarding whether or not Mr. Thomas had spent time here with you a week ago Sunday."

"That was a phony traffic accident wasn't it Detective. George would never have left the scene of an accident."

"You're correct, Mrs. Thomas. I was merely trying to verify his alibi without causing any undo stress on your relationship. Your answer to my inquiry puzzled us somewhat, and so here I am, trying to figure things out.

"You claimed that you weren't home that Sunday morning. May I ask where you were?"

"Moses Lake, looking for my wandering husband, Detective. He wasn't there."

"Would you like to explain further?" I asked.

"That damn job over there in the boondocks. For the first six months or so he would come home every weekend that he had off. He'd be hornier than a billy-goat and we even slept in the same bed.

"Then he told me he was buying a house over there and he wanted me to move. I wasn't going to leave all of this to live in the middle of nowhere, so I told him I was staying here.

"His visits became less and less frequent and the ol' billy-goat was gone. I knew he must be screwing some bimbo over there, so I hired a private detective to find out what was going on."

"When was that Mrs. Thomas?" I asked

"Last summer, around the end of July.

"What did your detective find?"

"He was seeing some hussy that worked in a hotel in Cariboo. She'd pick him up at a park and ride in Moses Lake and take him to her place on some farm down toward Royal City. Then after they had their fun, she'd take him back to his car, and he'd go home. That bastard was cheatin' on me!"

"What was the reason for your visiting him last week?" I asked.

"To confront him with what I had learned. I wanted to see his face when I told him I wanted a divorce and it was gonna cost him."

"What happened?" I asked.

"I went to his swanky waterfront place and he wasn't home," she said.

"When exactly was that, Mrs. Thomas?"

"Sunday morning about eight o'clock. I figured he must have still been shacked up with his slut."

"What did you do then?" I asked

"My investigator had told me where the bitch lived, so I decided to catch them together and really give them both hell. I drove all the way over to 12 SW and was checking off addresses approaching her's, when I saw an older SUV of some make pull into what turned out to be her driveway. There was only one person in it, so I decided she must be returning from taking George to the park and ride."

"Could you describe the individual in the SUV, Mrs. Thomas?"

"I can only tell you that it looked like a woman because of the long hair. These days though, who knows?"

"What did you do then?"

"I figured if he wasn't there, I'd look pretty pathetic to whoever was, so I drove back to his house on the lake. He still wasn't home, and by now I decided I was being foolish and should just come back here and contact an attorney."

I asked her to look at a photo I had. I didn't tell her it was of Cheryl.

"Did the person driving look anything like this?" I asked.

"No. Not unless she had grown her hair much longer since the photo."

"Thank you, Mrs. Thomas. If you should think of anything else regarding that day that may help me determine where Mr. Thomas was from Saturday night through Sunday afternoon, please call me'" I said as I handed her my card.

"I think George might have been here while I was in Moses Lake, Detective."

"Why do you say that?" I asked.

"Dirty dishes in the sink when I got home Sunday night. I cleaned up before I left on Saturday and no one else would have left a mess for me."

"You say you went to Moses Lake on Saturday," I said. Where were you Saturday night?"

"I stayed at the Best Western Lakefront. I figured it was the closest to George's place. Ate at something called the El Rodeo. Closest sit down restaurant I could find. Mexican food, but not too bad. I was back in my room at the hotel before eight, sipped a little bourbon and watched TV 'til I fell asleep."

"You didn't leave the hotel after you returned about eight?" I asked. "I can check their parking security cameras but it would be better if you can think of anyone who can back up your story."

"I don't know anyone over there and didn't pay any attention to anyone. Why do I need to account for my time anyway, Detective?"

"Miss Collins, the girl your husband was seeing, was the acquaintance whose death I am investigating. She was murdered, Mrs. Thomas. I have every reason to consider you a prime suspect.

"Now, if you will please give me the license number of the car you drove to Moses lake last week, it will save me a little time in checking your story."

She did, I jotted it on my faithful 8-1/2 x 11 pad and asked, "Is there anything you wish to change about what we've talked about this morning?"

"No, Detective. And if you wish to ask me any more questions please contact me through my lawyer."

She then dug a business card out of a drawer and handed it to me. Damned if the name on it wasn't Robert Langley, Attorney At Law.

"I hired him to handle my divorce but I understand he does criminal defense as well," she said.

I asked, "Do you know if he has ever met Mr. Thomas?"

"I don't believe so," she answered. "Now please show yourself out and don't come back."

Electronically guided, I found my way back to the hotel, went to my room, and before I threw stuff back into my overnight bag, called Sam and filled him in on Mrs. Thomas. I then asked if he would please call the Best Western Lakefront up in Moses Lake, find out what room Mrs. Thomas had been in, and have them secure any parking lot and hallway security footage they may have from the Saturday night in question. Hopefully they would be more thorough than the Chevron in Ellensburg.

I'm afraid I don't much believe in coincidences and when someone's name pops up too often in an investigation I think it's time to take a closer look. I pulled Mr. Langley's card from my pocket and checked the address. It was in Bellevue. My only hope of finding it was, once again, my GPS.

The voice coming from my dashboard had me turn south as I left the hotel, then east, then north on I-5 and then east on the 405. Thoroughly confused, I stayed on the 405 through its interchange with SR 522 and south toward Bellevue. I was given ample notice for my exit, and managed, after going around one block three times, to find a parking space near the Law Offices of Harper, Grogan and Langley, Attorneys At Law.

Not having any change in my pocked for the meter, I set the Adams County Sheriff placard on the dashboard and hoped for the best.

The building I entered was all glass and steel, and at least twice as tall as any of our grain silos in Cariboo. I saw a bank of elevators, and as I was about to push a button on the wall with an arrow pointed up, a door opened right in front of me. I stepped into the elevator and no one followed so I pushed button number ten. There was a 'whoosh' sound and in less than a second I was, according to the sign in the elevator, on the tenth floor. My first thought was that I hoped I wouldn't get the 'bends' from the rapid ascent.

There was a sign on the wall opposite the elevators that indicated that the office I was looking for was down the hall to my right. Finding the door closed, I walked in without knocking and was greeted by an empty receptionist desk and waiting area.

The door must have had something on it that alerted the folks inside because, almost immediately Mr. Grogan stepped through another door and asked, "May I help you?"

He must not have recognized me because he appeared a little startled when I called him by name and asked to see Mr. Langley.

"Do you have an appointment?" he asked.

I looked around the empty office with its empty desk and asked, "Do I really need one?"

He crossed the room, knocked on a door and said, "Robert, someone is here to see you."

Within seconds Mr. Langley was standing in his doorway, straightening his tie and, upon recognizing me asked, "What the hell are you doing here? Sean, why didn't you just tell him I wasn't in?

"You're becoming a real pain in the ass Detective."

"Nice to see you again as well, Mr. Langley. Shall we go into your office and talk, or would you prefer to do this in front of all these folks?"

We retreated to his office and he sat down behind a very clean desk. Without being asked, I sat in an upholstered chair against the side wall rather than the hard wood one in front of the desk.

"What the hell is this all about Detective?"

"Is Clarice Thomas a client of yours?" I asked.

"I don't have to tell you one way or another, but what if she was?"

"Do you know or have you ever met George Thomas?" I asked.

"Not yet. We haven't gotten that far in the proceedings," he replied. "Why?"

"I know you remember the gentleman that sat in the front row right at the memorial last Sunday."

"Uh oh," he said. "I'm getting a bad feeling about this."

"You should," I said. "Every time I turn around in this case I find myself looking at you. Why is that, Mr. Langley?"

Ignoring my question, he said, "I take it Mrs. Thomas has become a suspect."

"As I see it," I said. "She had the strongest motive of anyone I've looked at to date."

"You still haven't released the actual cause of death in this case, Detective. Will you tell me how you think she may have done it?"

"She would had to have help. As I recall, you claim to have been asleep in your room at the Wing at the time of the murder. Pretty flimsy alibi. You are right there on my suspect list with the others."

"Good day, Detective. Since we don't have a receptionist to do so, please show yourself out."

I didn't really suspect either Mrs. Thomas or Mr. Langley. I was just 'shaking the tree', maybe something would fall out.

I got back to my car and found a note under the wiper blade on the driver's side. It said, "If I wasn't a bird hunter I wouldn't even know where Adams County was. Next time put money in the meter." It was signed, J. Johnson, BPD Parking Enforcement.

Before I once again submitted myself to the traffic, I punched the button on my cell phone that connected directly to Sam's office.

"What's up, Hal," Sam answered.

"I was wondering how you made out with the hotel up in Moses Lake," I said.

"Good, they do a two week loop on their security cameras. If you want to come home by way of Moses Lake you can pick up a copy this afternoon."

"I'll do that," I said. "With any luck and, no snow in the pass, I ought to be there in about three hours."

"Just pick 'em up and head home from there, Hal. No need to come by the office. We can check 'em out tomorrow."

"Thanks, Sam. I'll see you in the morning."

For me, happiness was seeing the Seattle skyline in my rear view mirror while on I-90 going up the hill through Factoria. Just ahead were the mountains that keep most of the folks out of our side of the state. Seattle is pretty to look at, but to me its just too many people rushing to get someplace. Do you suppose they're happy when they get there?

Traffic thinned out nicely once I got through North Bend. The pass was bare and wet today and the speed limit was left at seventy most of the way. When I grabbed a burger at the Wendy's in Ellensburg, I was tempted to go to the Chevron on my way back to the freeway to see if they had repaired their security cameras. I didn't.

It was just starting to get dark as I hit the ramp for exit 176. I turned north and then took a left toward the Best Western Lakefront. I introduced myself to the desk clerk and he accompanied me to the manager's office located just behind the registration desk. He then handed me two thumb drives and followed me out to the lobby.

"I doubt if there's anything very exciting on those Detective. When things are slow, we pass the time here at the desk watching the live feed. We'll see people filling their ice chests with our ice occasionally or, a pet being smuggled into a room, but seldom see anything worth remembering."

I thanked him and promised that if I found anything worth remembering I would let him know.

I got back on I-90 right where I had gotten off, went east to the next exit and headed down SR 17 toward home. On the way I broke the law and called Shirley to warn her, just in case she was up to something I shouldn't know about.

12.
WEDENSDAY, NOVEMBER 8

Viewing the security recordings Wednesday morning confirmed my gut feeling that Mrs. Thomas was telling the truth. Her Lexus entered the parking lot at seven forty five Saturday evening and didn't move until about seven forty five Sunday morning. The hall camera located near her room recorded people in the area but no one entered or exited her room between seven forty seven Saturday evening and seven forty three Sunday morning. Unless Mrs. Thomas climbed out of her second story window and some one picked her up out of camera range, she was probably in her room as she claimed.

"What do you think about Mr. Langley?" Sam asked.

"I think he may know more that he is willing to talk about, and be more involved with my suspects than he claims, but I don't see him as a murderer. Actually," I said, "He's beginning to grow on me. If only he wasn't a smarmy lawyer we could be friends."

"Don't get all girly on me, Hal or I'll have to retire you," Sam said with a smile.

"So what are your plans for today?" he asked

"Mrs. Thomas claims she saw an older SUV enter Cheryl's driveway Sunday morning. I'm assuming that it was Cheryl's Blazer. Remember, when I went out there that Sunday morning, Jeff, the Grant county deputy said the hood of Cheryl's car was still warm. I'm sure the garage dusted it for finger prints but I doubt they found any matches. Maybe I can find some for them."

"How're you gonna do that?" Sam asked.

"To start with, I'll pull some photos of long dead perps out of our archives. I'll clean 'em up so there aren't any prints on 'em and have my suspects have a good look at photos of my, supposed, latest suspects. If they claim to have seen any of them around lately, it'll point a little finger in their direction, and I should be able to get good finger prints off of the photos that could match any from the car."

"You are one devious son of a bitch, Hal. I'm glad you're on my side. You are on my side, aren't you?"

I was thinking of two birds with one stone as I was driving back to the Mallory's again. Their proximity to Cheryl's home, and their seeming disregard for the truth had tweaked my interest. My mind, as, devious as it was, had started to plot out several possible motives that one, or both of the Mallory's may have had.

SR 26 was clear and dry, but County Road 262, and then 12 SW both had patches of ice and snow left over from the weekend storm. My county SUV handled well but I was glad to see that someone had cleared the downward sloping driveway that lead to the Mallory's home. I did notice that Cheryl's driveway was covered with snow without any tracks showing.

Once again I was greeted by Buck, their Golden Retriever, with his customary green tennis ball in his mouth, muffling his bark.

The front door opened as I approached the porch, and Mrs. Mallory, looking as chic as ever, said, "You again? Don't you have anything better to do than to keep bothering us?"

"I'll just take a few minutes of your time this morning," I said. "We have a new development in the case of Miss Collins' murder, and I would appreciate it if you would just look at a couple of photos, and perhaps help us to identify a suspect."

"Very well, Detective, but please make this visit brief. We have other things in our lives besides your case," she said.

"Peter, come into the kitchen," she called. "Detective Halverson has some photos he wishes us to see."

As we sat down at a small table I pulled two manila envelopes from my jacket pocket. "I want you to look at these separately so there is no accidental influence in identification," I said.

As they opened the envelopes Mrs. Mallory asked, "What, if I may ask, is your new development, Detective?"

"Someone was seen driving Miss Collins' car into her driveway on the Sunday morning of her murder. We think one of the people in these photos may be that person," I lied.

Not unexpectedly, Doctor Mallory said, "I don't believe I've ever seen any of these people, detective."

For the first time since I met him I knew he was telling the truth. All of the people in the photos were either deceased or presently incarcerated.

Picking his bunch up by their edges, I slid them back into his envelope.

"This one looks familiar, Detective," Mrs. Mallory said, pointing to a photo of a woman with medium long hair.

I had chosen that subject because of her resemblance to Mrs. Mallory.

"I'm fairly certain that I've seen her at the Swept Wing Hotel. Perhaps she works there."

"Very observant, Mrs. Mallory," I said as I gingerly placed her photos back in the envelope.

"Thank you for your help this morning. I'll leave you alone now and go see if I can find her." I wanted to say 'dig her up'. She's been dead for ten years or more.

I placed the envelopes that I had already written Mr. and Mrs. on back in my jacket pocket, shook hands with each of them and was shown to the door by Mrs. Mallory.

One thing I noticed on this visit, was that Peter, Doctor Mallory, appeared to be sober. Come to think of it, he seemed that way Sunday as well. I wondered how this affected Mrs. Mallory's extracurricular activities.

I called Sam and told him I was on my way to Ritzville with the Mallory's prints.

Cheryl's old Blazer was in the Sheriff's garage parking lot with about two inches of snow on its top. There was a near new BMW in the garage that looked like it was being disassembled piece by piece. The seats were sitting on the garage floor and the carpet was being removed by a technician when I walked in.

"Hey! What are you doing to my car," I yelled.

"What?" the guy pulling the carpet said as he looked up so fast he hit his head on the car's door frame.

"The guy that owned this car is dead and you will be too if you keep pulling shit like that," he said as he turned and saw me.

"I'm sorry you hit your head, but that's got to be the least used part of your anatomy."

"Up yours Detective. Anyway, Hal, what brings you to my domain?"

"How did you do, fingerprint dusting on Miss Collins' car?" I asked

"Not too good. Everything on the drivers side had been wiped clean. Steering wheel, shift lever, door handle, light switch, everything. The rest of the car had her prints, Mr. Thomas' and a few smeared areas where I really couldn't get anything clear enough to categorize."

"Well that is disappointing," I said. "I have a sample of prints that probably aren't in any data base. I was hoping we might find a match."

"I did get one good hit we could check," he said. "You know how those old Blazers had the exterior mounted spare back by the tailgate?"

"Not really, but go ahead."

"To open the tailgate you have to pull up on a lever between that and the spare tire. That allows the tire to swing off to the right and allow you to open the back of the vehicle. I got a partial of what I believe to be fingers of a left hand on the lever."

"Only a partial?" I asked.

"On the lever, yes," he replied. "However, I got a full right hand on the cover of the spare tire where someone leaned while pulling the lever with their left. They didn't match anything in the data base, but I have 'em on file."

"I take back the insult about your head, for now anyway.

"By the way," I asked. "How'd you do a match on Mr. Thomas?"

"Called Boeing over in Moses Lake. All their employees are printed. They E-mailed 'em within minutes."

He escorted me upstairs to a small lab and introduced me to a sergeant technician sitting at a computer station. She stood up, shook my hand and said, "Hi, I'm Susan. Please don't address me as Sergeant.

"That doesn't go for you wrench head," she said to my guide.

He saluted, clicked his heels together and said, "Damn you're mean! I like that."

He then executed a snappy about face and left the room.

"What've you got for me, Detective?" she asked.

"If you're Susan, then I'm Hal," I said

"Okay, and I just do that to get his goat. He's so bright he should be telling me what to do. I'm trying to piss him off enough to take the exams next time they come around. Doesn't seem to be working though, he likes it down there in the dungeon."

I set the two envelopes down on her desk and explained what I had in mind. She told me she'd look at them right now and we should know pretty quickly if we've got a match.

Thirty minutes later she told me to look at something on her computer screen. She moved her mouse a little and it became kind of blurry. She then moved it again and I could see where two images lined up with each other.

"Bingo," she said, and handed me one of the envelopes. "That's your match, Hal. I hope it helps. I'll keep the photos here and put both sets of prints into the national data base."

I grabbed the other envelope, thanked her and left the building. On my way to my car the garage tech stopped me and asked, "What do you think?"

I told him we had a match and he said, "No, what do you think of Sergeant Susan?"

"I think she's way too good for a 'wrench head'. Why don't you work your way up the pole a little. Maybe she might take a shine to you."

"Take a shine? What kind of ancient language is that? Can I help you get in your car gramps?"

So much for trying to help.

I decided to reverse my previous route and go bother the Mallory's once again.

This time, when I drove in the driveway the dog just stayed where he was and wagged his tail. Carrying that tennis ball around all day must have tired him out.

No one came out the door to greet me, so I stepped up on the porch and pushed the doorbell thing in the middle of the door. It sounded like an old time school bell and I'm sure it could be heard throughout the house. About ten seconds later I saw movement through the peep hole and then heard multiple latches being undone.

He didn't look happy, but he still appeared to be clear-eyed as he asked, "What do you want now, detective?"

"Just a couple more minutes of time from you and Mrs. Mallory. I've identified the woman Mrs. Mallory recognized in the photo this morning. May I come in and discuss this development with the two of you?"

"Grace, it's him again," he said toward an adjoining room. "Do you have a moment to see him so we can send him on his way?"

Mrs. Mallory came into the foyer where we were standing and led us once again to the kitchen table.

I started my story fast, hoping they wouldn't be able to punch holes in it if they didn't have too much time to think.

"Those photos this morning were from our files of convicted felons from this county." So far no lie necessary.

"The woman you picked out is out of prison and is believed to have been an acquaintance of Miss Collins." Lie number one.

"She is also believed to have driven Miss Collins' car from time to time." Lie number two.

"Apparently she did deliveries for several businesses in Cariboo, to folks out here in the countryside." Lie number three.

"Do you recall her ever delivering anything to you that needed unloading from the back of that car and you may have helped?" I asked innocently.

"I've never been near that car, much less unloaded anything from it and I'm sure Grace hasn't either," answered Doctor Mallory. "Have you Grace?"

She hesitated only a micro second before she replied, "No. Of course not."

Then she went on to say, "A convicted felon, Detective. There's your murderer. Arrest her and keep the rest of us safe."

"I'll be making the arrest soon Mrs. Mallory. Just you wait and see."

I headed back to my office where I planned to take the information I had accumulated to date and put it on the white board in our conference room. That way Sam and I, or any one else that might have fresh ideas, could try to sort the grain from the chaff. That's wheat rancher language.

My cell phone buzzed in my pocket as I was looking for the dry erase markers.

"Detective Halverson, how may I help you?" I answered.

"Detective, this is Grace Mallory."

"Grace is it now," I thought.

"Yes, Mrs. Mallory. Nice to hear your voice again. How may I be of assistance?"

"I've been thinking, trying to place the woman who's picture you showed me this morning," she said. "Do you have a list of the businesses for whom she did deliveries?"

Time for the ol' imagination to start working again. I rattled off as many fictitious business names as I could, and then asked, "Any of them sound familiar, Mrs. Mallory?"

"What was that fixit one again, Detective?"

"All Around Fixit Shop?" I asked.

"Yes, yes, that was the one. I had them repair my Hoover."

"Your what?" I asked

"My Hoover, Detective. My vacuum cleaner."

"I see," I said. "What does this have to do with that woman?" I asked.

"I'm certain she delivered the repaired vacuum to our home, and Doctor Mallory helped her remove it from the back of the car she was driving."

"Can you describe the car, Mrs. Mallory/"

"Why, I think it might have been Miss Collin's car, Detective."

"Why?" I asked, "didn't doctor Mallory recognize the woman in the photo or remember helping her?"

"You know why, Detective. He was stoned most of the last month. Only his fear of losing me has kept him sober for the last week. I reminded him of the incident and he does recall it now."

"As I remember a conversation of ours from last week, you may not be happy about his newfound sobriety," I said.

"Oh, I'm wavering on that detective. Peter and I are experiencing a refreshed closeness."

"I'm delighted to hear that, Mrs. Mallory.

"One more thing," I said. "Do you have a receipt from the fixit shop?"

"I'm sorry, Detective, I don't believe I was given one. Perhaps you should check with the shop. Although, I understand a lot of that type of businesses keep as little paper work as possible, if you know what I mean, taxes and all."

"Perhaps your canceled check, Mrs. Mallory."

"No, they insisted I pay in cash."

"Thank you for calling, Mrs. Mallory. You've been very helpful," I said before I hit the hang up button.

It was dark by the time I had all of my suspects listed on the left side of the board along with my reasons for suspecting them. On the right side I had listed the people interviewed who had contributed to my suspicions. I had drawn arrows connecting folks on the right to the appropriate suspects and reasons on the left. Today, Wednesday is commonly referred to as hump day, and I thought that might be true for this case. Time to go home and clear my mind with a little of our fine box wine and a perfectly microwave dinner. My night to cook.

13.
THURSDAY, NOVEMBER 9

I was sitting looking at my art work from yesterday afternoon when Sam came into the conference room, coffee in his right hand, chocolate doughnut in his left.

"What'cha got goin' here, Hal?"

I explained my organization of the white board and pointed out the names I had written in red.

"Both Mallory's, you think they did it working together?" he asked.

"I think she did it and he may have unwittingly helped."

" What was her motive?" he asked.

"Jealousy, the oldest one in the book," I replied.

"You have that nailed down, Hal?"

"That's my plan for today. I want to ask Sylvia, one of the other waitresses over at the Wing a few questions, and if I get the answers I expect, I'll have every thing except how the murder was actually committed."

"You think you'll be able to figure that out?" he asked.

"I'm hoping someone will fill me in on that by accident," I replied.

The weather had taken a turn for the worse, so I buttoned up my coat and pulled on a wool knit hat before venturing out to my car. Fine flakes of snow had been falling for about an hour and the wind was blowing them into miniature drifts at the edge of the pavement. The wind rocked the car a little as I drove through town on my way to the Wing. I felt grateful that I didn't have an outdoor job on a day like this.

I waved to Karen as I walked through the lobby on my way to the dining room. Mrs. Perkins was reigning over her domain, and as I approached her I noticed that she looked a little less together than normal.

"You look a little less than happy this morning, Mrs. Perkins," I said.

"I am a little less than happy Detective. One of my waitresses didn't show up for work this morning, so everyone else is having to take up the slack."

"In that case, I almost hate to ask a favor of you," I said.

"Ask away, Detective. I'll help you if I can."

"When things slow down a bit, I'd like to talk with Sylvia, Mrs. Perkins."

"Can't do that here," she said.

"Why is that?" I asked.

"Because she's the one didn't show up," she said. "I've been trying to reach her to see why, but I've been unable."

"Perhaps I can help. I'll get her employee information from Jerome and go see if she's at home."

"Thank you Detective. And Detective, I'm a little worried. The last girl that didn't show up for her shift was Cheryl."

As I walked toward Jerome's office I called Sam on my cell and told him about Sylvia.

"Please have someone check the hospital, jail, accident reports and all that," I asked. "I'll get her address from Jerome and phone it in. Then if we have a patrol car nearer than I am, have them check her house. I'll be on my way there in a minute."

"Will do, Hal. You sound really worried. You have a bad feeling about this?"

"I do, Sam. She could be the key that unlocks the whole Collins case. I don't think her absence is coincidental."

Without mentioning any name but Sylvia's, I quickly explained my concerns to Jerome. He brought her personnel file up on his computer and printed a copy for me. I punched Sam's number on my speed dial as I ran, well trotted, toward my car and gave him her address.

Her residence turned out to be a non-attached garage that had been converted into a rental on 9th Avenue, near Lion's Park. A patrol car had apparently just arrived and the officer I recognized as Ron something, was in the process of putting on his coat as I pulled up. I still had mine on so we got to the door of the apartment at the same time. There was no button for a bell so he rapped loudly on the door.

"What's this about, Detective?" he asked.

"The person living here, Sylvia Baker, may be an important witness in a murder case," I told him, "and she didn't show up for work this morning."

"I don't see no car here in her driveway. S'pose she might have just gone somewhere?"

"I hope so," I said. "knock again, I'm going to take a walk around the building." Meaning, I was going to look in the windows and try the back door.

As I approached the rear, a man stepped out on the porch of a house behind the apartment and asked, "What the hell is goin on?"

"Are you the owner of the apartment sir?" I asked.

"What if I am?" he replied.

I pulled my shield from my pocket an showed it to him.

"I asked you, what the hell is going on?" he said again.

"We have reason to believe Miss Baker may be in danger, sir. We're trying to locate her."

"That damn girl and her strange friends. Wish I'da never rented the place to her."

"I'd consider this an emergency sir. If you have a key to the apartment would you please let us in?" I asked.

"Don't know if I should. Privacy laws and all."

"Very well sir. Officer, go ahead and kick the door in," I shouted. " Don't worry about damage."

"Wait, wait, I'll open the damn thing. Just hold on while I get my coat and the key."

When I got back to the front door of the apartment, Ron stared at me and said, "Break the door down? Don't worry about damage? What was that about, Detective?"

"Just my way of politely asking the owner to allow us entry into the apartment. I'm glad you didn't do it. Might've been hard to explain."

The apartment owner, mumbling to himself, let us in and stood by the door as we looked around. Three rooms, a not so great, great room, a bedroom and a three quarter bath. No room for a tub. No sign of a struggle, and a check of the closet reveled several waitress outfits but no personal clothes. The dresser was empty.

"Looks like she moved out, Detective," Ron said.

"So it does," I replied. "I might have an idea why. Hopefully I can find her."

"I hope you do too." the owner said. "She owes me two month's rent."

Just to bug our friendly landlord, I told Ron to put a crime scene tape around the house.

"No one goes in until we've cleared the place with CSI," I lied. "And I'll need to keep your keys."

"If anyone tries to get in the place, call me," I said as I handed him one of my cards. "But, don't try to apprehend them. They could be dangerous.

"Have a nice day." I told him.

"CSI, what the hell is CSI?" asked Ron as we walked to our cars.

"Don't you watch TV?" I asked.

"No, I drink when I want to leave reality," he replied.

Once back in my car I called Sam and brought him up to date.

"I need to find out the make and model of her car as well as the tag numbers, Sam."

" Already got 'em, Hal. And I'll put out an APB on 'em right now."

I wrote down the information and then asked Sam, "Where would you go if you were suddenly afraid for your life?"

"I'd go to someone I was absolutely certain was on my side," he replied.

"Such as?" I asked.

"My mom. But I wouldn't want to put her in any danger. I'd have to be pretty sneaky about it."

"Thanks, Sam. I'm gonna work with that."

Checking Sylvia's personnel file again, I found that she had listed her mother, Alice Baker, as next of kin. Her mother's occupation, as I had learned last Saturday, was teacher. According to the file, her school was Jefferson High, Portland Oregon. Her address was listed as on North Denver Avenue, Portland. I called the telephone number listed and was asked by a mechanical voice to please leave a brief message. I didn't.

My next call was to my new friend up in Moses Lake, CJ Morris, Captain of the transit cops.

"Hal, or should I say, Detective Halverson, thanks for the check. You didn't need to do that," he answered.

"My boss didn't think so either," I told him, "but he made it happen. Buy your wife something nice with it."

"Yeah. I was thinking she needed a nice new fly rod."

"Oh, she fly fishes?"

"No, but I do."

"Well, back to business," I said. "Do you still have any contacts in the Portland PD?"

"There are a few of us old farts left down there. What do you need?"

"Do you think someone could do a drive-by," I gave him the address, "and see if there is a Subaru there with a Washington plate," and I gave him the number.

"Don't see any problem with that. Something to do with the Collin's case?" he asked.

"That's right, CJ.

"Do they have a resource officer at Jefferson High?" I asked.

"As far as I know, Why?"

"If the car is there, I would like him to contact one of the teachers. Can you get me his contact information?"

"I'll get on it right now. This the best phone to call?"

"This is it. Thanks"

Since no new ideas were popping into my head, I drove back to the office to worry about Sylvia. I tried finishing up some of the paper, or rather computer, work from the last few days, but found I couldn't concentrate. If something bad had happened to Sylvia I 'd feel guilty for not moving faster on this case. If she had gotten scared off and was in hiding, I hoped I could find her and she could be convinced to open up and tell us why. I thought she was the key to this case and I was afraid the murderer might think the same. Forty five minutes after our last conversation, CJ's name showed up on my caller ID.

"What did you find, CJ?" I asked without saying hello.

"No car in the driveway but the house has a detached garage. Fortunately, the house next door is for sale and empty. My guy pretended to be looking at that house, wandered into the back yard and got a glimpse through the window of our garage. There's a Subaru in there alright but he couldn't see the plates. Want me to have him knock on the door?"

"No. I don't want to spook my witness. Did you get the information about the school resource officer?" I asked.

"Yes I did. His name is Roger Brown. He carries a cell with him and his number is 503..."

"I don't know how to thank you, CJ. You've been a great help right from the get-go. I'll let you know what happens with all this."

"Feel free to call anytime, Hal. I'm enjoying doing all this and not having my ass on the line."

I hit the off button and then punched in officer Brown's number.

"Officer Brown, how may I help you," he answered, just as I was afraid it would go to voice mail.

"Officer Brown, this is Detective Halverson of the Adams County Sheriff's Department up here in Cariboo, Washington. Do you need to verify my ID?" I asked.

"No need, Detective. I was informed, unofficially, that you might call," he said.

"Good. Do you know a Mrs. Baker that teaches there at Jefferson?"

"Yes sir. One of the good ones."

"Do you think you would be able to talk with her casually some time in the next hour or so?" I asked.

"No problem Detective. Her room is just down the hall and it'll be break time in ten minutes."

"Please ask her to call me at this number immediately. Tell her it is extremely important and is regarding her daughter Sylvia's safety. Then, stay with her until she makes the call. Do you have any questions, officer Brown?"

"No sir. If anything goes wrong I'll call you right away, Detective. Now I better head to her room so I can be waiting in the hall at the break."

More waiting by the phone. Only twelve minutes this time.

"Detective Halverson, how may I help you?"

"This is Alice Baker. What is this about my daughter's safety, detective?"

"Sylvia may be an important witness in a murder case, Mrs. Baker. I believe she's frightened and has come to you to hide from both the murderer and the authorities.

"Is she at your home, Mrs. Baker?"

"If she was, what would you have me do, detective?'

"I'd have you explain to her that until we have apprehended the murderer she'll never be out of danger. And, that without her help we might not be able arrest that person."

"And then, Detective?"

"If she is at your home, please have her call me. I'll try my best to leave her right where she is until arrests are made. That is, unless she has disclosed to the suspect your place of residence. If that is the case, I'll have her put under twenty four hour guard for as long as the suspect is free."

"Hopefully, you'll receive a call from her within two hours, Detective. I can't tell you what Sylvia may do. Now I must go to my last class of the day.

"And, Detective?"

"Yes?"

"Thank you, and please take care of my baby girl, if she'll let you."

"I await her call, Mrs. Baker, and I will."

This time, while waiting I decided to ask Sam to go over my reasoning as I had posted it on the white board.

1. The Mallory's had the best accessibility to the victim.

2. They have told the most lies about their relationship with the victim.

3. Their alibis didn't match each other for the time of death.

4. Doctor Mallory's finger prints are on the spare tire cover and the release lever of the victim's car and the reason given for that is a complete lie.

5. Someone bearing a resemblance to Mrs. Mallory was seen driving the victim's car into the victim's driveway after the murder.

6. I believe, and hope to soon have proof that Mrs. Mallory had become jealous of the victim, believing that her lover was interested in her.

7. I believe also, that either Doctor or Mrs. Mallory have threatened Sylvia Baker causing her to flee the area.

"But what about the carbon monoxide poisoning, Hal. How did that work.?" Sam asked.

"It had to have something to do with that pool heater. It's running almost constantly, putting out great quantities of carbon monoxide as well as almost debilitating heat. If I could just figure that out, I wouldn't need Sylvia's statement. Mrs. Mallory has a degree in Mechanical Engineering. I'm sure she knows how to get more than just heat out of that pool heater.

"I do know this," I said. "Doctor Mallory, one of the times I had visited him, claimed that some one had messed with the heater's venting system. He was correcting the problem while I was there."

"Well, if we don't get enough from Sylvia, I guess we could get an engineer in here to help figure it out," Sam said.

"I'd probably go see Leon down at his garage first. He's smarter than most engineers I've known'" I said.

My phone finally buzzed at four thirty.

"This is Detective Halverson. Is that you Sylvia?" The caller ID Showed a 503 number.

"This is Alice Baker, Detective. Sylvia has agreed to talk to you but is afraid to do so on the phone. I can't tell you why. Too much TV I guess. Can you come here and see her in person?"

"I'll drive down in the morning Mrs. Baker. I'd leave tonight but we've got a pretty good snow storm goin' right now and I'd rather fight it in daylight."

"That should work out fine, Detective. When you get to Portland, come to my school and contact officer Brown. He'll know where I am. Then I can tell you where Sylvia is. She is one frightened little girl, Detective. See you tomorrow."

With that she hung up.

I told Sam what had transpired and said, "I'll leave at sunup. I hate people that scare little girls."

14.
FRIDAY, NOVEMBER 10

In good weather the drive from Cariboo to Portland would take four to four and a half hours. The weather this Friday morning was not good. It had snowed most of the night and was drifted against my garage door. From what I could see when the sun finally slid over the horizon, there were about six to eight inches of snow on the road in front of my house and the Cariboo DOT plows hadn't been here yet. No surprise. I checked to be sure there were tire chains in the county SUV, threw my overnight bag on the back seat and went back to my nice warm kitchen to fill my thermos with coffee. Shirley was in full battle dress ready to meet the day regardless of the weather. Look out students, here she comes!

The electric opener easily pulled the garage door up in spite of the drifted snow, and after a quick kiss, we each got in our own vehicles. She backed out first, skillfully tracking through the new snow without a slip or a slide, blinked her lights when she got to the street and took off toward the school.

I backed out reluctantly, knowing I was destined for a few hours of tight pucker driving. I doubted that there were many folks driving from here to Portland today, so at least the traffic should be light. I only hoped that the plows would have the worst of the snow pushed out of the way before I hit the highway. Once on the street, I watched the garage door close and turned south.

Leaving town, highway 24 west had been plowed and I could feel the all wheel drive system doing its job transferring power to the wheels with the most traction.

After crossing the north edge of Hanford Reach National Monument, I picked up Washington 241 South. Then 223 West, then onto 22 West which took me across I-83 and finally got me to US 97 south of Toppenish. I was once again thankful for the built in GPS system in the car.

The one hundred sixty miles or so on US 97 took me across the Yakima Reservation and some of the most sparsely populated country in the state. Make a mistake and slide off the road into a drift out there, they wouldn't find you 'till the spring thaw.

As I went through Goldendale and started downhill toward the Columbia River the snow began thinning out, and by the time I crossed the Bridge near Maryhill and got on I-84, the road was bare and wet. The last hundred miles of this trip should be a breeze. At least until I hit Portland traffic, then more tightening of the posterior.

In The Dalles, wind surfing capitol of the world, I made a pit stop at McDonalds and bought a hot cherry pie to restore my energy. Then, on to Portland.

It was a shade before two o'clock when I parked my vehicle in the Jefferson High School parking lot, just off Emerson street. I entered the school and following the signs

that said 'All visitors must register at office', I found the office. After showing my ID and signing in, I asked to see Officer Brown. They must have had some type of silent paging system because within ten seconds,
officer Brown was standing next to me.

"Officer Brown, I'm Detective Halverson. We spoke yesterday regarding Mrs. Baker."

"Roger sir."

"Roger?" I said.

"Yes sir, My name is Roger, Detective.

"Well, My name is Hal." I said.

Then I asked him, "Have you read Catch Twenty Two, Roger?"

"No sir. I don't believe I have. Why?"

"Oh, no reason," I said.

"Shall we go find Mrs. Baker, Detective? I believe she's expecting you."

"Yeah, let's do that, Roger."

Walking down the hallway of this old school with its smells of varnish, cafeteria cooking, old gym socks, a little fear and maybe some mold, brought back memories of my high school years in a fifty year old building. That was almost sixty years ago and the building is still standing. The schools they slap together these days will be lucky to be here twenty years from now and they just don't have that smell.

Mrs. Baker was teaching in room 108. Officer Brown tapped twice on the windowed door, stepped into the room and nodded. Mrs. Baker excused herself from the class and stepped into the hallway, leaving officer Brown in the class room.

"Detective Halverson?" she asked.

"Yes ma'am," I replied.

"This is my last class of the week, Detective. I'd like to finish it before I take you to see Sylvia. May I?"

"Of course, Mrs. Baker. I'll wait in my car out in the parking lot. I have to check in anyway. You can't miss the car. It's got the Washington plates and all those antennas and things."

"Thank you Detective. I'll be with you in about forty minutes."

She may have thought I was napping when she tapped on my window, but I was actually in a deep thinking mode. Recovering from my intense concentration I rolled down the window.

"Sylvia is staying with my sister and her husband over on Willamette Boulevard, not too far west of I-5. Follow me, we'll go down to Killingsworth to get across the freeway."

After crossing the freeway and US 99, we took a left on Concord and then a right on Willamette, ending up in a pleasant appearing, older neighborhood. She pulled into the driveway of a well kept brick home, and I parked at the curb. Sylvia's car was nowhere in sight, so I assumed it was behind the door of the non-attached single garage, just behind and to the left of the house.

I caught up to Mrs. Baker as she began walking toward the rear of the house.

"She thought that by bypassing my married name, my maiden name and staying with my sister, who of course, has a different married name, she could loose anyone who may try to find her," she said as we reached the back porch. "Right now, you are the only person from Cariboo she trusts. Someone up there has terrified her beyond reason. I hope you can find that person and see that they are put away for a very long time."

By this time she had taken a key from her purse, inserted it into a dead bolt lock and then into a knob lock, opened the door and let us into the house. We passed through a short hallway with a closed door to the left, and through another door into a kitchen.

Mrs. Baker put two fingers to her mouth and gave a shrill whistle. Then she called, "Syl', I'm here, and I have Detective Halverson with me. Please come to the kitchen so the two of you can talk."

I know it wasn't very professional, but Sylvia looked so much like a frightened little bird when she came into the room that I had to put my arms around her and give her a big hug. This seemed to calm her a little and she responded by saying, "Thank you for finding me, Detective. Hopefully the Mallory's can't."

"You've done a very thorough job of covering your trail," I said. "Without the help of your mother and several others that have only your safety in mind, I wouldn't be here. No one else will receive that help."

We sat down on built in bench seats opposite of each other in an old fashion breakfast nook. The table and seats had been painted a bright cheery yellow and must have been a great place to start a day.

Mrs. Baker asked, "Would you like me to leave the room Syl'?"

"No, mom," she replied. "I'm not keeping my life a secret from you any longer. I like girls."

"So did your father, dear. That's why I divorced him."

"I mean, my sexual orientation is toward females. I'm a lesbian," she said.

"Hon', I've known that probably longer than you have," Mrs. Baker said. "I love you and want you to be happy, Just someday, adopt me a grandbaby, that's all. Now, let's get down to business about what has frightened you so."

I set my trusty recorder on the table, started it, recited the date, time, place and the names of us who were present, then turned to Sylvia and asked, "What would you like to tell me?"

She started, "I guess you know by now that Grace, Mrs. Mallory, and I were lovers.

"For me it was just a fun fling with a very beautiful woman. Someone so different from me in her sophistication. She seemed to know something about everything and was never at a loss for words to express herself. I admired her greatly, but soon grew impatient with all those words when all I wanted was, I'm sorry mom, raw sex.

"Then I started noticing Cheryl. I was becoming more and more attracted to her each time we met. She was so full of life. She worked hard and played hard. And she had a beauty that couldn't be defined. Men were attracted to her like moths to a porch light. I was too. I knew she wasn't going to switch sides, but I thought we could still be good friends.

"I guess Grace saw us together a few times, as did her friend Mr. Langley. I think he was jealous of my relationship with Grace and wanted it to end. I'm fairly certain that he told her things that weren't true, and soon Grace gave me an ultimatum."

"What was that?" I asked.

"She told me that if I didn't stop seeing Cheryl she would see to it that Cheryl would stop seeing me.

"I just thought of it as so much bull shit and ignored her."

"When did this take place?" I asked.

At this point she broke down and cried so hard that she couldn't go on. I turned off the recorder, got up from the table and asked where the bathroom was. Mrs. Baker pointed to a door in the wall opposite the breakfast nook and then pointed left. I took my time and when I returned to the table, Sylvia looked to be under control of her emotions again so I sat back down.

I asked Sylvia if she was ready to go on. She nodded yes, so I started the recorder again.

"You were saying that Mrs. Mallory told you she would see to it that Cheryl would stop seeing you," I said. "When was that, Sylvia?"

"On the Saturday afternoon just before she was killed. I didn't think that much about it at the time.

"Then that night I was kinda' dozing in front of the TV when there was a knock on my door. I looked through the peep hole and saw it was Cheryl, so I let her in."

"About what time was that?" I asked"

"It was after the eleven o'clock news, but I didn't look at the clock."

"Okay," I said. "Go on."

"She had been crying, and she said she needed a friend to talk to. Apparently she and her lover were having some kind of problems.

"I told her I wanted to be her friend but there were complications and we really couldn't be seen together. When I explained about Mrs. Mallory, she said she'd go see her right now and straighten out the situation. That was the last I saw of her."

"Why didn't you tell me before now?" I asked.

"I didn't want to get involved. I just wanted people to leave me alone. And, I thought it was just an idle threat. In fact, it didn't seem significant until Mrs. Mallory called me this last Wednesday evening."

"What did she say when she called?"

"She told me that you were about to make an arrest in Cheryl's case. She said that you suspected Cheryl's friend that borrowed her car to make deliveries.

"I know that Cheryl never loaned her car to anyone, and I had never heard of a friend that did deliveries.

"Then, Mrs. Mallory told me to just keep quiet about any arguments we may have had. She said not to muddy the waters.

"I was okay with that until she said that if I talked to you about any of it, I could end up just like Cheryl."

An hour later, with the help of Mrs. Baker and her sister's computer I printed a copy of the complete interview. Sylvia signed it as did her mother, as a witness, and I faxed it to my office.

I called Sam, who was home by now, and asked him to please take the fax to the County Prosecutor, along with the reports I had on the case, and ask if we had enough now to arrest the Mallory's.

He asked me if I was coming home tonight and I told him I didn't want to take a chance on falling asleep behind the wheel, but that I'd leave Portland early enough tomorrow morning to get there around ten or so.

"I'll call the prosecutor right now, Hal," he said. "Then, go by our office, pick up the fax along with your reports and take them to his home.

"Great work, Hal. I'll call you as soon as I've heard what the prosecutor has to say."

I asked Sylvia if she would be able to stay here at her aunt's for a couple of days while we took care of things in Cariboo.

She said, "I'm pretty much through with Cariboo, Detective. Mom and I decided that I'd stay with her and try Portland Community College for a while. It's right next to Jefferson so we can drive back and forth together."

"You'll need to come back to Adams County to testify at the trial, if the Mallory's plead not guilty. Are you up to that?" I asked.

"As long as I'll never have to be alone with that woman again."

"I'll be with her all the way," her mother said. "She'll be Okay.

"Will you stay for dinner, detective?" she then asked. "I've got a wonderful new tofu recipe I want to try out."

"Thanks, Mrs. Baker, but I'll just grab something quick at my hotel and get to bed early."

I left them then and found a hotel near I-84 that had a dining room. After two glasses of single malt scotch and a thick juicy steak I'd be ready for sleep. Tofu my ass.

I had turned off my cell phone while in the dining room. I hate it when people answer them in a place like that and then carry on a one sided conversation loud enough for all to hear. I turned it back on as I walked the hallway toward my room and saw that I had two messages. Oh, oh, I'd forgotten to call Shirley and tell her where I was. I called Sam back first.

"Hal, the prosecutor has the stuff. He read it over while I was there and said it was all pretty much circumstantial, but enough to bring 'em in and have them arraigned. Of course, they are in Grant County so we'll have to clear it with them."

"If it works with Grant county, see if we can have Officer Cruz from Moses Lake PD in our office when I get there tomorrow. That should be around ten o'clock. Then we can meet one more of our guys out there and make the arrests.

"Oh, and Sam?" I said. "We better have at least one of our guys be a female officer."

I hit the off button and then called Shirley.

15.
SATURDAY, NOVEMBER 11

I left the hotel at five the next morning with a Styrofoam cup of lobby coffee and a bagel that must have been left from the last convention to hit town. The McDonalds in The Dalles was open, so I grabbed an Egg McMuffin and some much better coffee, got back on I-84 and went east until I hit US 97, crossed the river into Washington and headed north. The road was clear and wet all the way to Cariboo and I pulled into our parking lot at nine thirty four.

Carlos arrived about five minutes later, as I was planning our method of arrest.

I had Claudia Murphy, a very sturdy looking lady at about five foot ten and two hundred pounds, for our female officer. She would ride with me and do the pat down of Mrs. Mallory. Jim Bailey, a patrol officer would meet us at the intersection of 12SE and SR 262, and Carlos would be with us to represent Grant County.

Carlos was to park in Cheryl's driveway across the road from the Mallory's, and walk down around their home to block escape via the back door. Officer Bailey would park on the roadway and stand by in case of any problems. Officer Murphy would accompany me to the door and assist me with the arrest of Mrs. Mallory. I didn't anticipate any problems in arresting the Doctor.

Since Carlos had never been to the Mallory's, I Googled it, and showed him a three hundred and sixty degree view from the top of their driveway. This gave him good prospective of the relationship of their driveway to Cheryl's, which was located about twenty five yards to the west.

We left our office at eleven o'clock and at eleven twenty five hooked up with officer Bailey. I once again went over our plan of attack and at eleven forty five sent Carlos on his way. Five minutes later the rest of us headed west toward the Mallory residence.

When we arrived at the Mallory's driveway I could see no sign of Carlos' car so I figured he had hid it well over at Cheryl's, or had gotten lost. Officer Bailey stopped on the road short of the driveway and officer Murphy and I drove on down toward the house.

Old Buck just looked up from where he was lying, tennis ball in mouth, and wagged his tail this time as officer Murphy and I approached the front door. I pushed the bell button and we waited about thirty seconds. Just as I reached to push the button again, Doctor Mallory opened the door and we walked into the front hall.

"Detective Halverson," he said, none to enthusiastically. "What on earth is it now?"

"Good afternoon, Doctor. Is Mrs. Mallory in?" I asked.

"She has given me instructions that if you came to bother her again I am to tell you that she doesn't wish to be disturbed. And," he continued, "if you were persistent I was to tell you that all future contact would take place through her attorney."

"I'm sorry to hear that, Doctor. We wanted to tell her about the arrest of a suspect in the Collins case. Surely she would be interested in that. Why don't you ask her? We'll wait right here."

"Very well," he said. "She'll probably be grateful to hear the news"

Doctor Mallory went through a door on our left and I was hoping that Carlos was alert in the back yard, just in case.

It was about a minute later that Doctor Mallory reappeared through the door accompanying his wife.

"So you have good news for us, Detective," she said just before officer Murphy had her turned against the wall with cuffs on and being frisked.

"This is an outrage!" shouted Doctor Mallory as I performed the same maneuver with him.

"You are both under arrest for the murder of Cheryl Collins," I said. Then I read them their rights.

We walked them out the front door and I had Officer Murphy lock Mrs. Mallory in the back seat of my car with her hands cuffed behind her back and her seat belt fastened securely.

I then had Doctor Mallory sit on the driveway with his hands cuffed behind his back. I didn't see any way for him to stand up and make a quick get away, but for good measure, I told officer Murphy to shoot him if he even tried. The doctor looked as if he might loose control of his bowels.

Officer Bailey was standing at the top of the driveway, so I waved him down to where we were and gave him instructions pertaining to the crime scene. He would stand guard here, touching nothing until relieved by another officer or the crime scene investigation team from Ritzville.

I then walked around the left side of the house and saw Carlos standing far enough away so he could see both sides of the house as well as the rear. I waved him over and told him that he would be taking Doctor Mallory to Ritzville, and we would be following with Mrs. Mallory. I told him that under no circumstances were Doctor and Mrs. Mallory be allowed to communicate with each other.

"One question, Detective?" Carlos asked.

"What is it?" Carlos.

"What about the dog?" he asked.

"I guess I'll have to call Animal Control and have him picked up," I answered.

"I'll come back and get him after I go to Ritzville," Carlos said. "We just had to put our old dog down and we've got every thing to keep him happy, including kids."

"I don't know if it's exactly the right protocol," I said, "but it works for me."

I called Sam, told him we had the Mallory's in custody and were heading to Ritzville to book them into the jail there. I also told him I had officer Bailey securing the crime scene and would like the county crime scene investigators to come and check the place over.

"Especially the heating plant for the pool," I told him.

"Maybe we should have Sander's Heating and Cooling, send a tech over," I said. "According to a sticker I saw the last time I was here, they've been doing the maintenance. I'd like to know if anything has been tampered with since they were here last."

Sam assured me that he would take care of everything, so we took off for the County Seat

Except for the continuous threats for everything from law suits to my being fired emanating from the back seat, the trip to Ritzville was uneventful. Mrs. Mallory said she was going to call her good friend and powerful Bellevue attorney, Robert Langley and have him, "Hang my ass from the highest tree in the county!"

I thought, "Good, then we won't have to go get him." I still wanted to nail him with some of the responsibility for Cheryl's death.

When we arrived at the jail, Carlos took Doctor Mallory to the men's side for booking while we escorted Mrs. Mallory to the women's booking desk.

"I insist on seeing my husband before we go through this unnecessary procedure, Detective," Mrs. Mallory said. "Furthermore, if I may call my attorney, I feel certain that he will tell you to release both of us or expect dire consequences."

"You will not be having any contact with your husband so long as you are in this facility," I told her. "Furthermore, you will be allowed one phone call after you are booked, de-liced and in a nice orange jumpsuit and flip-flops. Now, if you will excuse me, I will leave you in the care of officer Murphy and these other fine ladies while I go talk with your husband."

Doctor Mallory was being booked, not so gently, on the other side of the jail. He appeared pale and was shaking so much he was almost blurred.

"Detective," he asked. " Why am I being persecuted so?"

"Because we believe you had a hand in the murder of Cheryl Collin's," I answered.

"Truthfully Detective, I have no recollection of the week she was killed, let alone what ever day or night it may have been," he said. "I'm certain that once our attorney, Mr. Langley, contacts you, my release will be immediate."

"I have some advice for you Doctor," I said. "Find another attorney."

"But why, detective? He is a very good friend of Grace's. I'm certain he will do everything possible to defend us against this horrible misunderstanding."

"Think about it Doctor. He is a very, very good friend of your wife's. He is not your friend, and I suspect, has every reason to wish you harm."

"My wife wouldn't let anything bad happen to me detective, " he said.

"She already has, Doctor. That's why you're here. Your finger prints weren't left on Cheryl's car by accident. Think about it."

I left him there and went back to the women's area to collect officer Murphy for the trip back to Cariboo.

According to officer Murphy, Mrs. Mallory used her one allowed phone call to leave a message on Mr. Langley's cell. This being a Saturday during bird hunting season, Mr. Langley was already in the area and showed up at the jail a half hour later, still wearing his cammos.

He fussed and fumed, as lawyers do, about our incompetence and his clients virtue. "Backwoods, hick town, wannabes," came out of his highly educated mouth at one time. He told Mrs. Mallory to refuse to answer any questions we may ask, no matter how insignificant they may seem, and he would see her at the arraignment hearing on Monday morning.

"Monday morning? Get me out of here right now Robert! I don't intend to spend one more minute in these clothes or this horrible place," cried Mrs. Mallory.

"I'm sorry Grace, but these small town police and their judges are all prejudiced against people with any sophistication. My hands are tied at the moment, but come Monday, we will have our day in court and you will be freed."

As soon as Mrs. Mallory was led back to her cell, Mr. Langley asked to see his other client, Doctor Mallory.

When he arrived at the men's side of the jail, he was told Doctor Mallory had not made his allowed phone call as yet and that he had informed no one that he wished to see Mr. Langley. The thoughtful staff then offered Mr. Langley the use of an empty cell, if he had nowhere else to stay. He declined their offer.

It was dark, and officer Murphy was on overtime when we finally pulled into our parking lot in Cariboo. It had been a long and somewhat stressful day, so I told her she could take care of her paper work tomorrow. Then I realized tomorrow was Sunday and said, "I'm sorry, but we need to have everything recorded in case it's needed at the arraignment on Monday. Do you have plans for tomorrow?"

"Yeah," she replied. "I'll be in the office taking care of my report for today. I wanna show that snooty bitch and her sleazy lawyer just how 'back woodsy' we non-sophisticates are. Besides, it's a regular work day for me."

I watched as she got in her car, started it and drove off. Then I hit my speed dial for our home phone, and when

Shirley asked who was calling, re- introduced myself and said, "I'm coming home. Send all your boy friends away."
"All of them?" she asked.

16.
SUNDAY, NOVEMBER 12

Shirley was very understanding about my need to get everything ready for Monday morning. After I served her breakfast in bed, cleaned up the kitchen and got the dishwasher going, I made sure the Seahawks game would be recorded. Then, as I was about to leave for the office, she came into the kitchen and gave me a big hug and a kiss.
"I'm worried about Sylvia and her mom," she said.
"Me too, Shir'. I gotta make sure the Mallory's, her at least, stay where they are. Otherwise, we'll have to put both of 'em into some kind of protective custody. "
"That would be awfully hard on Mrs. Baker," Shirley said. "She's probably just gotten her classes into full swing. Couldn't you leave her in school during the day?"
"That 'd put the whole school in jeopardy," I replied. "I don't want to set something in motion that could cause harm to any kids. Hopefully, the judge will deny bail because of Mrs. Mallory's threats to Sylvia."
"What if he doesn't?" she asked.
"Plan B," I replied.
"You have a plan B?" she asked.
"Not yet. Kiss me. I gotta go make one."

The place was Sunday morning quiet and officer Murphy was at a desk entering her report on yesterday's activities into our computer as I arrived.
In my office I had begun putting everything I had in my notes and reports regarding the Mallory's together in one chronological file, when my desk phone rang.

"Detective Halverson, how may I help you?" I answered.

"Detective, this is Candice Mead from the Prosecutor's office. I'm representing the county tomorrow at the arraignment for Mr. and Mrs. Mallory."

"That's Doctor and Mrs. Mallory, Ms. Mead."

"Okay, I stand corrected. Do you have time today to meet with me and go over the case?"

"I need some more time here to complete my personal reports," I told her. "And I'm waiting to hear from the crime scene guys. Hopefully they'll have some additional evidence for you. I would expect to have everything by three or four o'clock."

"I'm in Ritzville, Detective. If you have an office there in Cariboo where we might meet, I'll see you there at four."

"Thank you Ms. Mead. I'll be here and ready for you at four."

Once I had all of my stuff organized and had made copies of my taped interviews with Doctor Mallory and with Sylvia, I called Sam to see about the report from the crime scene guys.

"Christ, Hal, the Seahawks are just about to kick off. your timing is impeccable."

"Good afternoon to you too, Sam. I hope you've got some way of recording the game. If not, come on over when I get home tonight and we can watch it together."

"Okay, I get your point. By the way, have you any idea how expensive it is to get a pool heater tech to make a house call on a Saturday night?" he asked.

"Nope," I said, "That's your department. Will there be any money left to make payroll next week?"

"Yeah, I guess so."

"Did they find anything interesting out at the Mallory's yesterday? I asked.

"No sign of Miss Collins ever having been there, Hal. But, then again, everything was super clean. The only prints to be found belonged to the Mallory's. Before they let the tech into the room with the pool heater they dusted it pretty good. Everything had been wiped down except the flue and a chair that was in the corner. Doctor Mallory's prints were on the flue and the chair. Someone had done a hell of a job cleaning all the other surfaces. The tech, when we let him in the room, said he'd serviced the heater at least four times. None of his prints were to be found."

"It looks more and more as if Mrs. Mallory is trying to shift any blame over to her husband," I said. "And so far, all of our physical evidence points his way. I just hope she doesn't come out of this unscathed with him being found guilty of something he was too stoned to know about."

"I know. Sometimes justice is just too damn blind. The complete report is in the system, Hal. Just go to the case number in the documents file."

"Thanks, Sam. I'll be meeting with the prosecutor here around four to go over everything."

I brought the report up on my computer and printed a copy. I find I can absorb much more information from a printed sheet than I can from a computer screen.

Reading the report, I found nothing interesting until I got to the part describing the pool heater and the room in which it was located. At this point the observations of the heating tech were introduced as he wrote them, complete with his signature.

"There are signs of tampering with the flue mechanism," he wrote. "It appears that at some time it had been misadjusted. There is a carbon build up in the pipe that could have occurred as a result of a blockage. Such a blockage could force the heater to exhaust into the room creating an extreme warmth, and an atmosphere laden with carbon monoxide. The heater would have become quite inefficient as far as the pool was concerned. Someone apparently noted the inefficiency and made an attempt to correct the problem. What they did would have helped considerably, but without the use of the proper tools and gauges, could not have brought the unit up to peak efficiency."

I wished he had used the word "would" in place of "could"' in a few places, but his report pretty much supported my theory of how Cheryl was killed.

Ms. Mead tapped on my door frame at three forty five. Once again I may have appeared to have been snoozing, but in reality was deep in thought. I seem to get deep in thought more and more often as I get older.

"Detective Haroldson? " she asked.

"Halverson," I corrected. "I presume you are Ms. Mead?"

"Candice would be better," she said.

"In that case I'm Hal. Welcome to Cariboo, Candice."

Candice was probably in her late thirties, about five foot five and nicely proportioned. She was wearing blue jeans and a white sweater under her coat which she hung on my coat tree in the corner.

"How did you become a prosecutor in a Podunk place such as this, Candice?" I asked.

"I grew up in Ritzville," she replied. My folks had a restaurant there that provided for my education at 'Wazoo' and Law at 'Udub.'

"I worked for a mega firm in Seattle helping sleaze bags shirk their responsibilities for ten years and hated it. So I came back home, married my high school sweetheart, who had hoped to be a bachelor wheat rancher the rest of his life, and here I am."

"Are you mean enough for this job?" I asked.

"Just try me, you ugly old fart," she said.

"I guess you'll do," I admitted.

As I was setting out my reports, I asked her, "Do you know if Doctor Mallory has chosen a lawyer yet?"

"He hasn't, so the judge appointed a public defender for him," she said. "Old Clayton Ogden. Better known as 'You know you did it so plead guilty and take your lumps 'cause I've got a tee time.'"

"Well, that's still better than having his wife's very, very good friend Mr. Langley pretend to defend him.

" Besides," I said, "the golf courses are all closed for the winter around here. Why hasn't old Clayton gone south with the rest of the snow birds?"

"I don't know," she said. "I'll ask him tomorrow. Now, tell me how and why Miss Collins was murdered."

"Mrs. Mallory and our best witness, Sylvia Baker were carrying on an affair. Sylvia was becoming increasingly bored with the situation and wanted to end the relationship.

"Sylvia was a waitress at the hotel as was Cheryl. They became friends, but according to Sylvia, were not sexually involved.

"Some how, Mrs. Mallory became convinced that Sylvia and Cheryl were lovers and that Cheryl was the reason for Sylvia wanting out. I believe Mr. Langley, Mrs. Mallory's friend and 'wanna be' lover was responsible for this.

"When on the night of the murder Cheryl thought that her actual lover, a Mr. Thomas of Moses Lake, was going to drop her, she sought reassurance from her friend Sylvia."

Candice broke in here. "I understand Cheryl was pregnant. Is, or was, Mr. Thomas the father?"

"We should have the results of DNA testing tomorrow, but," I said, "I believe he was."

"If he was," she said. "I think we want to keep it to ourselves. We don't want Mr. Langley to have any additional ammunition he can use to cloud the waters. In fact, I don't want you to find out the results of the DNA test until after the arraignment. Now, go on."

I continued with my theory. "Sylvia had already become fearful of Mrs. Mallory and told Cheryl about the misunderstanding regarding her and Cheryl.

"Cheryl unwisely decided to inform Mrs. Mallory personally of the error in her thinking and drove out to the Mallory's home.

"Mrs. Mallory, acting all understanding and motherly took Cheryl to the pool heater house where it would be warm and comfy, and they would not be disturbing Doctor Mallory. Or, should the Doctor be sober, make him aware of Mrs. Mallory's extramarital activities.

"I believe that she had Cheryl sit in a chair that was in the heater room while she adjusted the flue to make it more comfortable. Then she told Cheryl she was going to get some tea, or something, and for Cheryl to relax and enjoy the heat.

"After she was sure Cheryl had 'relaxed' sufficiently, she had a perhaps stoned, Doctor Mallory help her carry her to her own car and deposit her in the back.

"The Mallory's then drove out to a deserted section of Fletcher Road and dumped Cheryl into the roadside ditch.

"Then they drove back to their home, where Mrs. Mallory cleaned all the surfaces in Cheryl's car that she had touched, leaving Doctor Mallory's prints on the spare tire mechanism.

"She then cleaned the pool heater and the heater room completely, erasing all finger prints.

"Sometime after eight thirty Sunday morning, Mrs. Mallory drove Cheryl's car across the road and parked it in Cheryl's barn. She once again cleaned all the surfaces she had touched and returned home."

Ms, Mead sat there for a few minutes thinking about what I had said, "You have evidence supporting every thing you just related?"

"I have statements from the Mallory's that are full of obvious lies. I have Sylvia Baker's statement about what happened leading up to the murder and also the threats she received from Mrs. Mallory this last week.

"I have the prints from Cheryl's car and the prints on the flue. Unfortunately, they belong to Doctor Mallory, but they do prove that at some time at least one of the Mallory's had had contact with the car. The lack of other prints speaks even more loudly to me, but I don't suppose anyone else can hear that."

"You have no witness putting Cheryl at the Mallory's on that Saturday night, though," she said.

"Only Sylvia's statement saying Cheryl was going there to see Mrs. Mallory," I replied.

"I believe it probably happened much as you think," she said. "Let's hope the judge sees it your way too."

I gave Candice copies of everything I had accumulated.

"I'll take all of this home with me now," she said, "and go over it several times tonight. Then I'll do it again in the morning.

"The arraignment is at ten thirty in court room two. Judge Orlon will be presiding."

"Is that Mathew Orlon, the old womanizer?" I asked.

"I always do well in his court, Hal."

"Just so Mrs. Mallory doesn't," I said.

Candice put on her coat, shook my hand, said, "See you in the morning, Hal," and was gone.

I called Shirley and asked her what kind of take-out I should bring home.

17.
MONDAY, NOVEMBER 13

It was five thirty AM when I looked at the bedside clock. I knew I'd been awake for at least an hour and it was unlikely that I'd fall asleep again this morning. I was concerned about today's arraignments and I was also hungry.

Hoping not to disturb Shirley, I rolled out of my side of the bed, put on my robe and slippers and went to the kitchen. Once I had the coffee maker going, I opened the door of the fridge and found the package of leftover chow mien from last night. It wasn't cold pizza but it was still damn good.

I was certain that I had the right people behind bars but I couldn't know how a judge, having seen nothing of the case or the people involved, would rule.

I went over and over my materials for about two hours, grabbed a shower, put on my 'going to court' clothes and left for Ritzville just before eight o'clock. I just vaguely remembered Shirley giving me a peck on the cheek and going out the door some time earlier.

At precisely ten thirty the bailiff announced," Court is in session. The honorable Judge Mathew Orlon presiding. All rise."

The judge then came into the room from his chambers, sat in his place behind the bench, and said, "Please be seated."

He then asked, "Bailiff, what've we got here this morning?"

"Adams County versus Doctor Peter Mallory. The charge is : Aiding and abetting the second degree murder of Miss Cheryl Collins and her unborn child."

"I see counsel is present," the judge said peering over the top of his half glasses. "How nice to see you, Ms. Mead.

And Clayton! What the hell are you doin' here this time of the year? All the golf courses are closed down."

"Lost my Arizona condo in a poker game last spring, Your Honor," was the reply from the defense attorney.

"Well, come see me after we get through here today, Clayton. I know some judges down there. Maybe we can find some legal way to get it back."

"That's just it, Your Honor. I lost it to a judge."

"Well come see me anyway, Clayton.

"Now, how does your defendant plea?" he asked.

"Not guilty, Your Honor. Against my advice, of course."

"Ms. Mead, does the county have a requested amount for bail?" the judge asked.

"One million dollars," she replied.

"We're in Ritzville, Ms. Mead, not Seattle. Five hundred thousand and a urine test each Monday morning at the public health clinic in Cariboo to check for the use of controlled substances," said the judge. "Don't even eat any poppy seed muffins, Doctor Mallory, or you'll be back in jail until the end of your trial.

"Next case."

Ms. Mead turned around and gave me a big wink. We had discussed earlier this morning the mount of bail to request for Doctor Mallory and, as I didn't believe him to be a danger to our witness, settled on five hundred thousand dollars.

As doctor Mallory was being escorted out of the court room toward the jail, Mrs. Mallory made her entrance.

Somehow she made the orange prisoner jumpsuit she was wearing look like next year's fall fashion. It was a little tight in the right places and the legs were short enough to reveal a glimpse of her dainty ankles. The flip-flops were off-set by the orange polish on her toe nails and she had an orange flower of some kind in her long golden hair.

The judge didn't take his eyes off of her as she had everything in motion walking to her place beside Mr. Langley at the defendants table. Then she smiled at the judge and he smiled back.

"We're sunk," I thought to myself. Ms. Mead once again turned to face me and slowly, and somewhat sadly, shook her head.

"What do we have here, bailiff?" the judge asked, still looking intently at Mrs. Mallory.

"Adams County versus Mrs. Grace Mallory. The charge is: Murder in the second degree of Miss Cheryl Collins and her unborn child. Also, threatening a witness."

"I see you have counsel present, Mrs. Mallory. Will you please introduce yourself, sir?" the judge asked.

"Thank you Your Honor. I am Robert Langley of Grogan, Harper and Langley. Our law offices are located in Bellevue Washington."

"Oh, I'm quite aware where Bellevue is, Mr. Langley. Did Mrs. Mallory feel that we had no competent attorneys in this part of the state?"

"I happen to be a very good friend of the defendant, Your Honor. And I was in the area hunting when she was taken into custody."

"Oh, a very good friend eh. Well good for you young man, good for you.

"Well, enough of this chit chat counselor. What does your very good friend plea this morning?" the judge finally asked.

"Not guilty, Your Honor. And since Mrs. Mallory is such a well known and well loved member of the community as well as being very active in many of the charity organizations here, we ask that she be released immediately on her own recognizance. This has been a tragic mistake due to..."

The judge broke in or Mr. Langley's speech with, "Hold on there, counselor. I'll be the one to determine if a mistake has been made.

"Ms. Mead, what is the county's view on bail for this lady?" he asked.

"Because of several threats Mrs. Mallory made to one of our witnesses, the county believes Mrs. Mallory poses a threat to the entire community. The county, therefore requests that she not be given bail at any price."

Before the judge could comment, Mr. Langley jumped up and shouted, "Alleged threats, Your Honor. Only the witness, who had been attempting to become Mrs. Mallory's lover and was turned away repeatedly by Mrs. Mallory, has claimed such threats. Their existence is questionable to say the least.

"In fact, Your Honor," he continued. " I believe that so called witness was the last person to see Miss Collins alive and should be sitting where Mrs. Mallory is right now."

"So you think that our local law enforcement folks are incompetent and have arrested the wrong person. Mr. Langley?"

"I believe judge that you are intelligent enough to see that this is a travesty of justice."

"Why thank you, Mr. Langley for your vote of confidence. However, I think I see several of the observers in the court room rolling up their pant legs. Detective Halverson," he shouted. "Why are you doin' that?"

"I just don't want to get any of that stuff on them," I said. "Shirley says it makes a mess in the wash."

"May I ask you something, Mr. Langley? the judge asked.

"What is it, Your Honor?"

"You were sitting in the front row there when Doctor Mallory was arraigned a little while ago. Why, if this is such a travesty, didn't you say anything when I set his bail at five hundred thousand dollars?"

"Because I'm not his attorney, Your Honor."

"Aren't you his very good friend also, Mr. Langley?

"I'm better acquainted with Mrs. Mallory, judge," he replied.

"I'll just bet you are.

"Bail is set at five hundred thousand dollars. Mrs. Mallory, a condition of that bail is that you do not leave Grant or Adams county. And, if there is even a rumor of any threats being made by you, or anyone associated with you," as he said this he looked pointedly at Mr. Langley, "toward anyone, your bail will be forfeited and you will remain in the county jail until the conclusion of your trial.

"As you and your husband will be tried separately, your trial will be held first for obvious reasons. Your trial will begin fourteen days from today in this court room. Doctor Mallory's trial, should it be necessary, will start two working days after the conclusion of Mrs. Mallory's trial.

"One more thing. Mr. Langley, are you tryin' to grow a beard?"

"No, Your Honor. I'm just being..."

"In that case," said the judge, "show some respect for this court and shave before you show up here for trial.

"Next case, Bailiff!"

"That's it, Your Honor. Like you said earlier, 'this ain't Seattle.'"

"Okay," I said to Candice when we reached her office upstairs ."How did the judge know about the Doctor's drug problem?"

"I may have let it slip this morning while I was having coffee with my cousin," she replied

"Your cousin?"

"Yeah, he's the judge's clerk. Old Orlon was forced to hire a male clerk after several ladies complained about being uncomfortable when they were alone with him in chambers," she said. "Personally, I think he's quite harmless but sorta' easy to lead around, if you get my drift."

"Aren't we all," I said.

"All except the 'swishy' ones. They're more difficult to control."

We talked about how we thought the arraignment went and decided, that except for the possibility of Mrs. Mallory making bail, things went well. Then we went over our list of witnesses for the prosecution and wondered who Langley would find for the defense. Mostly we were killing time, waiting for a call from the jail to tell us if either or both of our prisoners were being released.

Her desk phone finally rang at one fifteen.

"Mead here," she answered. "What've you got? Okay, got it. Thanks.

"Mrs. Mallory had no trouble putting up enough collateral for a bond. There wasn't enough left to spring Doctor Mallory."

"I don't suppose the Doctor is any too happy with that," I said. "That might work to our advantage."

"How so?" she asked.

"I think as we talk with him prior to her trial, we could open up a bit of a rift between them."

"But," she said, "he doesn't have to testify against her."

"No, but if Langley is thinking of using the Doctor as a defense witness, the door will be open for you to get the Doctor angry enough on the stand to help incriminate his wife."

"But how do we get him to put the Doctor on the stand," she asked.

"You sorta' lead him there. If you get my drift."

Now that Mrs. Mallory was being released, I had a couple of things to attend to. I hoped she wouldn't miss the dog, but in case she does I had to warn Carlos. I called his cell.

"Hey, Detective, what's up?" he answered.

"How's the newest member of your family doing," I asked.

"You mean my five year old?"

"No, Carlos, the dog, Buck."

"Oh, he's in doggie heaven, Detective."

"He's dead?" I exclaimed.

"No, no, He's just very happy. And the kids love him."

"Well I have bad news, Carlos. Mrs. Mallory has made bail. If she asks about her dog, I don't know what to do."

"Tell her animal control found the dog wondering on the road and, because he had no license, took him to the shelter where a family came and adopted him."

"What ever happened to the only honest man in the world?" I asked

"That's not completely a lie, detective. It just didn't happen exactly that way."

"Well I hope she doesn't pursue it. If she does you may have to give him up."

"If she does, have her come to my house to get the dog. After she sees him with my kids she'd have to be completely heartless to take him home."

"She is a murderer, remember."

"Murder is one thing. Separating a dog from kids who love him is way worse."

My other worry was how to protect Sylvia now that Mrs. Mallory was free. It was actually a greater concern than the dog but I put it off because I wasn't sure how to handle it.

We were still in Candice's office, her going once again over my reports and recordings and me ready to answer any questions she may have had.

I interrupted her by asking, "What about depositions? I'm sure Mr. Langley is going to insist on deposing Sylvia, and I want to protect her from both him and Mrs. Mallory. We'll need to have her available, but I don't want either of those two near her without one of us being present.

"I'm also concerned with Sylvia's mom, Mrs. Baker. I'm afraid we'll lose Sylvia if she feels her mom is in any danger."

Candice said, "You heard the judge, Hal. Any hanky-panky and Mrs. Mallory's ass is in jail until this is over."

"That's all well and good, but we can't keep track of her actions, or Mr. Langley's twenty four seven. One slip and our whole case goes to hell as well as Sylvia's well being."

"What do you suggest?" she asked.

"Protective custody for both. Put 'em up in one of those nice hotels up in Moses Lake. Have two officers with them at all times and all phone calls are monitored and recorded."

"You think the threat is that great?"

"I think Grace Mallory is such a cold blooded killer that she is trying to implicate her husband in the murder. I also think that Robert Langley would do anything she asked, to get in her pants."

"Don't sugar coat it, Hal," she laughed. "Tell me what you really think of those two."

"I'm serious, Candice," I said.

"I know you are, Hal. I'll check with my boss and see if we can set something up. Meanwhile, you better contact Sylvia and see if she'll agree to do what you're asking. Protective custody can be a little like prison."

I thanked Candice for her efforts on the case and told her that on my drive back to Cariboo I'd try to think up a way to convince Sylvia and her mom that we knew what we were doing.

I had just entered my office and was hanging up my coat when Sam appeared in my doorway

"I hear your murderer made bail this morning. What you want to do about your prize witness?" he asked.

"What would you suggest? I've got to keep her safe and unafraid to testify."

"She's pretty well hid at the present, isn't she?"

"Yeah, but if she ever told Mrs. Mallory about her mom, where she lives and what she does for a living it could be a problem."

"How so?"

"Say, she knows that her name is Alice Baker, and that she is a teacher in Portland. Having that information, it took me three phone calls to locate her. If you know your way around a computer you could probably do it faster."

Sam said, "Go on,"

"Someone, not necessarily Mrs. Mallory or even her lawyer friend, meets Mrs. Baker in the school parking lot, the supermarket or, even knocks on her door and asks where her daughter Sylvia is.

"Now, even if Mrs. Baker didn't know where she was, or that she was a valuable witness in a murder case, she would try to contact her daughter and by doing so make Sylvia fearful for her mother's safety.

"But the fact is, she does know where her daughter is, and she knows about the murder case. This would make Mrs. Baker then fear for her daughter's safety as well as her own. If Sylvia even senses this, we've lost our witness and Sylvia lives in fear for the rest of her life."

"Okay," Sam said. Call your contact officer at the school and tell him to have Mrs. Baker call you ASAP.

"Then, tell her officer Murphy, in street clothes, will head down to Pasco this afternoon and catch the Horizon flight to Portland. Portland PD will pick up Mrs. Baker and her daughter Sylvia in the morning and take them to meet officer Murphy and board the eight AM flight back to Pasco. Officer Murphy will then drive them to The Inn At Moses Lake where she will be met by two officers, as yet to be determined, who will help our guests to check in and provide twenty four hour security as long as it is needed."

"Wow!" I said. "You sure came up with that in a hurry. We better clear it with the prosecutor though. Ms. Mead was going to see what they could do."

Sam smiled and said, "Candice called while you were driving down here. She put the whole thing together. Now you better make your call. When the Baker's have agreed to the program, Portland PD will call them to make the pick up arrangements."

I called Roger Brown, the resource officer at Jefferson High in Portland. He remembered me and said he would contact Mrs. Baker immediately and make sure she followed up on calling me back. I thanked him, hung up my phone and sat there wondering just how I was going to explain our inability to keep Mrs. Mallory in jail and how badly we needed Sylvia's testimony.

Eight minutes later, my phone buzzed.

"Mrs. Baker, thanks for returning my call," I answered.

"Not that I had much choice, Detective. Officer Brown is very persuasive, being armed and all."

"Well, tell him to holster his pistol and stand down while we talk."

"Oh, I think that's just a squirt gun he carries anyway. Why the urgent call?"

"Mrs. Mallory was arraigned this morning, Mrs. Baker, and the judge allowed her to post bail," I said.

"You mean she's free?" she asked.

"Free with some restrictions. She isn't allowed to leave Adams or Grant county and she isn't allowed to threaten anyone."

"Well I'm sure she plans to obey those restrictions. Hell, she's a murderer. She doesn't believe in restrictions!"

"That's why I called. We have a plan in motion right now that will keep you and your daughter under a twenty four hour guard until this whole ordeal is over, but we need your cooperation to make it work."

"What is that plan, detective?" she asked.

I told her the plan that Candice had devised and asked her if she thought she and Sylvia could live with it.

"I'd have to take three or four weeks off from my teaching," she said.

"My wife is a teacher, Mrs. Baker. She told me how difficult that would be for you."

"We stay in a hotel and have to eat our meals in a restaurant every day?"

"I'm afraid so, Mrs. Baker. Unless you want meals brought to you."

"We can use the hotel spa and pool?"

"As long as we can adequately guard you there," I said.

"And the county pays for everything?" she asked.

"Yes ma'am."

"We'll do it even if I have to hog tie Sylvia to get her on the plane. Hell, I need a vacation."

"May I have Portland PD call you on this number to finalize the schedule?" I asked.

"Yep. And I'll go tell the principal to find a substitute. I guess we'll see you tomorrow."

"Well that was a hard sell," I thought, as I hung up.

"Sam, it was difficult, but I finally talked them into it," I said as I leaned heavily on his door frame.

"Thanks, Hal. I'll call Portland PD. Why don't you take the rest of the day off?"

"Just what I was thinking, Sam. And, it's still only a little bit dark out."

18.
TUESDAY, NOVEMBER 14

At seven o'clock Tuesday morning I called the office and was provided with officer Murphy's cell number. At seven oh five I called her.

"Morning detective," she answered

"Good morning Claudia," I said. How are your charges this morning?"

"We're about ready to board. Sam didn't tell me I'd be riding in a toy airplane. It even has a couple of those fan things on the motors."

"Propellers. They don't fly many 747s into Pasco, Claudia."

"Yeah. Sam said it was the only flight without a layover, and those land way up in Wenatchee.

"Anyway, these nice ladies are acting as if they're goin' to Hawaii. I hope they packed their long underwear.

"Who's gonna' meet me at the hotel," she asked.

"I'll be there along with Candice Mead the prosecutor, and the first shift of guards."

"Is that hunk from Moses lake PD gonna' be there?" she asked.

"Come on Claudia. He's a married man with kids, a dog and everything. Besides, my wife says she's first in line if all that doesn't work out for him."

"Okay," she said. "I'll see you in Moses lake. You can buy me lunch."

"You got it," I said and hung up.

Yesterday had been so hectic that I had all but forgotten about the DNA results we were due to receive. I called my friend Ross over at the WSP lab in Seattle on my personal cell.

"This is Ross," he answered. "I've been wondering where you've been, Hal."

"Hi, Ross. It's been busy over here. We've made a couple of arrests in the Collins case."

"Good to hear that," he said. "Are you still interested in the DNA results?"

"Yes and No. I don't really want to know if Mr. Thomas was the father, and I don't want him to know as yet either."

"I understand, Hal. Do you want the results to be lost somewhere in the system?" he asked.

"No, just delayed a few weeks. I understand you guys are awfully busy over there."

"That we are. It may be a month before we have the results," he said.

"I can live with that," I said. "Just maybe tell me one thing."

"What's that?"

"Are you able to tell me that Mr. Thomas wasn't the father."

"No Hal. I can't."

"Then I guess I still don't know who the father was. I can only guess."

"You're one devious son of a bitch, Hal. I'm glad you're on our side."

Candice had arranged to have our guests in a top floor room at the far end of the hall from the elevators. There was a door connecting it to the only adjoining room, and our guards would use that room for a rest area. Carlos and a deputy from our office in Ritzville were standing near the check-in desk as I entered the hotel carrying three large steaming pizza boxes.

"Detective Halverson, this is officer Jensen," Carlos said by way of introduction.

We shook hands all around and I asked if the rooms were ready.

"Yes sir," said officer Jensen, "327 and 329."

"I'll take these up then," I said. "Ms. Mead from the prosecutor's office should be arriving any minute, as well as our guests. If she shows up first, send her up. You two escort officer Murphy, Sylvia and her mom to the room."

"Just you, Ms. Mead and three pizzas. I'm gonna' tell Mrs. Halverson," Carlos said with an evil smile on his face.

"That's Old Lady Halverson to you, officer Cruz. And look out for officer Murphy, she's got the hots for you."

I left Carlos standing there with his ears growing red and our deputy chuckling.

Rom 329 had two queen size beds, a small fridge, a microwave, a forty inch TV, two upholstered chairs a small table, a couch, a mini bar, and a large dresser. The bath had an oversized Jacuzzi tub and a marble shower big enough for a basketball team. Not exactly home, but not too bad.

I stepped through the connecting door to room 327 and found a king size bed, a hida bed sofa, a desk, a table with four chairs, a thirty inch TV, and a mini fridge. The bath had a five foot tub-shower. Definitely the room for the peons. I set the pizzas on the table and tried to ignore the aromas riding the steam out of the boxes.

When I heard voices in the hall way, I opened the door and was greeted with an unexpected hug from Mrs. Baker. Carlos looked at me with a silly grin and shook his head.

"Come on in and let's have some lunch before we get down to business," I said.

Being her usually sharp self, Candice said, "I don't see any beer so I'll hit the soda machine in the hall. What do you all like?"

When everyone had voiced their preference, officer Murphy piped up with. "You really know how to treat a lady to lunch, don'cha detective."

Carlos still had that silly- ass grin on his face.

After we ate, I told officer Murphy that she had performed her duties well and was relieved until her shift as a guard here at the hotel.

She looked at Carlos, mentally undressed him in front of us, smiled and said, "See ya."

Carlos' grin was replaced by the once again reddening of his ears.

Candice and I went with Sylvia and Alice into their room while Carlos and officer Jensen cleaned up from our lunch. I noticed that several pieces of left-over pizza were grouped into one box and stuffed into the fridge.

Candice pulled a tape recorder, a copy of my notes and a legal pad from her briefcase and set them on the table. She switched the recorder on.

"I know you have gone over all of this with Detective Halverson," she said. "But, I'm afraid you're going to have to do this a number of times before the trial is finished.

"I want you to think back to your earliest encounter with Grace Mallory, and tell me everything you can remember, starting at that time and up until today, about your relationship with her. Include conversations you shared in person and over the telephone, as well as any e-mail or texting. I may interrupt your narrative from time to time to ask you questions. If at any time you become uncomfortable with your mom or Detective Halverson being present, tell me and we will have them leave the room. If you become tired, we can stop and begin again when you are ready. Once we have finished this part of our preparation, we may need to go over parts of it again to be certain we have you ready to be deposed by the defense and testify at the trial.

"Now, try to relax, despite what I just said, and start at the beginning."

"I started working as a waitress at the Wing on the first of July, this year," Sylvia began. I had just moved to Cariboo from Spokane where I had done the same job at the Davenport Hotel. I had been getting increasingly uncomfortable with the crowd I was running around with there, and felt that in a small town I could do my thing and not be involved with all the political bull shit.

"The good part about the move was that no one here knew me, or had preconceived ideas about who or what I was. The bad thing was that I had no friends and was quite lonely.

"Some time toward the middle of August, this beautiful, elegant lady, Mrs. Mallory, began sitting at one of my tables two or three mornings a week. We soon were conversing beyond the diner-waitress level and I was becoming infatuated with her beauty and sophisticated manor. You can imagine my surprise and then excitement when one morning she asked if I preferred women as lovers rather than men. Before I could gather my wits and give her an answer, she said, 'I know I do. I'm in 205. Come by after you finish your shift and we can discuss this further.'

"She was an experienced lover." Here Sylvia turned to her mother and said, "Sorry mom. If this bothers you I'll wait until you leave before I go on."

"Honey," Mrs. Baker said. "I love you and nothing you can say will ever change that. I'm here because I want to support you, and I'm not leaving unless you want me too."

Sylvia began again, "Anyway, I learned a lot from her and for about six weeks we had outrageous sex.

"Then I began to grow a little tired of the arrangement when what I had once thought of as sophisticated conversation became the price I had to pay for her sexual favors.

"I wanted out, and she thought it was because I had found a new partner.

"I was attracted to Cheryl, but she made it very clear that she would be a close friend but that, for her, sex with another woman was out of the question.

"I respected that, as she respected my life style.

"Mrs. Mallory thought Cheryl was the reason for my reduced ardor, and demanded that I quit seeing her. She said that her friend, Mr. Langley had seen us stealing kisses in the back of the dining room, and had once seen Cheryl use a key to open the door of my home.

"I got a little mad and accused her of sleeping with her boy friend in the next room, the same Robert Langley.

"She told me that she never intended to sleep with a man again unless there were great gains to be had. She said Mr. Langley was nothing but a sleazy second rate lawyer and she kept him panting and drooling on a string so she could use him when she divorces her husband. But no sex now, and no sex then.

"That's when she told me to stop seeing Cheryl or she would see to it that Cheryl would stop seeing me."

"When was that?" Candice asked.

"That Saturday. The Saturday Cheryl was killed," Sylvia said.

The rest of what Sylvia told Candice was pretty much the same as what I had heard before. About six PM, Candice stood up and said, "Thank you, Sylvia, for being so strong here today. I expect to talk with you several more times before the trial but relax for now and enjoy your unusual vacation.

"I'll be submitting my list of witnesses to Mr. Langley tomorrow, and I would expect him to give me a list of his intended witnesses for the defense before the end of the week.

"I'm sure Mr. Langley will want to depose you soon, but I won't allow that to take place prior to receiving his list. I will insist that any contact between you and Mr. Langley will take place in my office or in one of the county court rooms with myself being present. I discussed this earlier with judge Orlon, and because of the alleged threats, he agrees with me as to that arrangement."

She then gave Sylvia and her mom each a hug and said, "Detective Halverson, please escort me to my car. I'm tired and I want to go home."

I followed her out the door to the hall and found Carlos sitting in a chair that he had apparently brought from the room next door. He looked up, grinned his smart-ass grin and said, "You all go straight home now, ya' hear?"

As I walked away from him and down the hall with Candice I discretely put my right hand behind my back and extended my middle finger.

19.
WEDNESDAY, NOVEMBER 15

Back in my office on Wednesday morning, I was feeling the let down that occurs, for me at least, at the end of a case. I knew it wouldn't be completely over until we actually had convictions, but for now there was nothing that I could think of to do before the trial began in twelve days.

"Both those lawyers picked up copies of your reports while you were living it up in Moses Lake yesterday," Sam said as he leaned against my door frame.

"I interviewed a lot of people during the last few weeks," I said. "I wonder how many they'll call as defense witnesses."

"I don't know about ol' Clayton, but I'd think that Langley guy would call Mr. Thomas and maybe Doctor Mallory."

"Ms. Mead and I were kinda' hoping he'd have the doctor on the stand. If we can depose him with the right questions we might be able to drive a little wedge between him and his wife."

"But can you have him testify against her, Hal?" he asked.

"We can't force him, but once he's on the stand for the defense, Ms. Mead may just allow him to vent a little about how his wife is trying to push the blame in his direction."

"What about Mr. Thomas?" Sam asked. "You think Langley's gonna' try to get the jury lookin' in his direction?"

"Hell, he's already told the court that we should have arrested Sylvia Baker. Who knows what he'll do next?

"What about Clayton?" I asked. "What do you think his strategy is?"

"I think he's just gonna' watch Mrs. Mallory's trial and see what happens. If she's found innocent, God forbid, He'll ask for the charges against the doctor to be dropped.

"If she's found guilty, he'll advise the doctor to do the same. If the doctor still wants to plead not guilty, I'll wager that ol' Clayton pleads poor health and goes to Arizona."

"Nah," I said. "He lost his condo in a poker game."

"He told me yesterday that he got it back, Sam said. "Judge Orlon knew the judge that won it off him and called him after the arraignment on Monday. Seems he had tried to sell it but the market is so bad down there that no one even called to look at it. Then, he tried to rent it out, and again, no takers. Still, he was responsible for all the condo association dues as well as upkeep on the unit. He told judge Orlon that it was the worst damn thing he had ever won and he wanted to give it back to Clayton."

"That being the case, I'm surprised Clayton was still here yesterday to pick up the files," I said.

"Me too," said Sam. "but if the goin' gets tough, you can be sure ol' Clayton will be goin'."

Our conversation reminded me that it was about time for me to make a phone call and eat a little crow.

"This is George Thomas' phone. Please leave a message after the beep."

"Mr. Thomas, this is Hal Halverson from the Adams County sheriff's office. I have some good news for you. Please call me back at this number at your earliest convenience."

My call back came at eleven thirty AM. "Detective Halverson, this is George Thomas. What is your good news? Do you have a terminal illness or something else that may cheer me up?"

"I was calling to tell you that we have made arrests in the Cheryl Collins case and I wanted to take you to lunch as part of my apology for putting you through the ringer."

"Lunch? Where, at the county jail?"

"No sir. You name the place and I'll even meet you there so you won't have to worry about riding in my car and being locked in.

"Your ordeal isn't quite over, Mr. Thomas. I want to talk with you before a certain lawyer does."

"Would you mind coming to our training facility about noon tomorrow, Detective? I would appreciate it if you could help me dispel some of the rumors around here. People have avoided me like I had the plague since you visited me last."

"My pleasure, George. One thing though."

"What is it?"

"Don't talk to any lawyer, no matter who they say they represent until we have had a chance to meet."

"Sounds serious, but okay"

"See you at noon tomorrow."

I spent the rest of Wednesday sharpening pencils, drinking coffee and pretty much driving everyone in the office nuts. Before I left for the night, I told Sam I was going up to Moses lake tomorrow for a little early Christmas shopping.

"Bull shit, Hal. I don't know what you're up to, but you better take your county SUV in case we need you to do something while you're up there."

"Thanks, Sam. By the way?" I asked. "What do you want for Christmas?"

"I want a conviction on your case and for you to remember who is s'pose to be the boss around here."

"I can't promise both boss, but I'll sure try every chance I get."

20.
THURSDAY, NOVEMBER 16

It was still a half hour to daylight when Shirley backed down the driveway on her way to school. I puttered around, picking up after our breakfast of toast and coffee, took the garbage out and generally tried to kill time without doing anything really useful. If I were into exercise and all that fitness stuff, this would have been a good time to relieve my stress with a workout on my nonexistent apparatus in the garage. Personally, I'd rather stress out than workout. I had another cup of coffee instead.

I did the New York Times crossword puzzles from the last three weeks, only Monday through Wednesday 'cause the rest were too frustrating, and hit the shower.

Dressed in a clean shirt and fairly clean tie and sport coat, I was ready at least a half hour earlier than was necessary, and decided I would drive at a nice relaxing pace and enjoy the scenery on my way to Moses Lake.

The scenery between Cariboo and Moses Lake in the winter was much like a black and white movie. The sky was gray, the patches of snow were gray and white and what vegetation you could see had all turned black from the freezing temperatures. The only color was the yellow line down the middle of the road and it was faded and scuffed from the snow plows.

I was fifteen minutes early when I told the receptionist I was here to see Mr. Thomas.

"Do you want to sneak up on him again?" she asked, "or, should I tell him you're here."

"I'll just wait over there," I said, pointing to a couple of plastic upholstered chairs on the opposite wall. "He's expecting me this time."

"You might be more comfortable waiting in the break room. That's the first door on your right down the hall. George has asked the staff to meet with him there at noon. I guess you might be involved with that."

On the wall of the break room were pictures of what must have been every model of airplane ever built by Boeing. They were interesting, but the best display was a series of photos of a 707 piloted by 'Tex' Johnson doing a barrel roll over Lake Washington in the late fifties. I had heard about that stunt at the time, but hadn't realized how impressive it must have been until I saw these pictures.

People began coming into the room just after noon. George Thomas was the last to enter as he followed the receptionist through the door. He wasn't looking as tan and robust as I had remembered him, and I assumed that I may have been somewhat responsible for the change. I walked up to him, and thankfully we shook hands. The chatter diminished and stopped altogether as he started to speak.

"Ladies and gentlemen, I'd like to introduce Detective Halverson of the Adams County Sheriff's department. I believe he has a few words to say that may explain the unusual actions of law enforcement officers here and at my home. Detective?"

"Thank you folks for taking time out of your busy day to meet with us," I started.

"Just less than a month ago, a close friend of George's was the victim of a homicide. It is a fact that most homicides are committed by people known to the victim, and in many cases, the people most closely associated to the victim.

"That being said, we did a vigorous investigation that I'm sure, at times, caused great discomfort for George as well you, his co-workers.

"We have made two arrests in the case and George should be considered completely exonerated by our investigation.

"I wish to publicly apologize to George on behalf of myself and the three law enforcement agencies involved.

"He has remained a gentleman throughout this ordeal and is to be commended for the actions he has taken behind the scenes.

"As this case is about to go to trial I will not be able to answer questions at this time.

There was a round of applause that I assume was intended for George, and then handshakes and hugs from his co-workers. No one shook my hand or hugged me.

I left the room and he soon followed.

"How about a good steak, George. You look like you could use some nourishment. I'm sorry the experience has been so hard on you."

"Just getting the winter time pallor," he replied. "No sun, no water skiing, not much time for fresh air."

As we left the building I said, "You can ride with me and I promise to bring you back right after lunch, or If you still don't trust me, I'll meet you at that steak house over on Strafford."

"I'll take a chance and ride with you, Detective. It might be that you're an honorable man, just doing his job."

The wraparound seat in the booth was a nice soft leather and the air carried the wonderful aroma of fine whiskey and beef being seared, that makes you think, "Cholesterol be damned. I'm glad I'm here.'"

The waitress had taken our orders and we each had a glass of single malt scotch in our hand when George asked, "Hal, I assume I can call you Hal since you have been referring to me as George for the last forty five minutes."

"I had hoped you would," I replied.

"So, Hal, what is the real reason for your visit today?"

"I wanted, off the record of course, to warn you about what will probably happen in the next few weeks regarding the trial."

"I have to admit," he said, "I wasn't aware of the arrests. I don't take the local papers or watch the local news on TV. One murder over here in the boonies doesn't make much news in Seattle where it seems to be an everyday occurrence. I finally went on line after your call yesterday and was none too surprised to see Doctor Mallory's name. But Mrs. Mallory as the murderer? I didn't see that coming."

"I believe she is one conniving bitch," I said. "Completely self serving and devoid of any conscience. "

"I'll take your word for that," he said. "But, why are we here?"

"Mrs. Mallory's lawyer, I believe you may have met him at the memorial, will undoubtedly try to muddy the waters of real evidence by attacking you, George. I'm sure he thinks you were the father of her unborn child."

"Well, am I?" he asked.

"I don't know and you don't want to know. We don't want to provide him with any extra ammunition to be used against you or to confuse the jury.

"The results of your DNA test have been delayed at the lab. That way, when he asks if you are the father you can truthfully, and under oath say that you really don't know."

The waitress then appeared with our orders and the only sound for the next five minutes was the clink of silverware and an occasional "Mmmm." After I had devoured the last scrap of meat on my plate and wiped any juices that may have remained from my mouth, I asked, "Did you know that Mrs. Mallory has retained Robert Langley, the same lawyer that your wife has said will represent her in your divorce?"

"I realized I'd heard the name before when he approached me at the memorial. I did enjoy how your young officer stepped between me and the sleazes. I thought for a moment that one or all of those three lawyers might soil their pants."

I went on, "I'm sure that he'll call for you to be deposed before the trial, as will the prosecuting attorney, Candice Mead. Answer only the questions he asks with complete honesty. Do not offer any information.

"Also, the prosecution will be calling for your wife to testify, not against you, but to help establish the chain of events on the Sunday morning following the murder. I advise you to have no contact with her until after the trial, and don't allow Mr. Langley to bait you concerning your relationships.

"Just between you and me, I've met and talked with your wife and while I don't condone your actions, I can't blame you either.

"Dessert?" I asked.

He declined saying he had to get back to work, and I left a wad of cash on the table. This meeting had never taken place.

When I dropped George back at the training facility, I told him to take care of himself. I wasn't convinced that it was only a lack of sun that caused his sallow complexion, and hoped I hadn't aggravated what ever strange condition he suffered from that had cost him his commercial license.

Since I had driven a county car to Moses Lake to do my 'Christmas shopping', I thought I should do something more visible for the county while I was in the area. The hotel where we had Sylvia and her mother stashed was only a couple of blocks off my route back to Cariboo, so I decided to see how things were going with our witness and our guard detail.

The elevator took me quickly to the third floor, and when I got to the end of the hallway Carlos was sitting in the same chair, in the same place as he was yesterday.

"Haven't you moved since I was here last?" I asked.

"Yeah, I have. I'm sittin' out here because I've already lost all my pocket change and half my walkin' around money to those card sharks in that room"

"Card sharks?" I asked. "What card sharks?"

"Sylvia, her mom and that Amazon you sent up here to help with the guard detail."

"Officer Murphy?" I asked.

"That's the one. When I told 'em I had to quit because I was running out of money, she suggested we play strip poker and the other two agreed."

"That could be grounds for a sexual harassment charge. Want me to run 'em in?"

"Nah, I might have lead 'em on a little. I haven't had that much female attention for a while."

"Other than that, how are things going?" I asked.

"Quiet. In fact, boring."

"Has Ms. Mead been by today?"

"She was here for an hour this morning, according to the log. I didn't come on until eleven so I missed her."

"Well I better go in and say hello, anyway," I said.

"I'd leave your wallet out here. I think you're probably safe as far as the strip poker goes."

"With any luck," I said. "You will be old some day too."

"Yeah, but I'll still have that Latin flair."

I turned, knocked on the door and was greeted by a chorus of, "Come on in Carlos."

"See?" he said.

When I opened the door I could see looks of disappointment on three faces, but I tried not to let it bother me.

"Officer Murphy," I said. "Officer Cruz has asked me to file charges of sexual harassment against you."

She turned deathly pale, and for a minute I was afraid she was going to faint.

"No, no, no," I'm only joking," I said. "Keep up the good work. It's good for his ego. Anyone can see he's lacking in self confidence as well as respect for his elders."

"But, as for the ordinance against gambling..."

Mrs. Baker, who had obviously been sampling some of the wine in the mini bar said, "You can't arrest me, detective, I'm an Oregon citizen."

"Damn, that's right," I said. "If everything is alright here, then I will leave you to your own devices."

"On your way out, send officer Cruz back in," Sylvia said. "He could be a mind changer."

"No way young lady. He's liable to ask for hazardous duty pay. If there is nothing else I can do for you ladies, I bid you adieu," I said on my way out the door."

In the hall, Carlos once again said, "See?"

"Just make sure for me that any alcohol consumed in that room is done so by our guests."

"You got it Detective. Your lady officer is just being friendly with 'em. She's actually a nice gal. Please don't let her know that I referred to her as an Amazon. She'd probably break my neck."

As I was climbing back into my car, I realized I really didn't want to go back to my office and count paper clips. Sam wouldn't be assigning me another case until this one was put to bed, so I'd just be driving myself and everyone around me nuts as I waited for the trial to start. So I called Candice to see how things were progressing, and to ask if I could do anything to help.

"Good afternoon, Detective. I was just about to call you."

"Well, here I am. What's up?"

"I've got the defense's list of witnesses, and a list of who he wants to depose from our list. You got time to look at 'em?"

"I'm in Moses lake right now. I should be at your office in less than an hour."

"Great. See you about three."

"Good," I thought. "Something to keep my mind occupied for the rest of the day."

I-90 is about a straight as a highway can be, running from Moses Lake to Ritzville. A sugar beet processing plant and a potato processing plant, both filling the air with foul smelling vapors, were about the only things to be seen other than mile after mile of wheat stubble. I ended up singing to myself in order to stay awake while that steak in my stomach kept telling me to take a nap. Since no one, including myself, could possibly fall asleep listening to me sing, I made it safely to the prosecutors office in fifty minutes. I had five minutes to spare and I thought about doing some deep thinking for that length of time, but decided against it. If I got too deep in thought and no one realized I was in this car, I could freeze to death before tomorrow morning.

Candice greeted me with, "Your eyelids are sagging, Hal."

"Must be from all the sleep I've lost worrying about the proper prosecution of my air-tight case."

"Air-tight it's not, but I'm working on patching it up the best I can."

"How are we doing on it Candice?"

"Maybe better than I had expected at this point. I have Langley's list of witnesses and it's pretty short."

"Really? Who's on it?" I asked.

" Doctor Mallory and Mr. Thomas. I think he's going to try and convince the jury that Mr. Thomas wanted to get rid of Cheryl to avoid an expensive divorce.

"Or that Doctor Mallory did it because he was angry that Cheryl had rejected his advances, both spiritual and sexual."

"Don't you already have Mr. Thomas on the list of prosecution witnesses?"

"Yeah, but he's just making sure he gets a shot at him in case we don't call his name at trial."

"Well this gives us a chance to depose the doctor and maybe have him see the error of his ways in defending his wife. Who of our list does he want to depose?"

"Sylvia, Mr. Thomas, the lead crime scene officer, the tech that inspected Cheryl's car and the pool heater guy."

"None of our Latino witnesses?"

"He said there was no point in my calling witnesses who didn't under stand or speak English. I agreed."

"So he doesn't know about Ramon's policy for his crew?"

"Apparently not. Too bad for the arrogant ass and his arrogant client."

"When are you going to depose Doctor Mallory?" I asked.

"I thought I'd wait 'till Monday. Have him enjoy another week- end behind bars while his wife is on the outside enjoying the good life."

"Splendid idea. Can I join you then?"
"See you here at ten thirty AM , Monday. Bring your rubber hose."

21.
FRIDAY, NOVEMBER 17

Friday morning found me sipping the last of my early morning coffee and reading the newspaper when Shirley gave me a peck on the cheek and announced, "I'll be home at three forty five. Be packed for a weekend in Leavenworth."
"Leavenworth?" I'm spending the weekend in a federal prison?"
"No, dummy. Leavenworth Washington. I've made reservations and you're gettin' out of Dodge for a couple days."
Leavenworth is a pseudo Bavarian village located on the eastern edge of the Cascade Mountain range on US Highway 2, a little over a hundred miles north of Cariboo. It has a Christmas like atmosphere the year around with tourists crowding the shops buying Alpine souvenirs, many of which are manufactured in China. To me, it's greatest asset is the abundance of German restaurants and beer.

I called in and asked Sam if there was anything I could do to help at the office today.
"Yeah, there is," he replied. "Stay the hell away. Until the trial I don't expect to see your sorry ass in here unless you have something important to do concerning that trial. But, thanks for asking."
"'Well," I thought. "I guess I'll get ready to go to Leavenworth."
Some time after lunch I began practice in preparation for the beer I would be consuming over the week-end. When

Shirley got home, she assessed the situation and volunteered to do the driving. I agreed.

We left home about four fifteen, and taking the flat land route through Quincy, Ephrata and Wenatchee, were at our Leavenworth hotel at six thirty. After unpacking, we walked the streets of town, peering in shop windows until an aroma wafting its way up the stairs from one of the cellar restaurants lured us to gastric oblivion.

As we waddled to our car after checking out on Sunday, we swore to each other that we would start dieting tomorrow. Or maybe Tuesday.

While in Wenatchee, we of course stopped at Costco, and as we grazed our way through the free food samples, bought cases of stuff that would last us at least a year.

Then, home again to start the final week before the trial.

22.
MONDAY, NOVEMBER 20

Monday morning I obeyed Sam's edict and left the house at nine o'clock for Ritzville and our ten thirty session with Doctor Mallory. I arrived at Candice's office at ten oh five, and asked her, "What is the procedure here this morning?"

"Doctor Mallory will be accompanied by his attorney Clayton Ogden as he is brought up here from the jail. The guard will wait outside the door while I depose his prisoner. Mr. Langley requested that he be present but since he is not the attorney of record, his request was denied. We'll do this in the conference room next door, and I want you to sit on one side of the table with me, while Doctor Mallory and his attorney sit on the other. You may not question Doctor Mallory directly, but you may write suggestions on a tablet for me to read. Any questions?"

"No ma'am."

"It sounds like they've arrived," she said. "Let's go mess with him a little."

Candice began with, "Good morning Doctor Mallory, good morning Mr. Ogden."

Their returned good mornings were not quite as cheerful as her's.

"As you both can see," she continued. "We have with us this morning a court stenographer, who will double as the court clerk, as well as a detective from the Adams County Sheriff's department. At this time the stenographer will have Doctor Mallory swear to be truthful during these proceedings."

"Please rise, Doctor Mallory," the stenographer said, " and raise your right hand.

Doctor Mallory did stand up, raise his right hand and did swear to tell the truth, so help him God.

"I will remind you, Doctor Mallory, that you are not obligated to make any statement that may incriminate yourself. Nor are you obligated to say anything that would incriminate Mrs. Mallory. However, if you do indeed say anything that incriminates either one of you it will be considered voluntary by the court, and may be entered as evidence against you or your wife. Do you understand?" she asked.

Doctor Mallory looked at his attorney who nodded and then nodded himself.

"As these proceedings are being recorded, Doctor, I need a vocal response to the question."

"Yes, I understand," he muttered.

"Doctor Mallory, can you tell me where you were three weeks ago on Saturday October 28th?"

"I was most likely at my home on 12 SW."

"Most likely?" she asked.

"Yes ma'am. At the time I was overmedicating and some parts of my recollections are little vague."

"Were you taking a prescribed medicine, Doctor?"

"Yes. I have a prescription for medical marijuana."

"Really? Can you tell me what kind of a condition you were treating?"

Here his attorney stepped in and said, "His medical history is protected information. Do not answer that question Doctor."

"Were you overdosing yourself, Doctor, or was the amount prescribed excessive?"

"I'm not sure," he answered. "I just used what ever my wife gave me."

"Are you using the medication at the present time, Doctor?"

"I stopped using it a week ago last Friday at the suggestion of Detective Halverson, and I wish to thank you, Detective. My mind is functioning much better since I quit."

"Doctor Mallory, when you were questioned about the time your wife arrived home on the night of the murder, you told Detective Halverson that it was after midnight. Yet, Mrs. Mallory claims she got home between nine thirty and ten PM."

"As I said before, I was somewhat impaired at that time. Her recollection is undoubtedly correct."

"Your fingerprints were found on the mechanism that opens the tailgate of Miss Collins' car. Do you recall at anytime, opening, or helping someone open the tailgate of Miss Collin's car?" she asked.

"I vaguely remember helping someone to remove our vacuum from the rear of some car, but I'm not sure who's."

"Do you vaguely remember doing it or do you possibly just remember someone telling you that you had?"

"Oh, I'm sure that I must have done it," he replied.

"Did you know that yours are the only fingerprints that were found in the pool heater room. The room where it is believed Miss Collins was killed?"

"I've been made aware of that."

"Are you aware that your wife is presently free on bail while you're still incarcerated?"

"So I've been told."

"Has your wife visited you or attempted to contact you since your arrest?"

"I was told that we were forbidden to communicate, ma'am, otherwise I'm sure she would have."

"Were you aware that your wife and her attorney often stayed in adjoining rooms at The Swept Wing Inn?"

"They've been friends since we lived over in Bellevue. I'm sure they just happened to be given those rooms. The doors between the rooms are locked."

"Did you know that we have a witness that claims to have had a homosexual affair with Mrs. Mallory?"

"I'm certain that she must be lying. My wife and I both believe that homosexuality is an abomination and forbidden by God."

"Mrs. Mallory claims that you are impotent. Is that true?"

Here old Clayton Ogden seemed to wake up and said, "You needn't answer that question Doctor. Do you have anything relevant to ask my client Ms. Mead? If not, we're leaving."

"Just one more question, if I may?

"Doctor Mallory, were you forced by unexpected circumstances to help remove Miss Collins' body from your premises late Saturday night, the 28th, or early Sunday morning the 29th of October?"

The doctor seemed to think for just a moment before his attorney said, "Doctor Mallory has nothing further to say. Good day Ms. Mead, Detective."

Candice then said, "Thank you both for your time this morning. I hope you are enjoying your stay, Doctor Mallory."

"Whew!" I said once we were back in Candice's office. "That ought to give him some food for thought. That is, unless he has completely mellowed his brain."

"Not exactly 'Macho Man,' is he. God what a limp dick."

I'm not used to hearing that kind of language from a lady lawyer. I think my jaw may have dropped a little.

"Well?" I asked trying to sound manly. "What the heck is next?"

Candice said she would be interviewing the techs that did the fingerprinting on the car, as well as the sergeant in charge of crime scene investigation, today. Then tomorrow morning, Mr. Thomas and the pool heater guy would be here for interviews prior to Mr. Langley's afternoon deposition of our witnesses. Tomorrow afternoon, providing that she shows up, will be Mrs. Thomas' turn. Wednesday, she planned being in Cariboo to interview our Latino witnesses as well as the two men who found the body.

"I'd like for you to be present during all of my witness interviews, Hal."

"No problem. When do we start?"

The sergeant in charge of the crime scene investigation was Bill Miller. I liked him because he was fatter and balder than me. I was probably ten years his senior though, so I guess it evened out.

He was sworn in and then Candice asked, "Sergeant Miller, will you please describe the scene of your investigation on Saturday, November the eleventh?"

"The Mallory home is an upscale residence in Grant County in the nine hundred block on the south side of 12

SW just west of State highway 262. Because the deceased was found in Adams County, the homicide investigation had been the initiated by the Adams County Sheriff. As such, we were authorized by the Grant County Sheriff to pursue the investigation into Grant county with the stipulation that any and all results of the investigation be made available to the Grant County sheriff if so requested."

"Good, but a little more information than is necessary, unless asked for by the defense," Candice said. "What were you looking for at this residence, where did you look and what did you find pertaining to this case, Sergeant?"

"We were looking for anything that would indicate that Miss Collins had at any time been on the premises. Also, any sign that there had been any kind of physical struggle or altercation on the premises. To do so, we dusted all likely surfaces for finger prints and looked for damage to, or unusual placement of anything in the house."

"Did you find anything of significance in the house, Sergeant?"

"No ma'am, but when we checked the pool heater room we found a lack of fingerprints on everything but a chair and the flue apparatus for the heater. All other surfaces had definitely been wiped down to remove any sign of prints."

"Were you able to identify the prints you found, sergeant?"

"Yes. They belonged to Doctor Mallory."

I interrupted here. "Bill, were there no other prints on that chair?"

Candice then interupted me, saying, "Must I remind you, detective, that any questions you have for the witness must be asked by me?"

"Sorry," I said. "May he answer?"

"Go ahead Sergeant Miller," she said.

"No, Hal. Why?"

"May I answer?" I asked.

"Yeah, what the hell,"' she said

"I moved it when I was interviewing Doctor Mallory. My prints had to have been wiped off after I left, then Doctor Mallory's were left some time later. That had to be very deliberate and was probably done after the Mallory's became concerned about our investigation."

"Do you think that affects your theory about how and why Cheryl was killed?" asked Candice.

"Probably not. It's interesting though."

"Is there anything else you wish to add?" she asked Bill.

"No ma'am. I think we've covered everything we found."

"Thank you Sergeant. I'm sure you've done this enough times in the past to know better than to volunteer any knowledge to the defense when you are deposed or on the stand. If we feel the need for additional information we will ask you for it."

"Yes ma'am. I'll see you at the defense deposition?"

"Detective Halverson and I will be there," she assured him.

Sergeant Susan O'Brien was followed through the door by the tech she called wrench head. He had opened the door for her and held the back of her chair as she sat down at the conference table.

"Ms. Mead," I said, "This is Sergeant O'Brien, our finger print tech and Officer Kent Williams who is in charge of the impound garage. Officer Williams did the inspection of Miss Collin's car."

"Officer Williams, did you find anything in or on Miss Collins' car that you felt was unusual?" Candice asked after they had sworn to tell the truth..

"Yes," he began. "The complete driver's area of the car had been wiped down destroying any traces of fingerprints in that part of the vehicle. The rest of the car had prints belonging to Miss Collins and Mr. George Thomas as well as other people that were known to have been Miss Collins' acquaintances. The driver's side door had also been wiped clean. We did find prints, later identified as belonging to Doctor Mallory, on the spare tire cover and the mechanism that releases the spare tire to enable entry into the rear of the vehicle. And the carpet on the floor of the rear compartment appeared to have been spot cleaned recently. However, we did find traces of body fluids still present in those spots."

"Body fluids, Officer? "

"Yes ma'am. A recently deceased body will seep fluids as the muscles relax. I believe these fluids were a result of that happening."

I spoke up, "You didn't mention that part of your findings when we talked, Kent."

"Detective!" Candice said as she threw her hands in the air in a gesture of despair.

"It was in my written report, Hal. I never brought it up because I figured you had already concluded that she had been transported in the vehicle."

"My fault," I said. "I should have been more diligent in my reading. Did you identify those fluids as belonging to Miss Collins."

"Yes we did. At the time, Miss Collins' body was still in the county morgue so the Coroner was able to do the matching."

"We do have the coroner on our witness list, don't we?" I asked Candice.

"Of course. I read all of the reports thoroughly. You must have gone into one of your deep thinking sessions when you read this one."

Ouch! That would have hurt if I wasn't occasionally guilty of that happening. "Maybe," I thought, "I am getting too old for this job."

"Do you have anything else to add, Officer Williams?"

"Only this, ma'am. Detective Halverson may be older than God but some times he comes up with good ideas. His obtaining samples of the Mallory's fingerprints is one example."

"Thanks, Kent," I said. "Now I guess I owe you one."

"Yes sir," he replied.

"Sergeant O'Brien," Candice asked, "do you have anything to add to Officer Williams' report?"

"Only that I processed the data that Officer Williams collected and did the fingerprint analysis."

"You are confident in your fingerprint work?"

"My computer and I are quite capable, Ms. Mead. I look forward to the trial."

"Thank you both for your time. You know the routine for your depositions. Answer only the questions you are asked. Do not volunteer any additional information. Detective Halverson and I will be there to advise if necessary."

Officer Williams jumped up and helped Sergeant O'Brien with her chair, then opened the door and followed her from the room.

"Poor guy," I said. "She hardly knows he's alive."

"Wrong again, Detective. Didn't you see how she watched him out of the corner of her eye. She's playing him like a prize fish. Once he passes his sergeant's exam she'll land him and he'll think it was all his idea."

"So he finally signed up and is going to take the exam. Good for him," I said.

"She signed him up and he can't back out or he'll look like a wimp."

"How do you know that?" I asked.

"Girl's network. Be careful 'cause we're all around you."

"And scary," I replied.

"Well that's it for today," Candice said, "want'a join me for a drink across the street at the Library Lounge."

"Thanks, but your Girl's network has me worried. If my girl hears about me having a drink with you it could be uncomfortable at home."

"We all think of you as a harmless old man, you know," she said.

"Okay, one drink. But, if you make a pass at me, I'm out'a there."

She winked and said, "Fair enough."

I managed to leave the bar without having been accosted by any of the female patrons and was feeling a little unappreciated. This feeling evaporated when I walked through the door from my garage to the kitchen and Shirley gave me a big hug, a little kiss and asked, "What were you doing having drinks with a woman half your age?"

Girl's network?

"Fix me a nice dinner," she continued, "and I might forgive you."

23.
TUESDAY, NOVEMBER 21

Tuesday morning the drive to Ritzville was uneventful but I did have some concern for my trip back home this evening.

During the night, the temperature had risen to about forty degrees and a gusty wind was driving a heavy rain from the south. It doesn't rain much in this part of the state, and when it does this time of the year, look out. Often the temperature will suddenly drop below the freezing point while the rain is falling. This can create a layer of ice on everything, making roads all but undrivable, and cause power lines and trees to snap under the accumulated weight.

It was five minutes to nine when I entered Candice's office.

"Good morning Hal. I trust you were appropriately admonished for your sinful ways when you arrived home last evening."

"I'm not even goin' to ask how Shirley knew about our drink," I said.

"Better that you don't."

She then walked to the coffee pot, poured a large mug full and handed it to me. "How'd she know I wanted a cup of coffee," I thought.

George Thomas entered Candice's office at nine thirty. He appeared thinner and with less coloring even than when I was with him last week.

"We're going to do the interview in the conference room next door," Candice said. "Would you like to bring a cup of coffee with you Mr. Thomas?"

"No, thank you. I've pretty much quit drinking coffee. It no longer sits well in my stomach," he replied.

"Are you ill, George?" I asked.

"I seem to be having a reoccurrence of the ailment that caused my commercial pilot's license to be revoked. I feel certain that it will go back into remission again soon."

We sat down at the conference table with Candice and me again on one side and our interviewee on the other. The court reporter did her job swearing Mr. Thomas to be truthful and the deposition began.

"I'm Candice Mead, and I will be representing Adams County in the murder trial of Mrs. Grace Mallory. The reason I have called you as a witness is solely to establish a time line for the series of events that occurred on the night of Miss Collins' death. I have no reason to delve into your relationship other than to establish the reason for, and the time of your last meeting.

"However, we believe that the defense will attempt to convince the jury that you should be considered a viable suspect even though the investigation by the sheriff's detective has cleared you from suspicion. You must be prepared for an assault on your character today during the defense's deposition, as well as in the actual trial. You need to tell the absolute truth here this morning, this afternoon and during the trial.

"Do you have any questions for me at this point, Mr. Thomas?" she asked.

"No ma'am. I just want to get this over with and go on from here."

"Very well.

"Mr. Thomas, when did you last see Miss Collins?"

"Saturday the twenty eighth of October, at about eleven PM."

"Where were you at that time?"

"The Park and ride at SR-17 and I-90."

"Why were you there, Mr. Thomas?"

"That was where we would meet. I didn't want my car to be seen at her home, so I'd leave it there and ride to her place in her's."

"Mr. Thomas," Candice warned, "if the defense asks you the same question, don't say anything more than it was where you would meet. If they ask why you met there, be as brief in your explanation as possible."

"Yes ma'am."

"Did you leave the park and ride together that night?"

"No. We left separately and I never saw her again"

"Again, Mr. Thomas, a one word answer was all that was called for. Do you understand my reasoning?"

"Not really. I no longer have anything to hide from anyone, Ms. Mead."

"The defense will attempt to twist everything you say into something that makes you look like an unreliable witness, or even worse, a murder suspect. Please don't provide them with any unnecessary ammunition."

"Okay, I'll try not to do so."

"Did you see which direction Miss Collins went when she left the park and ride?"

"No. I assume..."

"Hold it. No assumptions!"

"Yes ma'am."

"Where did you go after she left the lot?"

"To my home in Moses Lake."

"That's better, Mr. Thomas.

"Did you know at that time that Miss Collins was pregnant?"

"No."

"Were you the father of the unborn child?"

"I don't know."

"Was a DNA sample taken from you for the purpose of determining whether or not you were the father?"

"Yes."

"Have the results of that test been made available?"

"Not that I am aware of."

"Thank you Mr. Thomas. I have Detective Halverson's recording of his interviews with you. Is there anything in those interviews you wish to correct?"

"Only what I said on the first time we met about my wife being home in Mill Creek when I was there on that Sunday. I believe that was corrected during our second meeting."

"Yes it was, Mr. Thomas. Thank you, and we'll see you here again at one thirty this afternoon for your deposition. Take care of yourself."

As he went out the door I could see how his clothes seemed to hang on his frame like they would a hanger in a closet. Once again I hoped that I wasn't partly responsible for his relapse.

Ten minutes later there was a man clad in dark blue coveralls, sworn in, and sitting across the table from us. He did not appear to be happy.

"Do I really have to do this?" he asked none to quietly.

Candice looked at him like Mrs. Perkins would an unruly patron of her coffee shop and said, "Yes you do Mr. Sanders. This will be the easy part because you are to be a witness for the prosecution and we wish to have everyone believe your testimony. However, this afternoon you will be deposed by the defense and they probably won't like what you have to say, and will try to discredit your testimony and even your character."

"What if I just get up and leave right now?"

"Detective Halverson, who is sitting on my right, will arrest you for violation of a court order to appear, and put you in a cell downstairs until you have decided to cooperate."

"Can't I just pay a fine or something and be on my way?" he asked.

"Mr. Sanders, an innocent woman has been murdered and we believe you possess the skills and information to help put her killer behind bars."

"But the Mallory's have been nice to me. Big tips when I serviced their heater. Why would I want to do anything that'd hurt them?"

"We believe that Mrs. Mallory is a cold blooded killer. Without your testimony she could be set free to kill again. Do you have a family, Mr. Sanders? How safe would they be with someone like Mrs. Mallory in the area? Who knows how easily Mrs. Mallory may be offended to the point where she kills again? If she gets away with murder once, why not again?"

"Okay, okay. What do I need to do."

"Simply answer my questions honestly," she said. "and heed my instructions for the deposition and trial. Then you'll be able to live with yourself knowing you did the right thing."

Her first question was, "What qualifies you to be an expert on the Mallory's pool heating system?"

"One hundred eighty hours of class room work while I was apprenticing for two years."

"How long have you been doing this type of work?"

"Eight years as an employee and two years as the owner of my own company."

"Are you presently owner of that company."

"Yes ma'am."

"How long have you been doing maintenance on the pool heater at the Mallory' residence?"

"For two years, but the Mallory's have only lived there for about six months."

"How many times have you serviced the pool heater since the Mallory's have lived there?"

"Twice. Once right after they moved in to make sure it was functioning correctly and to familiarize them with the equipment. Once again about two months ago as a regular four month check up."

"While familiarizing them with the equipment, did you caution them about the dangers associate with the heater?"

"Yes. I warned them about possible carbon monoxide poisoning if the flue became damaged, and I cautioned them not to attempt any repairs, if the unit appear to not be working properly. I told them that someone from my company was available twenty four seven should the unit fail in any way."

"Did your company receive any calls for repair of this unit during the last six months?"

"No. We did only the routine four month service. Everything seemed in good working order at that time."

"On the evening that you were called by the Adams County Sheriff's department, did you find anything unusual when you examined the heating unit?"

"Yes Ma'am. The damper on the flue had been bent and appeared to have been jammed in the pipe recently. As a result there was a build-up of soot inside the flue."

"If the damper had been jammed as you say, in what way would it have affected the operation of the heater?"

"It would have become quite inefficient in heating the pool."

"Is there anything else that would have resulted from such a jam?"

"There would have been an increase of heat in the heater room and it could have caused the carbon monoxide level in the room to reach a critical level."

"A high enough carbon monoxide level to cause asphyxiation?"

"That is a possibility," he answered.

"Thank you Mr. Sanders. The lawyer for the defense will most likely ask you the same questions during your deposition. Answer him just as you have answered me here this morning. He may pretend to be your friend but, he is not. Do not volunteer any additional information and do not allow him to get under your skin. Detective Halverson and I will see you here at three, this afternoon."

"Who pays for my time while I'm up here doing all this?" he asked. "This is costing me."

"Here is my card Mr. Sanders," Candice replied. Submit an invoice from your company for travel and time at your normal rate, to me at the Adams County Prosecutors office. I will see that you're properly compensated."

We shared a delivery pizza while we reviewed what our witnesses had said to date. Both of us felt confident that our case would hold up in court, barring some unanticipated disaster.

George Thomas walked into Candice's office at one o'clock and I asked him if he'd like a piece of the pizza.

"No thanks, Hal. I just don't seem to have much of an appetite these days. Hopefully it'll come back when all this is over. Well this and my divorce. I guess I'm lucky that this

Langley character is busy here with this trial 'cause I've been told that he and my wife are intending to take me to the cleaners."

"I'd sure like to find a way to nail him for some of the responsibility for Cheryl's death," I told him. "I'm certain he was telling Mrs. Mallory lies about Cheryl and her friend Sylvia in an effort to get Mrs. Mallory in the sack."

"If I can help you in any way, Hal, let me know. You were pretty hard on me at the start of this thing but I deserved it. You were doing your job and you're good at finding the truth. I've quit lying to myself now as well as to you. I guess that's one good thing coming out of this whole mess."

I picked up the nearly empty pizza box and took it out into the hallway to find a garbage can when Mr. Langley spotted me.

"Hey!" he shouted. "Don't throw that away. I'll eat it."

"Poor starving lawyer," I thought as I dumped it into the garbage.

"C'mon," he said. "We're all friends around here. Why'd you do that?"

"Oh, I'm sorry," I said. "I didn't think you were serious. It's still on top in there if you really want it."

Back in the conference room again, we were seated this time on the same side of the table as George Thomas. He was on the far left, then Candice, then me on the far right. Across from us sat Mr. Langley and at the end of the table to the left, sat the court clerk. The clerk swore Mr. Thomas in and the afternoon began.

"I am Robert Langley, the attorney representing Mrs. Grace Mallory in the case of Adams County Vs. Grace Mallory who is charged with murder in the second degree of Miss Cheryl Collins and her unborn child. Remember, Mr. Thomas, you are under oath and must truthfully, and to the best of your knowledge answer all questions I ask you pertaining to this case this afternoon. Do you understand, Mr. Thomas?"

"I do."

"Please state your full name and city of residence."

"My name is George Clarence Thomas and I am now residing in Moses Lake Washington."

"How long have you lived in Moses Lake, Mr. Thomas?"

"Nearly two years."

"Is it true that your commercial pilot's license was revoked, forcing you to take a much lower paying job as an instructor?"

"No."

"But you are an instructor now and your license was revoked?"

"Yes."

"Wasn't that demeaning, Mr. Thomas? Didn't that make you angry?"

"No."

I'm thinking about now that George is one cool individual under pressure. The kinda' guy you want piloting the plane you're on.

"Were you having an affair with Miss Collins, Mr. Thomas?"

"Yes."

"Did you know that Miss Collins was pregnant?"

"When?"

"I'm asking. You answer, Mr. Thomas."

"I do know now. I did not know prior to her death and the resulting autopsy."

"Are you the father of her unborn child?"

"I don't know."

"Didn't Detective Halverson make you submit to DNA testing for the purpose of identifying the father?"

"Yes, but the results of that testing are not yet available."

"When and where did you last see Miss Collins?"

"About eleven PM on Saturday the twenty eighth of October, at the park and ride lot near the intersection of SR-17 and I-90."

"On the night of Miss Collins death, you were initiating an end to the affair, were you not, Mr. Thomas."

"No."

"Why had you met at the park and ride."

"That was our customary meeting spot."

"Why was that your customary meeting place, Mr. Thomas?"

Candice broke in here and said, "You don't have to answer that question, Mr. Thomas. It Isn't relevant to establishing a time line."

"But I think it is important in establishing the type of relationship Mr. Thomas had with the victim, Mr. Langley replied."

"If you believe that, ask the question at trial and see if the judge allows it," Candice said. "He will not reply to the question at this time."

"You obviously don't know how this is supposed to work, Ms. Mead. You must not do much of this in your little court," Mr. Langley retorted.

"You obviously are wasting our time here, Mr. Langley. Ask Mr. Thomas relevant questions only or this deposition is over. If you have a problem with that, complain to Judge Orlon."

"What time had you arrived at the park and ride that night."

"About ten forty five"

"Did you and Miss. Collins arrive there in the same car?"

"No."

"What time did Miss Collins arrive?"

"I'd say, about ten minutes later."

"You met and left separately?"

"Yes."

"Was that customary.?"

"No."

"Why did you leave separately that night, Mr. Thomas."

"Because I was going to drive to my home in Mill Creek that night."

"Why was that?"

Once again Candice spoke up. "Irrelevant, Mr. Langley."

"Who left the lot first, Mr. Thomas, you or Miss Collins?"

"I did."

"Did you see which direction Miss Collins went when she left the lot?"

"I didn't see her leave."

"You left her all alone and unprotected in that lot at that time of the night, Mr. Thomas? Was that the responsible thing to do?"

"Probably not."

"So you don't know if Miss Collins left the lot alive do you?"

"No. No I don't."

"Do you think that her death may have been caused, in part, by your negligence, Mr. Thomas?"

"That will be all Mr. Langley," Candice said. "We'll be back in this room with Mr. Sanders at three."

George came back into Candice's office with us.

"I loved that girl and I'll never forgive myself for leaving her that night," he said. "I could never have hurt her, but I still feel responsible for her death."

"We all live with regrets, George," I said lamely. "Hopefully time will take some of the sting away for you."

"It may," he said.

It was a little after three, we were back in the conference room with Fred Sanders this time, still dressed in his

coveralls. He had been sworn in by the clerk and Mr. Langley began with, "So, you are here as an expert witness, Mr. Sanders?"
"Yes."
"Did you have a college degree, Mr. Sanders?"
"No."
"Did you even finish high school, Mr. Sanders?"
"No."
"What was the last year of high school that you attended?"
"Part of the twelfth grade. I joined the Navy as soon as I turned eighteen."
"You didn't even finish high school and yet you claim to be an expert witness. Is this the best you can do Ms. Mead?"
"Mr. Langley, Candice replied. "Probably half the people in this county, including your jury pool, consider Mr. Sanders to be an expert in the field of HVAC. Belittle his real accomplishments with care."
"What qualifies you to be an expert in the field of, what you call HVAC, other than the adoration of your customers, Mr. Sanders?" he asked.
"Twenty years of experience aboard atomic powered submarines, operating and maintaining heating, ventilating, cooling and propulsion systems. Also, one hundred eighty hours of class room instruction while I was completing my two year apprentice in order to qualify for my civilian card. Then there are the ten years I have been servicing HVAC units for people in this area."
"Why did you join the Navy, rather that complete high school?"
"I felt it was my patriotic duty, and I thought I was wasting my time with all the crap in school. I wanted to get on with my life."
Candice interrupted with, "Can we please end this pissing contest Mr. Langley, and get to something meaningful?"

"I'm only trying to establish Mr. Sander's degree of expertise, Ms. Mead. I may bring an expert in the field over from the University of Washington, to refute Mr. Sanders findings."

"You better get him on your witness list quickly, Mr. Langley, so I can depose him. And, good luck with the jury on that idea. If you want to bring in a university type, I'd suggest WSU. Remember, you're not in Bellevue anymore."

The rest of the deposition consisted of basically the same questions and answers as our interview that morning, until Mr. Langley asked Fred, "Do you own a suit, Mr. Sanders?"

"Yes I do," he replied. I wear it to weddings and funerals. Do you own a pair of coveralls, Mr. Langley?"

Once back in Candice's office, we both thanked Fred, and Candice asked, "Do you plan on wearing your coveralls to court, Fred?"

"I'm not sure," he answered.

"Please do," Candice said. "I think they upset Mr. Langley a little because he doesn't think he's getting the respect he deserves."

I stood in the doorway after once again thanking Fred and said, "It looks as if Mrs. Thomas is a no-show. What do you want to do?"

"Just interview her, she's right behind you, Hal."

About that time I realized there was a strong cigarette odor invading the office. I turned around and there she was, looking as charming as the last time we met.

"Good afternoon, Mrs. Thomas."

"Detective," she said. "Hell of a day for a drive over the mountains. I need a drink."

"After we finish here, Mrs. Thomas, you can do as you wish until you're called at the trial," I said and the three of us walked into the conference room.

"Was that my lawyer I saw as I was coming down the hall.?" she asked.

"Who would that be, Mrs. Thomas," Candice asked.

"Robert Langley," She replied.

"Could have been," Candice said.

"What the hell's he doing here?" asked Mrs. Thomas.

"He's the defense attorney in the murder trial you have been called as a witness for," Candice said.

"Damn small world and I didn't witness no murder."

Candice sat down, had the court reporter swear Mrs. Thomas in, said, "I'm Candice Mead."...and she went on telling Mrs. Thomas why she was here and what to expect today as well as in the days to come.

"Mrs. Thomas, were you in the Moses Lake, Royal city area on Sunday the twenty ninth of October?"

"Yeah, I was trying to find my no good husband."

"Please, Mrs. Thomas. Unless I ask you to explain an answer, a simple yes or no will suffice. Do not give the defense attorney or me any extra information. As you are in a position to be a viable suspect in this case, you best take my advice."

"Yes Ma'am."

"Did you drive from Moses Lake that morning looking for a residence on 12 SW in the Royal Slope area."

"Yes."

"Please tell me what route you took to do so."

"I went south on SR 17 until I reached SR 262. I went west on 262 until I turned right onto 12 SE which soon became 12 SW. The address I was looking for would be very close, in the 900 block on my right."

"Did you stop at the address you were seeking?"

"No."

"Why not, Mrs. Thomas?"

"A car suddenly appeared coming from the opposite direction and turned into the driveway of the house I was looking for."

"Suddenly appeared?"

"Yes. The road is straight with very few ups and downs. You can see a car for at least a half mile before you pass. I went through this little dip and there it was, right in front of me."

"Can you describe the car. Mrs. Thomas?"

"It was an older SUV. One of those with the spare tire mounted on the rear door."

"Could you see the occupants of the car?"

"There was only the driver."

"Are you able to describe the driver?"

"Only that it appeared to be a woman with long hair."

"What did you do next?"

"I drove back to Moses Lake."

"Thank you Mrs. Thomas. Let me remind you that even though Mr. Langley may be representing you in your divorce, do not make the mistake of thinking he is on your side in this murder case. He will do everything he can to discredit you and your testimony. He may even try to incriminate you. Short answers only, unless I indicate otherwise. And you must be truthful."

When Mrs. Thomas had left, Candice asked, "Join me and the girls for a drink, Hal?"

"Thanks," I said, "but I'm a little concerned about the weather. It could get icy before I get home. Or, with the girl's network operating, my home could be a little icy when I get there.

"See you at our offices in the morning?"

Fortunately it hadn't started to freeze the rain that was on the road as yet, so my drive back to Cariboo was unexciting. Shirley had dinner cooking and a box of fine red wine was sitting on the kitchen counter. Life has it's good moments.

24.
WEDNESDAY, NOVEMBER 22

Sometime during the night the temperature had dropped below freezing and every surface that was wet yesterday was soon covered with a sheet of ice. The city, county and state DOTs had their crews out sanding the roads, starting about three thirty this morning, and the light snow falling now, at six thirty, was supposed to let up before noon

I asked Shirley if, because of the conditions, she wanted me to drive her to school. She looked at me as if I were demented and said, "You gotta be kidding!"

Okay, so she's the better foul weather driver. It just seemed like the right thing to say at the time.

"If you get into trouble trying to get to your office this morning, call me at school," she said. I'll get one of the driver's-ed students to come pick you up."

We each had one more cup of coffee and then I watched as she deftly backed down our driveway and slid to a stop facing the right direction. I decided to clean up the kitchen and wait until daylight before I began my white knuckled trip.

I was at my desk by eight thirty and Candice walked in my office door just before nine.

"How are we going to do this today?" I asked her

"We'll start with the maid that's in charge of room 205, Mrs. Mallory's usual room. She should help us to establish the fact that Mrs. Mallory and Sylvia Baker had some type of relationship and that they argued on the day of Cheryl's death.

"Then we'll interview the parking lot attendant that saw Sylvia and Mrs. Mallory arguing. He also saw Sylvia returning to the hotel after her shift on the day Cheryl was murdered. He won't be able to tell us what she did after returning, but it coincides with the maid's observations. He will also be able to tell us when Cheryl left the parking lot the night of her death.

"This afternoon we'll talk with Jeremy Wilson to establish how, when and where Cheryl's body was found."

"You won't be doing Nate, his partner?" I asked.

"I don't think Nate's recollection of the night would be too clear, and It could muddy the waters. Langley doesn't have him listed so I'm ignoring him at this time."

The maid, who I knew only as a number on my notes and recording, arrived right at nine o'clock accompanied by Ramon, and we moved next door, into the conference room

Candice greeted her. "Buena dais senorita, I'm Candice Mead and I will represent Adams County in the trial of Grace Mallory, who has been accused of murdering Cheryl Collins. I'm going to ask you a few questions this morning about what you may have observed while you performed your duties at The Swept Wing Inn. Please answer them truthfully and without fear. It is highly unusual, but, I will allow Mr. Martinez to be present if it will make you more comfortable. Do you have any questions?"

"No."

After the witness was sworn in by a local court official, Candice asked, "Please state your full name and your occupation."

"Sonya Marie Questro. I work as maid at Swept Wing Inn hotel."

"Sonya, did you know Cheryl Collins?"

"Si."

"Do you know Sylvia Baker?"

"Si."

"Do you Know who Mrs. Grace Mallory is?"

"Si."

"Was Mrs. Mallory a frequent guest at the Swept Wing Inn?"

"Si."

"Did she often stay in the same room?"

"Si, room 205. One of my rooms."

"Did you ever see Sylvia Baker enter room 205 while Mrs. Mallory was staying there?"

"Si. For a while, almost every time Mrs. Mallory stay at hotel."

"Do you remember when this started?"

"Some time late summer. Sylvia come to room after her shift in coffee shop."

"How long did this go on, Sonya?"

"Four, five weeks. Then not so often. I think lessons finished."

"Lessons?" Candice asked.

"Mrs. Mallory very sofisticado, I think she help Sylvia to be same."

"Do you remember the last time you saw Sylvia visit Mrs. Mallory?"

"Si ,tres samanas. Three weeks ago on Saturday. Sylvia come later in day and they argue."

"Would that be Saturday the twenty eighth of October?"

Sonya thought a moment and then said,"Si,28 de Octubre."

"Could you tell what they were arguing about, Sonya?"

"No. I go to other end of hall. Not my business."

"Sonya, I will be calling on you as a witness in Mrs. Mallory's trial for the murder of Cheryl Collins. Are all of your documents in order?"

Here Sonya looked at Ramon who said, "If not now, they will be before Monday."

"At the trial, Sonya, I will ask pretty much these same questions. I expect your answers to be the same as this morning.

"Then, the lawyer representing Mrs. Mallory will question you. He may try to confuse you and he probably will call you a liar. Please, do not let him bully you into changing your answers. I will be there and will do everything I can to help you through this.

"Do you now have any questions?"

"Will Ramon be there?" she asked.

"I'll be there. And, so will many of your friends from the hotel," Ramon answered. "Do as Ms. Mead asks and do not be afraid."

Ramon accompanied Sonya back to the hotel and returned with the parking lot attendant. Again, I knew the young man only as a number, so I couldn't make the proper introductions. We all entered the conference room and sat at the table.

"Buena dais senor, I'm Candice Mead. I will be representing Adams County in the trial of Grace Mallory, who has been accused of murdering Cheryl Collins. I will be asking you questions about things you may have observed while working at the Swept Wing Inn. Please answer my questions honestly and without fear. Do you have any questions?"

"No."

After the swearing in, Candice asked," Please state your full name and occupation."

"Juan Ricardo Veltez. I take care of the parking lot at the Swept Wing Inn."

"What do you do to 'take care' of the lot, Juan?"

"I watch to see that cars are not stolen or vandalized while parked there. I keep the lot clean and watch for cars that may be left by people who are not doing business with the

Inn. I often see women employees to their cars during hours of darkness."

"Did you know Cheryl Collins?"

"Yes ma'am."

"Do you know Sylvia Baker?"

"Si."

"Do you know who Mrs. Grace Mallory is?"

"Si, we all do."

"Please, just answer , si, or yes, or no to my questions, unless, I ask for more.

"Si, okay."

"Did you ever see Cheryl and Sylvia arrive or leave together, in the same car?"

"No."

"Did you ever see them meet or carry on a conversation in the parking area."

"Si."

"Did that happen often?"

"No."

"Please, this time tell me more if you wish, Juan."

"They only meet if they get there same time. Sometimes they talk while walking from the hotel to their cars."

"Did Sylvia ever meet anyone else in the parking lot?"

"Si."

"What other people have you seen her meet?"

"Only Mrs. Mallory."

"How often?"

"Uno, dos, one, two times a week maybe."

"Did you ever overhear any of their conversations, Juan?"

"No. None of my business. Last few times they meet it sounds like arguing. I go to the other end of the lot."

"Did you ever see Sylvia return to the parking lot later, after she had completed her shift and gone home?"

"Only once. On Saturday, three weeks ago."

"Can you tell me the date that occurred?"

Like Sonya, Juan thought a moment before saying, "Si, 28 de Octubre, October twenty eighth."

"Did Cheryl ever return later in the day, after she had left following her shift?"

"Si."

"Often?"

"Si."

"Tell me more if you wish, Juan."

"She like to dance. Come back Saturday nights sometimes. For fun, not work."

"Did she come back on that Saturday, three weeks ago?"

"Si, then she leave about ten thirty that night and head east. She live to the west. Too bad she not go home."

"Thank you Juan..." and she told him the same things she had told Sonya earlier.

When Juan and Ramon had left, I asked Candice if she wanted to catch a quick lunch before this afternoon's session. She said, "Sure, I skipped breakfast this morning so I could get an early start on the icy roads."

There was a KFC down the block from my office and as we walked through the lightly falling snow she asked, "Do you like it hot and spicy."

I looked her in the eye and said, "That, and original."

I think she blushed a little.

"Don't mess with dirty old men," I told her.

Jeremy tapped on my door frame at about one fifteen, I introduced him to Candice and we walked into the conference room. He didn't look very comfortable there at the table.

Candice asked him, "Jeremy, you seem a little distressed. Are you okay?"

"I'm just not much used to talkin' to lawyers, ma'am."

"We're on the same side here, Jeremy. I only wish to prosecute Mrs. Mallory for killing Cheryl Collins. You're here only to establish when and where her body was found."

He looked questioningly at me and I told him, "You can trust her, Jeremy. I promise."

"If you're ready, I'll ask you some questions," Candice said. You only need to answer them honestly using as few words as possible. If a question makes you uncomfortable, tell us."

"Yes ma'am."

The court official did her job and Candice began.

"Please state your full name and occupation."

"Jeremy Wilson. I, uh, work a little farm land south east of here."

"You have no middle name, Jeremy?"

"Woodrow, ma'am. Jeremy Woodrow Wilson."

"Do you remember where you were and what you did on Saturday night, October twenty eighth and Sunday morning, the twenty ninth?"

"How could I forget it, ma'am?"

"A simple yes will do. No unnecessary words today or at the trial."

"Yes ma'am."

"Were you driving east on Fletcher Road, early on that Sunday morning?"

"Yes ma'am."

"Where had you been and where were you going?"

"We'd been at the Thirsty Dog Tavern in Cariboo, and were headed home."

"We?"

"My buddy Nate and Me."

"Had you been drinking at The Thirsty Dog?"

"Yes ma'am."

"Approximately how many drinks had you consumed before you started to drive home?"

"Maybe six, or so."

"And you decided to drive anyway?"

"Yes ma'am."

"What had you been drinking, Mr. Wilson?"

"Busch NA"

"Non alcoholic beer?"

"Yes ma'am."

"What time did you leave the tavern, Jeremy?"

"When they closed the bar. Around one thirty Sunday morning."

"How was it you stopped on the way home and found Cheryl's body?"

"My buddy, Nate, was feeling a little out of sorts so I stopped the truck and let him out."

"Was Nate inebriated at the time?"

"Yes."

"Who saw the body first?"

"Nate."

"What did he do?"

"'He called me over to the side of the road and asked what I thought it was."

"Did you realize what you were seeing?"

"I grabbed a flashlight out of the truck and slid down the bank to get a closer look."

"Then what?"

"I saw it was the body of a female and checked for a pulse and breathing. There was still some body heat present so I tried CPR but gave up after about ten minutes."

"Are you qualified to administer CPR, Jeremy?"

"Yes ma'am."

"How so?"

"I spent four years as a Navy Medical Corpsman. Most of that time I was attached to a Marine Corps company in a war zone. I had saved lives in the past but I was too late to help her."

"After you decided you couldn't help her, Jeremy, what did you do?"

"We drove east about a mile to old man McPhee's place and woke him up so we could use his phone to call the sheriff."

"You don't have a cell phone, Jeremy?"

"I didn't then. I got me one now."

"Did you return to the site of the body?"

"Yes ma'am."

"How long did you remain there?"

"'Till Detective Halverson told us we could go home."

"Thank you, Jeremy, for your service, for what you tried to do for Cheryl, and for being here today," Candice said.

"When we get to court just tell the truth and you'll do fine. Mr. Langley, the defense attorney, may try to confuse you and even go so far as accusing you of harming Cheryl when you administered CPR. Don't let him get under your skin. He's not half the man you are."

"Yes ma'am. Thank you ma'am."

Candice and I had returned to my office when I asked her, "What about Nate?"

"I've removed him from my witness list and Langley didn't call him for deposition," she replied. "We're probably better off without him."

I grabbed my coat from the hook on the wall, handed Candice hers and asked, "Join me for a drink across the street at our local cop watering hole?"

"No thanks, someone warned me about you earlier today."

"Yeah, my mistake. So what happens now?" I asked.

"You go sit in your rocker, or what ever people your age do to pass the time. I'll probably visit Sylvia once more and then barricade myself in my office to do my final preparation for the trial. I'll call you if I have any questions or loose ends."

Then she actually gave me a peck on the cheek and said, "See ya gramps."

As I was passing Sam's door on the way out he waved me into his office.

"Are we ready for this ,Hal?"

"I don't know of anything more I can do, Sam," I replied.

"Then get the hell out of here. I'll ride with you to the courthouse on Monday."

When I walked from the garage through the kitchen door, Shirley was at the eating bar with a glass of wine in her hand.

"Well, if it isn't the original Mr. hot and spicy comin' through the door. What're ya making me for dinner tonight, gramps?"

25.
THURSDAY, NOVEMBER 23

Four days to kill, but with this being Thanksgiving weekend, at least I had Shirley's company to take my mind off the trial. She was busy in the kitchen this morning so I needed to entertain myself, at least until dinner This time of the year you couldn't do much outdoors, and indoors I became more claustrophobic by the minute. I finally went down to the public library to check out some of the classics that I always meant to read. They were closed of course, so I took a walk around our block. The snow had stopped falling sometime yesterday and the nip in the air was invigorating. Only ninety three more hours to go.

26.
MONDAY, NOVEMBER 27

At ten thirty Monday morning Judge Orlon walked through the door from his chambers into the courtroom. The gallery seats were filled with prospective jurors. Mr. Langley and Mrs. Mallory were seated at the defendants table on the left, near the jury box, and Candice and a young man I hadn't met were seated at the table to the right of center. The court clerk, Candice's cousin, sat at his desk in the center just below and in front of the judges bench. The court reporter was seated below and to our left of the judge and the witness box was below and to our right. Sam and I were seated behind Candice in the first row outside of the railing that separated the gallery from the participants.

"All rise," shouted the bailiff. "Court is now in session. Judge Mathew Orlon presiding."

Judge Orlon seated himself at the bench and said, "Please be seated"

Once everyone had settled in their seats, the judge said, "Good morning ladies and gentlemen. Today we are going to select twelve persons to be the jury and two persons to be alternates for the trial of Mrs. Grace Mallory, for murder in the second degree, of Miss Cheryl Collins and her unborn child. If, for some reason, we are unable to complete the selection by the end of today, we will continue tomorrow. The trial is expected to last no more than one week after the jury has been selected.

"Now," he went on, "do any of you think you should be excused from serving on this jury because you would be caused undue hardship?"

Twelve people raised their hands and the judge asked them questions one by one until he had dismissed six and kept the others in the jury pool.

"Is there anyone here that believes they may already have reached a verdict in their own mind and would be prejudiced toward the case?"

The six that hadn't been dismissed before raised their hands along with three others.

"You six don't give up easily, do you. Put your hands down, and if you are called to be questioned by the attorneys, I'll let them decide what to do with you. You other three, turn your badges in at the door as you leave."

"Is there anyone here who is related to either the defendant or the victim in this case. If you six raise your hands this time, I'm goin' to hold you for contempt of court."

No hands this time.

"Very well. You were each issued a number when you received your notice to show up here today. The clerk will call twelve of those numbers, and each of those twelve people will be given a seat in the jury box. The attorneys and I will then have an opportunity to ask each of you some questions. If they, or I, find you not to our liking, within reason for the attorneys, you will be dismissed and another prospective juror from the pool out there will be called to take your place. Does anyone have any questions at this time?"

Again, no hands were raised.

Voir dire, or jury questioning and selection, went as smooth as could be expected, with Mr. Langley using up all of his peremptory challenges when he couldn't convince the judge of potential bias. By four o'clock that afternoon we had a jury of eight women and four men, plus one man and one woman as alternates. The trial would start at ten thirty, Tuesday morning with the judge's instructions for the jury and the prosecution telling them why they should convict Mrs. Mallory of murder.

Before Sam and I headed back to Cariboo for the night we stopped by Candice's office to see how happy she was with the jury.

"I'll need help from you two in the court room. I've been given an assistant but he's such a newbie he'll just be handling paper for me and helping me stay on track. You're both experts at reading body language, so tell me if I start loosing anyone in the jury."

"Hal's really good at reading it but, he ain't been able to write for years," Sam said.

"Damn," Sam said as we walked to the car. "Wouldn't you like to be young and full of piss and vinegar again."

"Seems I'm full of piss more often than is comfortable these days and vinegar gives me reflux," I replied. "And the idea of being young makes me tired."

27.
TUESDAY, NOVEMBER 28

I was in my office a little before eight o'clock Tuesday morning when Sam walked in still wearing his coat.

"Ready to go?" he asked.

"Let me just empty my bladder and refill my coffee cup," I replied.

I drove my county SUV while Sam rode shotgun.

"I should be stayin' at the office instead of running up to Ritzville with you, but I want to see this thing through," Sam commented.

"I appreciate you being here Sam, and I know Candice does as well."

"Yeah, the three of us know damn well Mrs. Mallory killed that girl, but convincing a jury can be difficult. That weasel lawyer she's got is liable to try anything to get her off. I just hope the folks on that jury can see through his sophisticated bull shit."

We entered the Courthouse in Ritzville at nine oh five and took the elevator to Candice's office on the third floor.

"Good morning gentlemen," she said without looking away from her computer screen.

"I just received an e-mail from Judge Orlon, actually from my cousin, his clerk. The judge has appointed Carl Johnson to be the jury foreman.

"According to my cousin, the judge didn't want any 'willy-nilly popularity contest among the jurors.' Mr. Johnson is president of the local Rotary Club and Judge Orlon says 'if he can keep that bunch on track, he can sure as hell run a twelve person jury.'"

We talked a little about what was expected to happen today and by ten fifteen were in our seats waiting patiently for the start of today's proceedings.

At precisely ten thirty the judge walked in, we stood up, sat down, and court was back in session.

Judge Orlon began with, "Ladies and gentlemen of the jury, do any of you wish to be sequestered, that's a little like being imprisoned, for the duration of the trial?"

Almost everyone in the jury box shook their heads as if to say no.

"That being the case," the judge continued, "you must heed the following instructions.

"You will not discuss anything that occurs in this room with fellow jurors prior my instructions to do so. You will not discuss anything that occurs in this room with anyone else prior to my dismissal of you as jurors. That includes spouses, lovers, your barber or even your psychiatrist.

"You will not read any news reports about these proceedings. You will not listen to any radio or watch any TV news broadcasts prior to your dismissal.

"You are about to participate in a ritual that is the very backbone of our free society. Do your job here with dignity and diligence, for your decisions will profoundly affect the life of the defendant as well countless others, yourselves included.

"Is there anyone among the jury who does not understand these instructions?" At this point he looked at each of the jurors individually until each had locked eyes with him.

"Good," he continued, finally. "You may have noticed a number on your seat when you entered the box this morning. That is your juror number and you will sit in that same place throughout the trial. I have exercised my legal option of selecting a jury foreman and he is in seat number one at the left end of the front row as seen from the bench.

"Unless someone has something to add to or a question about my instructions, we will take a thirty minute recess and then hear what the prosecutor has to say."

The jury was led from the room by the bailiff and most of us sitting in the gallery left the room to take care of any personal needs.

Thirty two minutes later the judge walked into the courtroom again, and once again the bailiff announced his arrival. The trial was about to begin.

The judge nodded at Candice and said, "Ms. Mead, the floor is yours."

Candice rose from her chair and walked past the defense table so as to stand directly in front of the jury box. She swept the panel with a look to insure all were awake and listening, and began.

"Ladies and gentlemen, I talked briefly with each one of you yesterday during the jury selection. I am Candice Mead and I represent you, the citizens of Adams County against Mrs. Grace Mallory. It is my duty to prove to you that Mrs. Mallory, on the night of October twenty eighth or, early in the morning of October twenty ninth, murdered Miss Cheryl Collins and her unborn child, and then deposited her lifeless body in a roadside ditch.

"The reason for Mrs. Mallory's heinous act was one of the oldest and most common motives in the world: jealousy.

"Mrs. Mallory believed that Cheryl Collins was the reason her lover, Miss Sylvia Baker, wanted to end their once torrid but now lackluster affair.

"Miss Baker insisted that although they were good friends, there were no romantic or sexual ties between her and Miss Collins.

"Mrs. Mallory chose not to believe her, and in fact threatened Miss Baker, and through her, Cheryl Collins.

"Mrs. Mallory told Miss Baker that if she didn't stop her friendship with Miss Collins, she, Mrs. Mallory would see to it that miss Baker would not see Miss Collins again.

"There may be some of you who will find the lifestyles of individuals involved in this case distasteful. I remind you that you are not here to judge those lifestyles. You are here to determine only whether Mrs. Mallory did, or did not, murder Cheryl Collins."

Candice paused a moment here to let the jury absorb what she had said so far, and I suspect, to organize in her mind what she was about to tell them.

"On Saturday, October twenty eighth of this year Cheryl Collins worked the breakfast shift at the Swept Wing Inn as a waitress in the coffee shop. At two PM, the end of her shift, she drove to her home on 12 SW. In the evening she returned, as she often had done before, to the Swept Wing for an evening of dancing.

"At sometime between ten and ten thirty PM, she left the Inn and drove to a rendezvous with her lover at the park and ride lot near SR- 17 and I-90. She arrived at the park and ride at ten fifty four PM. During the rendezvous, her lover,

Mr. George Thomas, a married man, told Cheryl that he intended to drive home to Mill Creek, Washington that night to see his wife. Mr. Thomas exited the lot at eleven oh two PM and went north toward Moses Lake. Cheryl left the lot at eleven oh five PM and drove south toward Cariboo. Cheryl was despondent because she was afraid that her affair with Mr. Thomas was at an end. And, she was pregnant, something she was excited about but had not been able to tell Mr. Thomas.

"Needing the comfort and understanding of a friend, Cheryl drove to Miss Baker's home on Ninth Avenue in Cariboo, knocked on the door and was let in by Miss Baker. Miss Baker was frightened because of the threats made by Mrs. Mallory and related them to Cheryl.

"Cheryl, unwisely as we know now, told Miss Baker that she would stop at the Mallory's on her way home and assure Mrs. Mallory that she was not interested in a lesbian affair with anyone.

"When Cheryl arrived at the Mallory's home, Mrs. Mallory told her that she could see that something had upset her and took her out to the pool heater room, telling Cheryl she didn't wish to disturb Doctor Mallory who was meditating in the house.

"She then told Cheryl to take a seat in a chair that was in the room, and after Mrs. Mallory, who incidentally possesses a degree in mechanical engineering, adjusted the heater flue to make her more 'comfortable', told Cheryl she would go get tea for both of them. She left the room, closing the door behind her.

"Her adjustment of the heater flue caused extreme heat and a lethal amount of carbon monoxide to enter the room and Cheryl died there of carbon monoxide asphyxiation.

"Mrs. Mallory waited until she felt certain that Cheryl was dead, opened the door to the room and let the lethal atmosphere dissipate. She then, with the help of Doctor

Mallory, loaded Cheryl's still warm but lifeless body into the back of Cheryl's own car, and transported her to Fletcher Road, east of Cariboo, where they dumped Cheryl into a roadside ditch.

"The Mallory's then returned home where Mrs. Mallory wiped down all surfaces that either Cheryl or Mrs. Mallory had touched that evening. Those surfaces even included the driver's area of Cheryl's car, an area that should have been covered with Cheryl's prints. Mrs. Mallory did however, leave Doctor Mallory's prints on the mechanism that releases the spare tire of Cheryl's car, and later made sure that Doctor Mallory's were the only prints to be found in the pool heater room.

"At about eight thirty Sunday morning, Mrs. Mallory parked the car in Cheryl's barn, once again wiping all surfaces she had contacted free of prints.

"Cheryl's still warm body was found about two thirty Sunday morning. There was at that time, no pulse or signs of breathing. However, because there was still body heat an attempt was made to revive her. That attempt failed."

Candice looked at each member of the jury to be sure they were with her, and then walked back to her table and sat down.

After a moment of silence, the judge asked, "Does the defense wish to make a statement at this time?"

Mr. Langley stood and said, "That was a sad but completely untrue story, Your Honor. When the prosecution has finished with her unqualified witnesses I intend to ask that charges against my client in this travesty of justice be dismissed. For now, I look forward to cross exam."

"In that case," said the judge, "we will recess for lunch. Court will reconvene at one o'clock."

The bailiff had retrieved and seated the jury by one oh three and Judge Orlon entered the courtroom at one oh five." The prosecution may call your first witness," he said."

Candice stood up and said, "The prosecution calls George Thomas."

George entered the courtroom from the main entry at the back wall center, walked up the center aisle, stepped through the gate in the railing and proceeded to the witness box. He was met there by the court clerk, who administered the oath before he sat down.

Candice walked to a point between the witness box and the defense table and, looking at George, said, "Please state your full name, occupation and place of residence, Mr. Thomas."

"George Clarence Thomas. I am an instructor at the Boeing Flight Training Center in Moses Lake. I presently reside in Moses lake, Washington."

"Mr. Thomas, did you know Miss Cheryl Collins?"

"Yes."

"What was your relationship with her at the time of her death?"

"We were having an affair."

"For how long had you had this relationship?"

"It began as an innocent friendship back around the Forth of July."

"Innocent?"

"Yes. I took her for an airplane ride. We had dinner at her home several times. I was naive enough to believe it could stay that way."

"When did that change, Mr. Thomas?"

"We had eaten dinner at her home one evening and were enjoying a conversation with each other when a neighbor knocked on the door. Cheryl answered his knock and he began shouting at her, calling her names and accusing her of living with me in sin."

"What was Cheryl's reaction to this intrusion?"

"She closed the door smiled and said, 'If people think we're sinning, maybe we should have a go at it.' That night our friendship turned into an affair."

"Do you know who the neighbor was?"

"I have since learned that it was Doctor Mallory, her neighbor from across the street."

"When and where did you last see Cheryl, Mr. Thomas?"

"About eleven o'clock Saturday night the twenty eighth of October..."

From here on, his testimony was pretty much the same as our last interview. When Candice was finished with him, and had returned to her seat, the judge said, "Mr. Langley, your witness."

Mr. Langley rose, walked to, all but leaned on the witness box, and said, "So, Mr. Thomas, when you were no longer allowed to be a big time airline pilot, you moved over here to the boonies and got a job as a teacher. I'll bet you found the women over here to be pretty easy prey for someone as sophisticated and good looking as you."

Candice broke in with, "Objection, Your Honor. Mr. Langley isn't questioning the witness, he's badgering him."

"Sustained. The 'statement' made by the defense shall be stricken from the record and the jury is to disregard it. That is, if you can.

"Mr. Langley," the judge continued, " stick to questions relevant to this case."

"But, Judge," Mr. Langley sputtered, "I'm only trying to establish the mental state of the witness in regard to Miss Collins."

"You're no damn psychiatrist Mr. Langley. Let the jury determine such things without your help.

"Would you like to start again or are you finished with this witness?"

Mr. Langley said, "Thank you, Your Honor. I will start again with this witness."

He stepped back a little from the box and asked, "Are you aware, Mr. Thomas, that Miss Collins was pregnant at the time of her death?"

"I am now. I wasn't prior to being informed of the fact by Detective Halverson."

"Come now, Mr. Thomas. She must have told you. Weren't you the father?"

"I don't know who the father was."

"Were you angry with Cheryl because she was pregnant and you didn't believe you were the father?"

"No."

"Why were you angry with her then, Mr. Thomas? Angry enough to want to kill her."

"Cheryl was probably the only person in my life that I hadn't been angry with at some time or other."

"Why did you leave her alone in that parking lot, then?"

"I thought that I needed to talk with my wife before I made any decisions as to my affair and my marriage. I left her and drove to my home in Mill Creek."

"Did you go directly from your rendezvous to your home in Mill Creek, or did you first asphyxiate Miss Collins by obstructing her exhaust system and then dump her body in a ditch?"

"I went from the park and ride to my Moses Lake home, switched cars, and drove to Mill Creek."

"Why did you switch cars, Mr. Thomas, to destroy evidence?"

"I switched to my Land Rover because it would handle better if it snowed in the pass during my trip."

"Do you have any proof that you actually drove to Mill Creek that night?"

"No."

"I wonder, Mr. Thomas, why you are not on trial for this crime rather than Grace Mallory. This appears to be gross negligence by the Grant County Sheriff.

"I have no further questions for this witness, Your Honor."

The judge asked Candice, "Does the prosecution wish to redirect?"

"Please, Your Honor."

Candice returned to her place between the witness and the defense table and asked, "Mr. Thomas, did you make any stops between your Moses Lake home and your Mill Creek residence?"

"Yes. I purchased gas in Ellensburg."

"Did you retain a receipt from that purchase?"

"Yes. I gave it to Detective Halverson."

Candice walked back to the prosecution table and picked up a sealed plastic envelope similar to a one gallon zip lock bag.

"Your Honor, I enter the prosecution's exhibit "A" , Mr. Thomas' receipt dated October 29 at twelve forty eight AM, issued by the Canyon Road Chevron, as well as Grant County Transit System surveillance recordings of Miss Collins and Mr. Thomas entering and leaving the lot separately.

"Mr. Thomas could not have killed Miss Collins, dumped her body and driven to Ellensburg in the time between when the victim was known to have entered the park and ride and when the receipt was issued."

"Mr. Langley," the judge asked, "do you have nay further questions for this witness?"

"No, Your Honor."

"In that case, court is adjourned for the night and will reconvene at ten thirty tomorrow morning."

28.
WEDNESDAY, NOVEMBER 29

Sylvia and her mother were already in Candice's office when Sam and I arrived at nine o'clock. They had been driven there from Moses Lake by one of our female deputies from the Ritzville office and were also accompanied by Carlos who had followed the Sheriff's department car in his Moses Lake PD vehicle.

After we had said our good mornings all around, Carlos caught my eye and gestured toward the hall.

"What's up?" I asked him.

"What about the dog?" he asked. "Has anyone asked about him?"

"Not that I know of," I replied. "I think you've got yourself a permanent house guest."

"I sure hope so. The kids love him and I think he feels the same way toward them. I don't know how old he is but he acts like a puppy when the kids are around. Then when they're at school, he sleeps so soundly that a few times I thought he was dead."

"Well," I said, "I think you're in the clear. It's a good thing though, that you don't need to show a bill of sale and registration to get a dog license."

Back in Candice's office, Mrs. Baker and Candice were working to calm Sylvia's nerves. The three cups of coffee and a sugar doughnut she had consumed since arriving here an hour ago, probably weren't helping matters.

At ten o'clock, Candice suggested to Sylvia that she visit the restroom one more time, and by ten fifteen we were on the elevator headed down to the courtroom.

Following the usual stand up, sit down routine Judge Orlon said, "The prosecution may continue with their witnesses."

"Thank you Your Honor. The prosecution calls Sylvia Baker."

Once Sylvia had been sworn in and was seated in the witness box, Candice walked over to her and said, "As you are at present in protective custody, you are not required to reveal your place of residence. So, please state your complete name, and your occupation as it was on October twenty eighth of this year."

"Sylvia Alice Baker. I was at that time a waitress at the Swept Wing Inn, in Cariboo, Washington."

"When did you leave that job, Miss Baker?"

"I last worked there on Wednesday, the eighth of November."

"Why did you leave your job on that day?"

"I had been threatened by Mrs. Mallory that day, and I feared for my life."

"In what way did Mrs. Mallory threaten you?"

"She telephoned and said that someone was about to be arrested for Cheryl's murder, and that I shouldn't tell anyone about the quarrels we'd been having. She said it would only muddy the waters. Then she said, if I told Detective Halverson about anything that had happened between us, I could end up just like Cheryl."

"What did you do then?"

"I immediately packed up everything I could and left the state."

"Had Mrs. Mallory said anything threatening previous to that telephone call?"

"Yes."

"What had she said?"

"She told me to stop seeing Cheryl or she would see to it that Cheryl stopped seeing me."

"When did she tell you that?"

"On the Saturday Cheryl was killed."

"Can you please tell us the actual date, Miss Baker?"

"That would have been Saturday the twenty eighth of October."

"What was your relationship with Cheryl Collins?"

"We both worked as waitresses at the Inn, and we had become friends."

"Were you and Cheryl having a sexual relationship, Miss Baker?"

"No."

"What was your relationship with Mrs. Mallory?"

"We were lovers"

Candice had Sylvia explain, as she had to us previously, how the affair had begun and how it had completely disintegrated on the Saturday of Cheryl's death.

She then asked her, "When and where did you last see Cheryl?"

"That Saturday night after the eleven o'clock news, I guess around midnight. She knocked on the door to my home, and I let her in."

"That Saturday night Miss Baker? Can you clarify the date again for us, please?"

"Saturday, October the twenty eighth."

"What happened after Cheryl came into your home?"

"I could see she had been crying, so I asked what was wrong. She said she was afraid her lover was going to drop her and go back to his wife, and she just needed someone to talk to about it.

"I told her about Mrs. Mallory's suspicions, and that if anyone saw her come here, I'd have hell to pay."

"She pulled herself together and said, 'That's nonsense, I'll stop on my way home and set her straight'. Then she left."

Sylvia was tearing up at this point and Candice said, "Thank you Miss Baker. I have no further questions."

"We'll take a half hour break here," said the judge, "and then the defense may do cross."

Thirty five minutes later Sylvia was back in the witness box and Mr. Langley left his seat at the defense table and approached her, asking, "Miss Baker, are you a lesbian?"

"Yes," she replied.

"Did you attempt to establish a homosexual relationship with Grace Mallory?"

"No"

"Didn't Mrs. Mallory, a fine Christian women who abhorred homosexuality, repeatedly reject your clumsy advances with grace and try to teach you how to defeat the devil that dwelled within you."

"No."

"How can you think for even a moment that we would believe that a beautiful, sophisticated woman of the world like Grace Mallory would ever desire someone as plain and ignorant as you?"

"I don't know. It just happened."

"Well, It's easy for me to see that having been rejected, you are trying to have Mrs. Mallory punished for something that you yourself, may have done. Were you the last person to see Miss Collins alive?"

"No sir." Pointing to Mrs. Mallory, Sylvia said, "she was."

"You thought that you were about to be arrested for murder and so you fled. And yet, here you are testifying for the prosecution against someone who had tried to help you rise above your level and become a better person. Shame on you, Miss Baker."

By now, Sylvia was sobbing heavily. Candice stood up and said, "Judge, the defense has resorted to browbeating the witness. Does this need to continue?"

"Does the defense have any questions of relevance to ask the witness," the judge asked.

"I'm through with the witness, Your Honor."

"Ms. Mead?"

Candice stood and said, "Thank you Miss Baker, and I apologize for the rudeness. I have no further questions."

Judge Orlon said, "Court will adjourn for lunch and reconvene at one o'clock."

The afternoon session began with Candice calling Sonya Questro. When Mr. Langley saw her approaching the witness box he stood and asked, "Do we have an interpreter, Your Honor? This witness doesn't speak English."

Candice said, "The witness speaks English very well Your Honor. We have no need for an interpreter."

"Your Honor, I was told by the prosecution that the Latino witnesses listed did not speak English."

"Ms. Mead, is that so?" asked the judge.

"No Your Honor. Mr. Langley, after seeing the Latino names on my witness list said, and I quote: 'There is no point in my calling witnesses who didn't understand English.' I merely agreed with him."

"Please proceed, Ms. Mead."

Sonya, as she had when we interviewed her, told about the frequency of Sylvia's visits to Mrs. Mallory's room for, as she put it, lessons. She also told about the arguing she had heard and the intensity of the argument on Saturday, the twenty eighth of October.

When Candice finished her questioning, and the defense had their turn at Sonya, Mr. Langley rose from his seat and asked, "Miss Questro, while performing your job as a maid, do you hear a lot of things that people would not say if they knew you understood English?"

"Si, Senor 207."

"I have no further use for this witness, Your Honor," he said as he sat back down."

Next, Candice called Juan, the parking lot manager. Like Sonya, he told of arguments between Mrs. Mallory and Sylvia. He also told of the unusual return to the Inn by

Sylvia on Saturday the twenty eighth. The last question Candice asked was, "Mr. Veltez, do you remember seeing Miss Collins leave the parking lot on that same Saturday night?"

"Si. She left a little before ten thirty and go east, not west toward home."

"Thank you Mr. Veltez. I have no further questions, Your Honor."

"We'll take a fifteen minute break," the judge said, "and then the defense may cross, if you wish."

We were all resettled in our seats when Mr. Langley approached the witness box and asked, "Mr. Veltez, why didn't you ever tell me you spoke English?"

"You never talk to me to find out."

"I apologize amigo," Did you ever listen in on conversations between Miss Collins and Miss Baker?"

"No, senor."

"How often did Miss Collins and Miss Baker meet in the parking lot?"

"They would sometimes arrive for work at the same time and walk to the employee's entrance together."

"Did they seem, ah, close, if you know what I mean?"

"I think I know what you mean, and I would say no."

"Did they leave together often?"

"Nunca, never."

"No more questions," Mr. Langley said as he sat back down.

"Since that was so short and sweet," the judge said, "lets move on to your next witness Ms. Mead."

"The prosecution calls Jeremy Wilson."

Jeremy was wearing blue jeans with a razor sharp crease, clean shined boots and a blindingly white shirt open at the collar. He was tall, lean, tan and clean shaven, with a full head of neatly trimmed jet black hair. Sam whispered to me, "Do you suddenly feel like a really sloppy old fart?"

"Not suddenly," I replied.

After the swearing in, Candice started with the usual, "Please state your complete name, occupation and place of residence."

Glancing at the jury, I noticed that none of the eight women were knitting while he gave his responses. Candice began her questioning.

"Mr. Wilson, did you, during the early morning of October twenty ninth of this year, discover a body in the ditch alongside Fletcher Road."

"Yes ma'am."

"Please tell us how that happened."

"We was drivin' home from the Thirsty Dog Tavern, down in Cariboo, and my buddy felt the need to get out of the truck for a minute. When he went over to the side of the road, he thought he saw somethin' in the ditch and called me over."

"Who was we, Mr. Wilson?"

"Me an' Nate. Nate Stuart."

"So Mr. Stuart thought he saw something. Did you investigate?"

"Yes ma'am."

"What did you do, Mr. Wilson?"

"I grabbed my flashlight and slid down into the ditch."

"What did you find there?"

"A girl, a young lady I guess. I checked her vital signs and she wasn't breathin' and I couldn't find a pulse."

"What did you do then?"

"I could detect some body heat so I knew she couldn't have been in this condition for long so I tried CPR."

"What was the result of your effort?"

"No response. After about ten minutes, I gave up."

"Then what did you do?"

"We drove over to old man McPhee's place and woke him up."

"Why."

"So we could call the Sheriff."

"Don't you have a cell phone, Mr. Wilson?"

"I do now. I didn't then."

"What did you do next?"

"We drove back to where the body was and waited for the sheriff."

"Did you recognize the body?"

"I thought it might have been Cheryl Collins, a nice gal that worked at the Wing and sometimes came down to the 'Dog for Saturday night dancing."

"You weren't sure at the time?"

"Ma'am, when you're tryin' to save a life, you don't pay that much attention to who's it is."

Candice turned to Mr. Langley and said, "Your witness."

Mr. Langley, rose and stepped in front of Jeremy, saying, "So you , a drunken cowboy, returning from a night on the town, decided to attempt CPR on someone who may still have been alive and probably caused asphyxiation with your misguided attempt."

"No sir."

"Had you not been drinking at the Thirsty Dog tavern for several hours prior to finding Miss Collins?"

"Yes sir."

"Just how many drinks had you consumed prior to attempting to drive home?"

"Maybe six."

"Six? So you must have been inebriated."

"No sir."

"How can that be Mr. Wilson?"

"I was drinking non alcoholic beer."

Mr. Langley seemed a little less than happy with this revelation but continued his questioning.

"Mr. Wilson, what in the world made you think that you could revive Miss Collins? Do you know that you could do her great harm by incorrectly administering CPR?"

"Yes sir."

"Then why did you do it? You may have killed her yourself."

"Because I've been able to save lives before, sir. The risk of damage is much less than the risk of doing nothing."

"And yet there was a risk."

"Sir?" Jeremy asked Mr. Langley, "if your heart suddenly stopped, and you collapsed where you are standing, would you like for me to call 911 and wait for them to respond. Or would you want to have someone who has saved lives with it before, give you CPR? I'd probably break one or more of your ribs but it could save your life."

"No further questions, Your Honor."

The judge declared another fifteen minute break, and twenty minutes later Candice stood and said, "The prosecution calls the Adams County Coroner, Doctor Seth Marshal."

Doctor Marshal was tall and pale and had dark hair sprinkled with gray. His suit was rumpled and his shoes were scuffed. All in all, he looked as if he didn't get out much. You could almost hear his joints creak as he folded his body down on to the witnesses chair.

"Doctor Marshal, did you and your office identify and do an autopsy on the body of Miss Cheryl Collins?"

"Yes, we did."

"When was that, Doctor?"

"We picked up the body out on Fletcher Road at four thirty AM on Sunday the twenty ninth of October of this year, and did the autopsy that afternoon."

"How did you identify the body?"

"Several of the Sheriff' deputies responding to the DB call said they believed she was a girl that worked at the Swept Wing Inn as a waitress. We called the Inn and had the manager, Mr. Dumas come to our offices to do a positive identification. He was accompanied by Mrs. Perkins, who was Miss Collins immediate supervisor."

"What was the cause of her death, Doctor?"

"Asphyxiation caused by carbon monoxide poisoning."

"Were there any signs of physical trauma?"

"None, other than post mortem bruising of the chest caused by CPR."

"Could the CPR possibly have caused any damage prior to death?"

"No. All bruising was after she had been dead."

"What was the approximate time of death, Doctor?"

"Some time between one and two AM."

"Was Miss Collins pregnant at the time of her death."

"Yes."

"Did the carbon monoxide kill the fetus as well as Miss Collins?"

"Yes."

"How long had Miss Collins been pregnant, Doctor?"

"The fetus appeared to be in it's third month."

"Thank you Doctor.

"I have no further questions, Your Honor."

The judge looked at the defense table and said, "Mr. Langley?"

Mr. Langley stood at his table and asked, "Doctor, how can you be absolutely certain Miss Collins was deceased before Mr. Wilson attempted CPR? Medicine is far from an exact science and you are far from being a leader in your field."

"Mr. Langley," Doctor Marshal said wearily, "live patients are much more likely to be misdiagnosed than those we can cut open and explore at will. I invite you to come and observe the process this evening after you finish your day here."

"No further questions, Your Honor."

"Ms. Mead," the judge asked. "Will you be able to finish tomorrow?"

"Yes, Your Honor."

"Mr. Langley, I expect the defense to be ready the minute the prosecution finishes. Will you be ready?"

"Unless Ms. Mead does something unexpected, Your Honor."

"Court is dismissed until ten thirty tomorrow morning."

29.
THURSDAY, NOVEMBER 30

Sam and I followed a 'SANDER'S HEATING AND COOLING' van for the last few miles going to Ritzville Thursday morning, and parked beside it in the courthouse parking lot at eight forty seven AM. Fred Sanders, wearing a clean set of coveralls climbed out, locked the door behind him and went around to the back of his van and checked the doors there.

"Those tools are my livelihood," he said. "Some asshole steals 'em and I'm out of business."

"We feel the same way about our guns," Sam joked.

No response from Mr. Sanders.

There was coffee and some kind of supermarket pastries on a table in the corner of Candice's office. the pastries didn't look too good to me but Sam grabbed one and soon had a frosting ring around his mouth.

"My wife never lets me eat these things at home," he said as he wiped his mouth with a napkin and slurped down some coffee.

Sitting rather close to each other on the couch, were our techs from the Adams County Sheriff's Department,

Sergeant O'Brien and Officer Williams. I looked at them and then at Candice who mouthed, "I told you so."

Sergeant Bill Miller, the crime scene investigator arrived at nine thirty.

Candice cleared her throat and said, "I will call Sergeant Miller first this morning, followed by Mr. Sanders, then Officer Williams and finally Sergeant O'Brien. Your testimony will establish the fact that the Mallory home and Cheryl's car had been wiped clean of finger prints in all areas where Cheryl may have been, or where Mrs. Mallory would have been during the course of Cheryl's murder and disposal. Mr. Sanders will explain how the heater flue had been altered to cause carbon monoxide poisoning."

Here Fred Sanders interrupted saying, "I said could. I never said would."

"Okay, Mr. Sanders. I ask you only to answer my questions to the best of your ability. Your truthful answers are all we need.

"Any other questions?" she asked.

Off we went to the courtroom.

Once again we did the stand up sit down and swearing in process. Then Candice approached her witness and said, "Please state your name and occupation."

"I'm Sergeant Bill Miller and I'm in charge of the crime investigation unit of the Adams County Sheriff's Department."

"Sergeant Miller, on Saturday the eleventh of November of this year, were you and your unit sent to a possible crime scene located on 12 SW in Grant County?"

"Yes."

"Please tell us what you found."

"It was an upscale home on the south side of 12 SW in the 900 block. The residents of the home had been arrested just prior to our arrival, and we were there to find any evidence that the deceased, Miss Collins, had been in the home. We were also looking for any signs of a recent struggle, any furniture that may have been relocated and in general anything that seemed out of order."

"What did you find?"

"We found nothing in the home that would suggest that anyone, other than Doctor and Mrs. Mallory and the arresting officers had ever been there."

"Did you inspect the pool heater room?"

"Yes.?"

"What did you find there?"

"The same thing."

"So, you struck out, then?"

"No."

"Please explain."

"Every surface that would normally have been touched by any guest in the home had been thoroughly wiped clean. We knew that Detective Halverson had been in the home on Wednesday, November the eighth and, more importantly in the pool heater room on Thursday, November second."

"Couldn't the lack of fingerprints in those area been the results of normal house cleaning activity?"

"Not unless someone was obsessive about cleaning only in guest frequented areas. The rest of the home, including those areas usually kept the cleanest, such as the cooking area, bore fingerprints that were months old."

"Did you find anything unusual in the pool heater room, Sergeant?"

"Yes. The room had evidently been wiped clean of all fingerprints sometime after Detective Halverson's visit on November second. The only prints to be found were those of Doctor Mallory, and those prints were only on the chimney flue and the arm of the single chair in the room."

Candice said, "Thank you sergeant. I have no more questions," and returned to her seat."

The judge said, "Your witness, Mr. Langley."

Mr. Langley said, "Thank you, Your Honor," and merely stood at his table and asked, "Sergeant, can you be one hundred percent sure that you're inability to find fingerprints is not due to diligent cleaning methods?"

"No sir."

"Thank you Sergeant. That will be all."

Candice jumped up and said, "Redirect, Your Honor."

"Go ahead, Ms. Mead."

"Sergeant, how sure are you that the prints were wiped away so as to not reveal the identity of any visiters to the Mallory residence?"

"Ninety nine point nine percent sure."

"Thank you sergeant. No further questions."

"Mr. Langley?" the judge asked.

"No, thank you."

"Sergeant, you may step down. Ms. Mead, please call your next witness."

"The prosecution calls Mr. Fred Sanders."

Fred walked up the center aisle in his freshly pressed blue coveralls glancing neither right nor left as he approached the witness box. Mr. Langley seeing how Fred was dressed, looked questioningly at the judge who returned the look and just shrugged his shoulders.

Once Fred had been sworn in and was seated in the box, Candice asked him, "Will you please state your name, occupation and place of residence?"

"Fred Sanders. I'm a journeyman HVAC technician. I live in Cariboo, Washington."

"Mr. Sanders, were you called by the Adams County Sheriff's department on the eleventh of November and asked to help them in an investigation?"

"Yes."

"Were did you go to do so?"

"To the Mallory residence, out on 12 SW."

"What were you asked to do at that residence?"

"I waited around while their technicians dusted the pool heater room for fingerprints. Then I was asked to check the heater for any deficiencies or modifications that may have occurred since I had last serviced the unit."

"What did you find, Mr. Sanders?"

"Someone had screwed with the flue adjustments and had actually bent the damper out of shape."

"Is it possible that the flue adjustment had happened simply as a malfunction of the heater?"

"No."

"How would that have affected the operation of the heater?"

"I would have been very inefficient in heating the pool water, and could have caused a build up of heat and carbon monoxide gasses in the pool heater room."

"Could that combination have caused someone in the heater room to fall asleep?"

"Yes, easily."

"Would that have been a fatal combination to someone sleeping in the heater room?"

"It could have been."

"Mr. Sanders, did you ever warn the Mallory's concerning the possibility of carbon monoxide build up in that room if the exhaust flue wasn't functioning properly?"

"Yes. The first time I performed routine maintenance after they had moved in."

"Thank you Mr. Sanders, I have no more questions."

As Candice walked back across the room to her table the judge asked, "Mr. Langley?"

"Thank you, Your Honor," he replied as he walked around his table and approached the witness box.

"Mr. Sanders, are you being paid by the prosecutor to make this court appearance?"

"Yes."

"That is a practice normally applied to an expert witness. Are you an expert, Mr. Sanders?"

"Depends on the subject."

"Mr. Sanders, you come into this court room dressed like a janitor. Don't you respect this court?"

"I respect the process and most of the people here."

"Do you have a degree in mechanical engineering, Mr. Sanders?"

"No."

"How can we consider you as an expert on the mechanisms involved here if you don't even have a college degree in the field involved?"

Here, Fred looked up at the judge and asked him, "Your Honor, may I ask Mr. Langley a question?"

"It's unusual, but I'll allow it," he replied.

Fred turned back to Mr. Langley and asked, "Mr. Langley, do you have a degree in equestrian anatomy?"

"No," the lawyer answered.

"And yet," continued Fred, "You are able to replicate the hindquarters of a horse so accurately."

The room filled with laughter until the judge banged his gavel on the bench and called for order. Mr. Langley looked at the judge and said, "I object to the witnesses' comment and demand that he be held in contempt!"

"You don't demand anything in my courtroom, Mr. Langley!"

"But, Your Honor I..."

"The court recorder will strike from the record anything that Mr. Sanders said, relating to Mr. Langley being a horse's ass. The jury is instructed to disregard the same. Go on, Mr. Langley. Do you have more questions for this witness?"

"No,"

"Then I have a few questions for Mr. Sanders," the judge replied.

I thought "Oh, oh, here's were Fred gets his ass chewed."

"Mr. Sanders?" the judge asked. "Are you getting paid by the county to testify here today?"

"Yes sir. They are supposed to pay for my time and travel at my usual rate."

"That being the case, Mr. Sanders, please listen closely to what I have to say.

"My chambers are too damn hot in the winter and too damn cold in the summer. The people who do the HVAC here at the court house have been unable to correct this problem. Do you have any suggestions?"

"Do you have a thermostat in your chambers, Your Honor?"

"No. Otherwise I coulda' taken care of the problem myself."

"Do you have a window, sir?"

"Yes."

"Try opening the window. If that doesn't fix what's wrong, call my office and schedule a service call."

"Thank you Mr. Sanders. Anyone else have any questions for the witness?"

I wanted to ask him why my fuel bills were so high, but decided it wasn't the time or place.

The judge called for a fifteen minute recess and dismissed the court.

Twenty minutes later, Judge Orlon said, "Your next witness please, Ms. Mead."

"The prosecution calls Officer Kent Williams"

Candice began with, "Please state your name and occupation."

"I am Officer Kent Williams of the Adams County Sheriff's department. I am in charge of all investigation procedures on vehicles that are considered to be involved in a crime in Adams County."

"How long have you been doing this job, Officer Williams?"

"Ten years ma'am. Five years working with the sergeant that trained me and five years as department supervisor."

"Did you have a nineteen eighty three Chevrolet S-10 Blazer belonging Miss Cheryl Collins in your shop reciently?"

"Yes."

"When was the vehicle brought in?"

"It had been transported on a truck from Miss Collins' residence to our crime lab yard and secured there on Sunday afternoon the twenty ninth of October of this year. I began work on the vehicle at eight o'clock Monday morning."

"As you were investigating the vehicle, officer, did you become convinced that it had been involved in a crime?"

"Yes ma'am."

"Why?"

"All surfaces in the drivers area of the vehicle had been wiped clean of any fingerprints. Not even the owner's prints could be found there. Also, all surfaces of the tailgate area had been wiped and we found but one set of prints there. They were not the owner's. The rest of the car had prints belonging to the owner as well as several other people, that had been there for some time."

"Did you identify the finger prints found in the tailgate area?"

"We didn't find a match in our database, but Detective Halverson provided a match several days later."

"How did he do that, Officer?"

"He brought to our lab two photos that had been handled, after being cleaned, by only Detective Halverson and one other person each."

"Who were those persons, Officer?"

"According to the detective, Doctor and Mrs. Mallory."

"Did one of the sets of prints match those you found?"

"Yes. Doctor Mallory's prints were on the spare tire cover and release mechanism of Miss Collins' Car."

"Was there anything else that suggested the vehicle had been involved in a crime?"

"Yes. Although someone has thoroughly scrubbed the area, we found fresh bodily secretions in the carpet of the rear compartment of the vehicle."

"What did you conclude from that?"

"Recently deceased bodies release these secretions as muscles relax. I believe that a recently deceased person had been transported in the back of Miss Collins car within the last forty eight hours."

"Could you identify the person from who these excretions had seeped?"

"Yes ma'am. It was Cheryl Collins."

"Thank you Officer Williams. No further questions, Your Honor."

"Does the defense wish to cross, Mr. Langley?

"Just one question, Your Honor."

He stood behind his table and asked, "Officer Williams, did you find any evidence at all that you could tie in any way to the defendant, Mrs. Mallory?"

Officer Williams thought a moment and answered, "No."

"Thank you officer. That will be all."

"Do you wish to redirect, Ms. Mead?"

"No thank you, Your Honor," she replied.

"We'll take our lunch break now," the judge announced. "Court will reconvene at one o'clock."

We were eating our Sub-Way sandwiches in Candice's office, when Mrs. Thomas came in accompanied by Carlos.

"You didn't need to send a babysitter for me this morning," Mrs. Thomas complained.

"We only wanted to be sure you arrived here on time and not under the influence of any medication, Mrs. Thomas," Candice explained.

"Well, at least you sent a real gentleman. Not to mention his bein' a hunk," Mrs. Thomas replied. "Ya' got any extra sandwiches?"

"Help yourself. You too Carlos," I said. They're in that sack on the desk."

"The prosecution calls Susan O'Brien"

Sergeant O'Brien filled out her regulation Sheriff's deputy uniform to perfection and the eyes of all the male occupants of the room followed her up the center aisle and watched closely as she was sworn in and seated in the witness box. I heard someone in the gallery say, "Damn , she even has her own cuffs."

Candice crossed the room and stood in front of the box forcing Mr. Langley to move to the far end of his table in order to see the witness. She then said, "Please tell us your name and what your duties are with the Adams County Sheriff's Department."

"My name is Susan O'Brien, and I am the sergeant in charge of fingerprint identification."

"Were did you receive training for this position, Sergeant?"

"The FBI training center in Quantico, Virginia."

"Did you do the fingerprint analysis related to the murder of Miss Cheryl Collins?"

"Yes."

"Tell me what you found."

"We first worked with prints found on and in Miss Collins' vehicle. Miss Collins' were easily identified because we had printed the body soon after it was brought to the morgue."

"What about other prints found?"

"We entered all prints into the national database and found no matches."

"Did you eventually find matches?"

"Yes. Once we were informed that a Mr. George Thomas, an employee of the Boeing Training Center in Moses Lake, was a possible suspect in the crime, we contacted the personnel department there. They immediately sent a print card to us with Mr. Thomas' prints. We then matched those to the prints found in the passenger area of Miss Collins' car."

"What other prints did you find?"

"It was strange because we found no prints at all in the driver's area of the car or the area in the rear where most people transport things. But we did find prints of a hand on the spare tire cover and a partial set on the lever that releases the spare so that the rear of the car can be accessed."

"Were you able to identify those prints?"

"Not at first, but Detective Halverson obtained samples of both Doctor and Mrs. Mallory, and brought them to our lab. The prints on the tire release mechanism were a perfect match for Doctor Mallory."

"Are you certain that the prints supplied by Detective Halverson were actually those of Doctor and Mrs. Mallory?"

"Yes ma'am. They were both printed when they were arrested. We checked to insure that they were correctly identified."

"Thank you Sergeant O'Brien.

" No further questions Your Honor."

"Mr. Langley?"

Once again Mr. Langley merely stood in place as he asked, "Sergeant O'Brien, were any prints belonging to Mrs. Mallory found on or in Miss Collins' vehicle or in the pool heater room?"

"No," she answered.

"Nothing further, Your Honor," Mr. Langley said as he sat back down.

"Ms. Mead?" the judge asked.

"No, Your Honor."

"Please call your next, and I hope, final witness, Ms. Mead."

"The prosecution calls Mrs. Clarice Thomas."

Mrs. Thomas did not receive the same scrutiny as Sergeant O'Brien had as she walked the aisle, and when she had been sworn in and seated, she had the audacity to wave and wink at Mr. Langley.

"Ms. Mead, Mr. Langley, will you both please approach the bench," the judge requested.

The judge put his hand over his microphone so the rest of us couldn't hear, but Candice told us later that he was upset that Mrs. Thomas and Mr. Langley were acquainted, and more upset to find that Mr. Langley was expected to represent Mrs. Thomas in her upcoming divorce from a previous witness. He told the two attorneys that the whole thing felt like an incestuous relationship and he would disqualify Mr. Langley from cross at the slightest indication of impropriety.

Once back and addressing the witness, Candice said, "Please state your name, occupation and place of residence."

"I'm Clarice Thomas, I'm a housewife and I live in Mill Creek Washington."

"Mrs. Thomas, on Sunday morning the twenty ninth of October at approximately eight thirty, were you driving west on 12 SW looking for a particular address?"

"Yes, I was...."

"Please Mrs. Thomas, if a simple yes or no will answer my questions do not supply anything more.

"Was the visibility good that morning?"

"Yes."

"Is 12 SW s straight road where you were driving?"

"Yes."

"Could you have seen a car approaching from the west, coming toward you for a half mile or so?"

Mr. Langley stood and said, "Objection, Your Honor. The question calls for speculation."

"I'll allow the question for now. Let's see where this is going."

"In spite of the good visibility and the straightness of the road, were you surprised by the sudden appearance of a vehicle approaching from the west?"

"Yes."

"You hadn't seen this vehicle enter 12 SW, you hadn't seen it approaching you and yet there it was when you came up out of a small dip in the road?"

Mr. Langley stood again and said, "Objection. The prosecution is leading the witness."

The judge said, "Get to your point, Ms. Mead."

"Mrs. Thomas, did the approaching vehicle make a left turn in front of you and enter a driveway?"

"Yes."

"Was it the driveway you were looking for."

"Yes, according to the GPS in my car."

"Please describe the vehicle you saw."

"It was one of those older SUVs. Probably a Chevy Blazer. We had one years ago. It had the spare tire mounted on the rear door like ours was.

"Did you see the occupants of the vehicle?"

"There was only the driver."

"Can you describe the driver."

"Only to say that it looked like a woman with long hair."

Pointing to Mrs. Mallory, Candice asked, "Could she have been the driver, Mrs. Thomas?"

"She could have been. But, so could anyone else in here with longish hair."

"Mrs. Thomas, do you know who that driveway belonged to?"

"Yes. That slu..."

"A name Mrs. Thomas, please"

"Cheryl Collins, that..."

"Thank you Mrs. Thomas, that will be all."

"Mr. Langley, and be careful," the judge said.

He stood in place and asked, "Mrs. Thomas, did you see the oncoming vehicle enter the highway from a driveway?"

"No."

"Thank you. No more questions."

Candice stood and said, "The prosecution rests, Your Honor."

"We'll recess for fifteen minutes and then the defense may present it's side of the case."

Out in the hallway, Candice approached Sam and me and asked, "What do you guys think so far?"

Sam started with, "I think you did one hell of a job with the little bit of stuff Hal here gave you."

"Screw you, boss, I replied. "She did a hell of a job in spite of the fact that your contribution to this case amounted to about two phone calls."

"At least three calls," Sam said.

"Thanks guys," Candice said. "I needed that boost."

"Seriously, I think we've got her. But, the defense hasn't started and you never know about juries."

"You're right, Sam," she replied. It aint over 'til it's over. Let's go in and see what Mr. Smarmy has up his sleeve."

Everyone was back in their places when Mr. Langley stood and said, "Your Honor, the defenses requests that any and all charges against Mrs. Grace Mallory be dropped and Mrs. Mallory be allowed to return to her life as an exemplary citizen of this county. The prosecution hasn't presented enough evidence to charge Mrs. Mallory with the crime of murder, much less convict her."

"Two words Mr. Langley," the judge said, "Fat chance.

"Please present your defense."

"The defense calls Doctor Peter Mallory."

Doctor Mallory was wearing his county prison coveralls, but somehow he had rigged a clerical collar and almost looked reverent as he took his vow of truth. Once seated in the witness box he was asked by Mr. Langley to state his name, occupation and place of residence.

"I am the Reverend Doctor Peter Mallory, and much like St. Peter, I presently reside in prison."

"Doctor Mallory," Mr. Langley asked, "what can you tell us about Saturday, the twenty eighth of October of this year?"

"I decided on that morning to kill my wife," he said.

There were a few gasps from the gallery. One of them may have come from me.

"Go on, Doctor."

"I believed that she was having affairs with one or more people, and she was trying to keep me so stoned on marijuana that I wouldn't realize what was happening. I had quit using the drug a month before and had been faking a drug induced state so I could observe her actions.

"I decided that in spite of all I believed about our God and mortality, I had enough of her and her cheating.

"I knew enough about our pool heater and the room where it was located to modify the exhaust flue and create a gas chamber to rival any the Nazis created during World War Two.

"My plan was to let our residence cool down to an uncomfortable level, and when Grace returned home that evening from whom ever she had been with, I would suggest she stay warm in the pool heater room while I checked the house's heating system.

"My plan changed when Miss Collins, one of the people I suspected of being my wife's lover, knocked on the door and asked to see Grace.

"I thought, 'Here is a chance to eliminate someone who has made my life miserable for months,' so I took her to the heater room ostensibly to wait for Grace.

"The heater worked as planned and when Grace finally came home, I explained my plan and told her that she was next on my list.

"Well, she told me of the error of my ways and convinced me that she loved only me.

"We then put Miss Collins' body in her old truck and dumped it in a ditch somewhere east of Cariboo. Grace said she would clean up after me and I went to bed and prayed for forgiveness."

"The defense rests, Your Honor."

"Ms. Mead? the judge asked.

"I am shocked beyond comprehension, Your Honor."

"Yeah, so am I Ms. Mead. Do you wish to question the witness?"

"Doctor Mallory?" she asked, "do you, a man of the Christian Church, actually swear that the outrageous story you have just told is the truth?"

"Of course. Would I lie to you?" he asked.

"I have no further questions for this witness Your Honor."

"In that case, we will have a fifteen minute recess and then you both may present your final arguments."

Twenty five minutes later, when Candice was sure she had their undivided attention, she addressed the jurors.

"Ladies and gentlemen, the story just told by Doctor Mallory should have started with, 'Once upon a time' and ended with, 'And they lived happily ever after.' As interesting as it was, it was a fairy tale concocted to draw your attention away from the facts of the case as presented by our witnesses. The defense apparently believes that because you live in a non-urban area, you aren't sophisticated enough to see through his big city sham, and will begin to doubt that which you know to be the truth.

"The facts of the case are: Number one: Mrs. Mallory was involved in a sexual relationship with Miss Baker.

"Number two: Miss Baker was a good friend of Cheryl Collins.

"Number three: Miss Baker's feelings for Mrs. Mallory were of a sexual nature combined the temporary thrill of a relationship with someone she thought of as a 'real lady.' Miss Baker did not develop an emotional attraction, or, love, for Mrs. Mallory and soon became bored with her.

"Number four: Mrs. Mallory mistakenly believed that Cheryl Collins was the cause for Miss Baker's recent lack of ardor.

"Number five: Mrs. Mallory forbade Miss Baker to see Cheryl Collins saying, and I quote 'Stop seeing Cheryl or I will see to it that Cheryl will stop seeing you.'

"Number six: Cheryl Collins visited Miss Baker On Saturday night, the twenty eighth and was told of Mrs. Mallory's assumptions. She then made the fatal error of believing she could reason with Mrs. Mallory and drove to Mrs. Mallory's residence

"Number seven: After leaving Miss Bakers' home, Cheryl was not seen by anyone but the Mallorys before she was found dead in a ditch on Fletcher Road in the early hours of Sunday October the twenty ninth.

"Number eight: According to forensic evidence found in Cheryl's car, her body had been transported in that car.

"Number nine: Cheryl's car was seen being driven into her driveway, most likely from the driveway of the Mallory residence, and the car had been thoroughly wiped down so that even Cheryl's prints could not be found in the driver's area. However, Doctor Mallory's print were present on the mechanism used to access the area where the body had been transported.

"Number ten: The damper in the flue of the Mallory's pool heater had been purposely altered to cause a carbon monoxide build up in the pool heater room.

"You cannot, after hearing the witnesses tell, not a fairy tale, but the real truth, have any doubt in your mind that Grace Mallory is guilty of the murder of Miss Cheryl Collins and her unborn child."

Candice returned to her place at the prosecutors table and sat down.

Judge Orlon said, "Fifteen minute break, then the defense can wind this thing up."

Everyone was once again seated after the break and the judge said, "Go ahead, Mr. Langley."

Mr. Langley got up from his chair, walked to his right and faced the jury.

"Ladies and gentlemen, I'll make this brief," he said.

"The prosecution's entire case is built on the imaginings, or worse, lies of an hysterical girl who was rejected by Grace Mallory as a lover, and now wishes to seek revenge. There are no facts to support her claims of an affair with Mrs. Mallory, nor her claims of having been threatened.

"The prosecution's only physical evidence in this case is, if you will, a lack of physical evidence.

"And, Doctor Mallory has in fact confessed to having committed the crime.

"There is no possible way that you can, beyond a reasonable doubt, believe that Grace Mallory is guilty of murder.

"You cannot convict someone of murder if there is any doubt that they are guilty.

"You must therefore present this court with a verdict of not guilty."

Mr. Langley then looked at each juror, one at a time, then walked slowly to his place and sat down.

"Ms. Mead, do you wish to rebut?"

"Thank you judge, no. I believe this jury will see through the defense's smoke screen and return a responsible verdict."

"Mr. Langley?" the judge asked.

"I have nothing more, Your Honor."

The judge gave his instructions to the jury. He emphasized the need of a unanimous decision. "You must all be convinced beyond any reasonable doubt that Mrs. Mallory is guilty of the crime of murder, in order to convict..

"You will begin deliberations now, and continue until ten PM if necessary. If a verdict is not reached by that time, you will begin again at eight o'clock tomorrow morning. I would suggest that you bring your toothbrush and at least one change of clothing at that time. You will not be sequestered tonight. However, if a verdict is not reached by ten PM tomorrow, you will be sequestered until you have reached a verdict. God help you with the task you are about to begin.

"Bailiff, put your jury to work."

He banged his gavel on the bench, declared that court was dismissed until a verdict had been achieved, we all stood up and he retired to his chambers.

Some of us gathered in Candice's office after leaving the courtroom. There were Candice, Sam and me of course, and joining us were George Thomas and Sylvia and Alice Baker, accompanied by Carlos. Sylvia and her mother had attended the final day of the trial sitting in the back row behind and almost impossible to see from the defense table. George had attended every session since he finished testifying.

We were discussing the strange turn of events since Doctor Mallory took the stand only a short while ago when Clayton Ogden, Doctor Mallory's attorney of record, tapped on the frame of the open door.

"Come on in, Clayton," Candice said. "What do you think about your client now?"

"I really can't say, Ms. Mead. What do you propose to do regarding his testimony today?"

"Depends on the verdict. If Mrs. Mallory is found guilty, and I think she should be, Doctor Mallory's trial for aiding and abetting will start on next Tuesday.

"If, God forbid, she is found innocent, I'm not sure if I will charge him with the murder, since I don't believe he did it. I may stay with the original charges.

"Then again, if you as his attorney can convince him to cop a plea to either charge, you can head south and play golf with a clear conscience."

"If he doesn't plead guilty to at least the aid and abet," Clayton said, "I'm going to plead old age and bad health and head south anyway, clear conscience or not."

"I think that would be a wise choice," she said. "There's a bad smell to this whole thing right now. After all the years that you've helped the folks around here through their legal problems, don't let this case be a part of your legacy."

"Thanks for being open and honest with me, Ms. Mead. Off the record, I hope you get them both. Good night."

Clayton had left the office and we were once again discussing the possible outcome of the trial when Candice's desk phone rang.

"Mead, County Prosecutors office," she answered. "Oh hi. You're sure? Okay, thanks for the call.

"That was my cousin, Judge Orlon's clerk. The judge told him to 'leak' some information to me.

"According to my cousin, if a verdict is reached before ten tonight, the judge will take a vow of secrecy from each member of the jury and allow them to go home and return for court to be convened at ten thirty tomorrow morning. What he means is: Go home, because there will be nothing to learn here tonight. So," she said, "I'm turning out the lights and goin' out the door. You all gotta' leave too. See you here in the morning."

We'd traveled in silence for about fifteen minutes when Sam asked, "What ya' thinkin', Hal?"

"I think, no I know, Grace Mallory killed Cheryl Collins, but I'm glad I only have to find em' and arrest em'. I'm glad we have twelve other people to decide if I'm right or wrong."

"Well I think you're right on this one and I hope they don't get it wrong."

30.
FRIDAY, DECEMBER 1

"The jurors were back at it this morning when I came in at eight thirty," Candice said.

"Ya' think that's good or bad?" I asked.

"Well, at least they didn't go to the jury room," Sam replied, "decide we had the wrong person and come right back out. That's gotta' be good."

"I'd have felt a lot better if they made that quick a turnaround and came back with a guilty verdict," Candice said.

We talked about this case and others that we had experienced. We talked about the various witnesses and how the verdict may effect them. We ran out of things to say after a while and I thought, "I wish I still smoked."

The phone on Candice's desk rang about eleven thirty, startling us all. Candice looked at us and picked up the receiver.

"Mead, County Prosecutor's office. Okay, thanks."

She hung up and said, "Jury's decided. The judge will reconvene at one thirty."

"Anyone want lunch?" Sam asked.

"Nope," I replied, "but, at least it's something to do while we wait."

"Let's hit my folk's old place. It's my good luck spot and the owner's will give us a room to ourselves," Candice said. "And, I'll treat."

"Works for me," said Sam, "But I bet you get a discount."

"Nope," she said. "Verdict day is always on the house."

One thirty finally arrived and we were all back in our accustomed places when Judge Orlon reconvened his court.

"Has the jury reached a verdict." he asked.

Carl Johnson, the jury foreman stood up and said, "Yes we have, Your Honor."

"What is your finding?" the judge asked.

"In the matter of Grace Mallory being charged with the second degree murder of Cheryl Collins and her unborn child: We find the defendant not guilty"

A murmur rose from the gallery and I found myself saying, "That's bull shit." before the judge banged his gavel on the bench and called for order.

"Mrs. Mallory," the judge said. "You are hereby released from the charge of the second degree murder of Cheryl Collins and her unborn child. You are free to go."

Back in Candice's office I asked her, "What now? Are we going after Doctor Mallory?"

"You guys go on home," she said. I'll consult with my boss and give you a call. I feel like I really let you and the people of this county down and I need to do some thinking."

"You used everything we gave you as well as it could be done," I told her. "We should have provided more ammunition.

"Call me and I'll do what ever I can to put her away," I said. "If he did the deed, then she was his accomplice. Maybe we just need to switch the charges around. That way there's no double jeopardy, and he has already confessed to the crime in front of witnesses without coercion."

"Thanks, Hal," she said, "I'll call you."

Sam and I slipped out the side door of the courthouse and we could see that the TV lights an cameras were focused on the main entry where Mr. Langley was the center of attention.

It was a long silent ride back to Cariboo and I was finally settled in my recliner with a well deserved glass of single malt scotch, when my cell phone rang. I was tempted to ignore it but the CID said Candice Mead.

"Hi," I said. "What's goin' on?"

"I can't believe it!" she said. With Mrs. Mallory being released, they transferred her bail over to Doctor Mallory and they have both gone home."

"I'll call Sam," I said. "and we'll have a car at each intersection of 12 SW they'd need to pass through to leave their home. They'll stay put until Tuesday, or have a fully armed escort where ever they go."

I called Sam and he promised to take care of the situation.

Back to my scotch.

31.
SATURDAY, DECEMBER 2

It was eight thirty Saturday morning and the sun had just burned through the haze to the east revealing a cloudless sky overhead. The temperature was twenty four degrees Fahrenheit, the barometer read twenty nine point nine. The winds were negligible with only an occasional whisper from the north.

George Thomas placed the lacquered pine box on the seat of the plane and did his preflight walk- around.

This was the same Cessna 172 that he had flown when he took Cheryl for her first airplane ride. This would be her last.

At eight forty seven he was cleared for take off. He powered the plane free from the earth and was soon flying south, south west toward the Columbia River gorge. He flew over the river until he came to Crab Creek on the south side of the Frenchman Hills. He then turned east and near Royal City he banked and turned north. George didn't notice the box slide off of the seat and land between the seat and the yoke column. As he approached Cheryl's old double-wide, he gently pushed the yoke forward putting the plane in a slight dive for a close pass over her home before he scattered her ashes to the winds over the countryside she loved.

As he approached his desired altitude, he pulled back on the yoke and was surprised to find that it wouldn't move. He was still in a slight dive, and the hill was rising rapidly in front of him. George was also surprised at the feeling of peace that enveloped him as he saw the inevitable about to happen.

The calls came in almost simultaneously, one to Adams County Dispatch from a radio car stationed east of the crash site and one to Grant County Dispatch from a radio car stationed to the west of the site. A small plane had just crashed into a residence in the 900 block of 12 SW and the residence was on fire. As the two cars sped toward the crash, there was a gigantic explosion and the crash site became a flaming inferno. It would remain impossible to approach any closer than one hundred feet for the next two hours. No one at the site at the time of the crash could possibly have survived.

According the hourly news from the radio station in Cariboo, it was unknown if the home was occupied. The tax records indicated that it was owned by The Light and Truth, LLC, a religious organization headquartered in Bellevue, Washington.

Shirley and I were having lunch when we heard the news on the radio we listened to while doing chores around the house.

"What do you think, Hal?" Shirley asked after hearing the report.

"I don't know, Shirl. I'll wait until they find out who was flying the plane. I think I know, and if I'm right, God have mercy on his tormented soul."

"You want to go out to the crash site?" she asked

"It'll be too hot to see anything out there today but I'd like to go tomorrow and talk with the fire guys."

"Are you worried about who may have been in the house?".

"I'm more worried about who may not have been there. I don't want to wait until Tuesday morning to see who shows up for trial."

32.
SUNDAY, DECEMBER 3

Another clear crisp day. Except for the long shadows caused by the sun being so far south this time of the year and the temperature being in the low twenties, it was almost summery.

I left the house about ten and drove west on SR- 26, turned north on SR-262 and west again on 12 SW. Once at the site I saw people wearing jackets with ATF, FAA, GCFD, and RCFD combing through debris that still appeared to be emitting smoke or steam in places. An ATF guy stopped me just as I climbed over the crime scene tape.

"Hold on there," he yelled. "Where the hell do you think you're going?"

I flashed my shield and asked if anyone here was in charge of this apparent Chinese fire drill.

"Everyone here thinks they're in charge, all I need now is one more damn expert."

"My advice," I told him, "is for you to tell the two local fire inspectors to leave if they aren't being of any help. Then tell the FAA guys to find the plane that caused this and try to find out why it crashed. Then tell me what I want to know and kick my ass outa' here."

"Let me look at that God damn badge of yours again," he said.

"Adams County Sheriff. Ain't you a little out of your territory?"

"What if I told you who was flying that plane and why he crashed it into this particular house," I said.

"The FAA boys already know who the pilot was, but they don't yet know the reason for the crash."

"Was the pilot George Thomas?" I asked.

"Yeah, but why plow into this house?"

"Have you found any remains, or has every thing been too hot to know yet?"

"Yeah, we've found remains. Maybe you know who they were."

"They were still whole after this fire?" I asked.

"Yeah. It looks like when the plane hit it started a small fire. The occupants must have thought that jumping into the pool would keep them safe. Then that five hundred gallon above ground propane tank blew and so much heat was created that the water in the pool actually boiled. They were boiled alive, but are still intact. Ya' want'a' take a look?"

"No," I told him, "but I guess I need to."

He led me over to a black step van that had ATF painted on the side. Opening the rear doors, reveled two body bags strapped to the floor. These were pretty fancy bags, not like we have at the county level and he pulled the zipper down on one of them. Boiled red as a lobster but recognizable was Grace Mallory staring back at me.

"Why didn't you at least close her eyes?" I asked

"Afraid the lids would come off ."

I checked the second bag and it contained The Reverend Doctor Peter Mallory.

"Looks to me like they got a sample of hell before they went there," I said. "You got something you want me to fill out for the identification?"

I drove back home thinking about justice, vengeance and how many lives can be disrupted because of a one misstep, one smile at a lonely person, one seemingly innocent friendship.

Shirley was in the kitchen when I got home, putting the finishing touches on heating a dinner she brought home from the deli.

"I thought you might need something special hon," she said, so I brought in take out."

"Perfect," I said, just as my cell buzzed in my pocket.

"Can't you leave that go to voice mail?" Shirley asked.

I looked at the CID and it was Sam.

"No."

"Hello, Sam, what's up?"

"Got a DB out on a farm south east of here.."

"Want me to go take a look?" I asked.

"No, Hal. The coroner's got this one. Says it's another God damn stupid hunting accident. Seems some hunter was trying to climb through a barbed wire fence on property leased to J & N Growers."

"J & N Growers?" I asked. "I've never heard of them."

"They lease the land from R Martinez LLC."

"Wait a minute," I said, "That's not Jeremy and Nate leasing from Ramon, is it?"

"Yep. Apparently a couple of Game cops found the guy when they were investigating an anonymous tip about some poaching going on in the area. Looks like the guy's shotgun went off accidentally as he was squeezing between the strands of wire and blasted him in the groin. He ended up bleeding out before the Game cops found him."

"If you don't want me to check it out, why so much information?" I asked.

" Kinda' thought you might know the guy."

"Why? Who was it?" I asked.

"Fella' named Robert Langley. I thought you outa' know. See ya' tomorrow, Hal."

"What was that all about," Shirley asked.

"I guess I don't have to go to court next week after all."

"Candice will be disappointed," she said.

PROLOG

Life goes on in that part of area code 509 around Cariboo and Moses Lake.

On the Sunday following the news release regarding the death of Robert Langley, the Bellevue, Washington chapter of the NRA , staged a protest, immediately following brunch in the lobby of the Swept Wing Inn. They demanded a moratorium on the sale and use of barbed wire fencing saying, "It is a lethal product that is unnecessary this day and age." They requested a list of all present owners of such. The local Co-op said they'd work on that.

Marijuana has been legalized in the state of Washington and J & N Growers is now the state's largest legal producer of the product, selling to retailers in all thirty nine counties.

The property formerly owned by The Truth and Light LLC of Bellevue has been purchase and developed by R Martinez LLC. Combined with the other land purchases on the south facing slope of the Frenchmen Hills, it will be a destination vineyard and winery able to host concerts, weddings and other gala events. Cheryl's old double-wide suffered extreme heat damage during the fire. Nearly all of the vinyl siding had melted in place virtually encapsulating the entire structure. The property is now leased to R Martinez LLC and used for parking and storage.

The Swept Wing Inn has been transformed into a home for the elderly and is operated by The Truth and Light LLC.

Sylvia and her mother, who rumor has it has been seeing a lot of Ramon Martinez lately, have purchased the Thirsty

Dog tavern. They have completely redecorated it and plan to re-open as The Gay Caballero.

George Thomas had the forethought before his marriage to Clarice to have a prenuptial agreement drawn up and signed by Clarice, that stated: In the event that Clarice engages an attorney with the intention of divorcing George, all property accumulated by the couple, unless specifically earned by Clarice, becomes the property of George only, negating any community property laws by the state.

George's latest will, naming one Carlos Cruz as his executor, (The only truly honest man George had ever known) declared that all property, except the Moses Lake residence, be liquidated and all proceeds be placed in a trust fund for any and all of his grandchildren. The Moses Lake property was left to Clarice Thomas on the condition that she reside there for a minimum of forty eight weeks per year and has a full time job.

Mrs. Clarice Thomas is presently employed as a sales associate in ladies wear at the Moses Lake Wal-Mart.

Buck is the proud papa of a litter of Golden Poodles and is continuing to live in the lap of luxury.

Made in the USA
Las Vegas, NV
08 February 2022